Nothing Beside Remains

Jaysinh Birjépatil

Fomite

Burlington, Vermont

ISBN-13 978-1-942515-02-9
Library of Congress Control Number: 2015933091

Digital Illustration by Hilary Baker

Fomite
58 Peru Street
Burlington, VT 05401
www.fomitepress.com

Acknowledgements

I am grateful to my old friends John Drew and Tony Connor, who
reached out to catch me falling.

Emmy (née Lederer) Kulshrestha for planting the seeds of her lost
Vienna in my mind.

Markus Fellinger Curator, Belvedere Collection, for valuable insights
into Viennese art; Doctors Deborah and Julian Ferholt, Yale University
School of Medicine and Doctors Dulari and Jitendra Gandhi of Baroda,
for decoding the lost art of healing.

Luis Batlle for generously sharing his profound knowledge of music
with me, and Lore Segal for valuable tips on the Vienna interludes in
the book.

Jennifer and Joe Mazur, Geraldine Batlle, Eva Friedlander, Stan
Charkey, Lou and Paul Nelsen and Sherry Bromley whose friendship
is my 'Obama Care.'

And finally the Fomite team of Marc Estrin and Donna Bister for
their art of shaping a chaotic script into a fine book

The following works helped me reimagine Vienna as it was between
the Wars: *The Man Without Qualities* — Robert Musil, *Other People's
Houses* — Lore Segal, *A Nervous Splendour* — Frederic Morton, *The
Hare with Amber Eyes* — Edmund de Waal, *The Vienna Paradox* —
Marjorie Perloff and *The Setting Of The Pearl* — Thomas Weyr.

Cast of Characters

India

Dr Cyrus Sorabji	A British trained hhysician
Dr Gisela (née Hartmann) Sorabji	Viennese wife
Juniper (Juno) Sorabji	Their daughter married to
Terry Dyson	A BBC freelance scriptwriter
Sissi	Their Daughter
Lady Perrin Sorabji	Dr Sorabji's mother
Sir Jamshet Sorabji	Dr Sorabji's father and Dewan of the Princely State of Umeednagar
The Old His Highness	The Late Maharaja of Umeednagar
The Old Her Highness	His widow
The Current His Highness	Their son who lives in England
John Duckworth	Tutor to the Old His Highness when he was an underage prince
Mike Aspel	Senior BBC Correspondent in Delhi
Subhadra	Gisela's Gurkha cook and house keeper
Bahadur	Her watchman husband
Kirpal	Their son
Dr Gopal Trivedi	Sorabji's colleague
Savita	Matron at the Sorabji Clinic
Mr Kazmi	The compounder
Jehangir Sanjanwala	Retired Curator of the local museum
Behroz Sanjanwala	His wife
Pestan (Pessy) Sanjanwala	Their son, a builder by profession
Homai Sanjanwala	His sister
Laxmi	His wife
Col. Mehra	A retired army officer
Osman Chacha	A retired forest officer
Collector Chaudhary	The Collector of Umeednagar
Pereira	The bartender at Umeednagar Club
Pavanlal Lakhanpal	Irascible head of the building Mafia
Janab Valiulla	An impoverished aristocrat who runs a hotel in Bhopal
Parvez	A Tour guide

Vienna

Gustav Hartmann (Papili)	Gisela's father, runs a famous Viennese book shop called Marcus Aurelius
Mutti	Gisela's Mother
Rudi	Gisela's mentally challenged brother
Hilde	The Hartmanns' maid
Uncle Yakob	Mutti's older brother
Uncle David	Mutti's younger brother
Herr Franz Rumplemayor	Gustav Hartmann's cousin and violinist at the Vienna Philharmonic
Bettlemann and Schlick	Hartmann's assistants

England

Mam	Terry's mother
Uncle Tom	Her brother
Venables	Her lodger
Elsie	Her friend
Mrs Hardcastle	Her neighbour
Mike Bartlett	A freelance documentary maker
Aiden Whitcomb	A senior journalist
Sir Simon Derramore	A Conservative politician
Percival Simpson	BBC News presenter
Dick Craven	Senior editor at the BBC
Jeanette Markham	American professor teaching in the 'semester in London' programme
Shekhar	An aspiring Indian actor
Mr and Mrs Jenkins	Cyrus Sorabji's guardians during his schooldays in England
Tom Jenkins	Their son

USA

Gabriella Rumplemayor	Gisela's cousin
Leslie Singer	Her niece
Harry Knickerbockers	A camera and sound technician
Becky	His wife

BOOK I

(i)

March 1976

Hotel Excelsior teetered between decent and flyblown, depending on the rise and fall in guest occupancy. One day it would be a clean, well-lighted place with fresh linen and towels, next day all the bulbs fused with a dodgy simultaneity. In the morning cockroaches clung to the rusty drainpipe beneath the washbasin like rooftop commuters on a suburban train.

According to the mustachioed manager, the Emergency had put a stopper to foreign liquor being smuggled into Umeednagar.

The Emergency.

It was a blood-caked, maggoty word, especially with Michael Foot playing cheerleader to Indira Gandhi.

Trains ran on time, passengers buried faces in evening editions, ate catered food and turned in early while the Rajdhani Express — a city on wheels — thundered past wayside stations, drowning the screams of suspects in police custody.

A raggle-taggle bunch had blown up a bridge, disrupting rail traffic. They were so obscure the keenest minds in RAW, the dreaded wing of the secret service, were baffled. With the resumption of the rail service, Terry was on his way to probe the incident.

During the Sepoy Mutiny in 1857, the British had stormed Umeednagar on suspicion of its sheltering the rebel leader Nana Sahib, seen fleeing towards its ramparts. Since then, save for an occasional monsoon overspill the town had jogged along at the leisurely pace of a rinky-dink hackery down a country lane.

In fractious times its archers manning star-shaped bastions had repelled many a Mughal siege. Those coddled warriors from Agra had finally thrown up their bejeweled hands and marched off to retake the sumptuous sea-side town of Surat in the neighboring state, its walls obligingly breeched by marauding bandit kings from the Deccan Hills.

Pat Aspel of the BBC was struck by the incongruity of an old princely backwater like Umeednagar raising the flag of rebellion and asked Terry to go down and file a report.

London viewed Terry Dyson as a provincial-lad-making-it-in-the-metropolis, but Pat was apt to judge a freelancer's worth by action rather than accent. He had often found Terry hunched over his Olivetti for long periods of time, waiting for the right word to connect all the dots. A short bravura snap-shot of events was not his style.

Terry had spent six seesaw months between euphoria and despair, witnessing the blood-soaked birth of Bangladesh; people's sorrow slowly giving way to the collective joy of becoming a nation, visions of future plenitude assuaging present hunger. Overloaded ferries might keel over for many monsoons to come, food shortages through bureaucratic plundering couldn't be ruled out, yet hope not despondency was the prevailing mood in the new country.

"Mrs Gandhi would cry foul," Pat said, "if I were to be seen boarding the milk train from Delhi. 'Interference in domestic affairs' or some such tosh. She nearly bit my head off at the Press Conference yesterday for asking if the clampdown was temporary. Bellicose as the Red Queen, ever since our Michael put his foot (ha ha) into his mouth backing what is unquestionably the biggest cock-up of her career."

The manager was always on about the good and bad of the Emergency. Husbands had stopped beating wives; adulterers gone underground, milk in the bazaar had lost some of the watery quality and cooking oil its foul smell. On the other hand people simply disappeared walking down lonely roads. Hardened criminals growled at the sudden influx of political prisoners in cramped jails, reducing by half their already frugal ration. The hooch trade slumped and you had to produce a doctor's prescription for a few drops of whiskey measured out with coffee spoons. No wonder Pat had been reluctant to leave Delhi. He was no tippler but considered a Scotchless week an extravagant rectitude for a thinking man.

For a week Terry dutifully downed buckets of syrupy cups of tea pressed on him in the evasive bazaar, pounded alleyways smelling of asafoetida. The trail had gone cold. With Indira Gandhi staring down from giant posters Umeednagar was as tight-lipped as a phalanx of loyal eunuchs guarding a teeming harim.

He needed a drink; the manager directed him to Dr Cyrus Sorabji.

"The doctor is a Parsi married to a foreign madam who is also a doctor, always helping poor women bring babies into world. Dr Sorabji can give permit for Bombay Gin and Johnny Walker."

The application dictated by the manager was a hoot — *I am habituated to drinking every day and cannot, not do without it* — but the law brooked no emendation.

At the end of the week Terry found himself on Sorabji's fan-shaped veranda waiting to be ushered in.

His feet sank into a thick carpet; an elderly man materialized frowning like a veteran actor suddenly confronted with an understudy instead of his usual sidekick.

"Cyrus Sorabji, at your service," he said, adjusting a monocle. "My wife is taking a shower, and will join us in a few minutes. I finish clinic in the afternoon but she stays on if a baby is due."

The doctor seemed to be straight out of *The Second Mrs Tanqueray* with an accent that smacked of long walks by gurgling brooks, plop of ball on willow, tea and scones on the lawn. He wore a hacking jacket with a polka-dot cravat tucked under a gray beard. In contrast to the brisk James Robertson Justice manner his tone was exceedingly low.

"I must apologize," Terry said, "for this wholly unwarranted intrusion, but it seems one needs a certificate to buy liquor here."

The old gent laughed.

"Absolutely no need to apologize. Most awkward, I dare say. Please sit down and tell me what brings you to our puritanical State."

There was no India hand in Terry's background, no glass cabinet with medals in velvet-lined display cases. His dad had gone to Singapore with his regiment but never returned after the War.

In the Seventies, people came down following the trail of an ancestor; Uncle Charlie who'd served as District Magistrate in Katiawar, or worked on the railways, built bridges like Alec Guinness in that picture about British troops under Japanese occupation.

"Terry Dyson. I am here to find out more about this Dynamite Case."

"No, no, please come and sit by me. I shall be mother," the doctor said taking the tray brought in by a little Gurkha woman. "Nasty business that, the Dynamite Case I mean, quite astounding. Can't say I understand how that chappy Janardan got involved in it. He is in pharmaceuticals. Bit of a cold fish really. Fellow club member and that sort of thing."

Somewhere an air-conditioner hummed, Terry felt his body relax in the cool dank air. There was a faint outline of a bronze discuss-thrower in an alcove on the left. Other figurines leaned from marble table tops; here a scaled down Bernini Daphne morphing into tree, there a bronze Krishna in an unconventional posture, eyes closed, resting his head calmly on one raised knee, a calf nuzzling his nape.

The house was almost a Museum.

Catching the young man's bewildered look, his host smiled.

"Mostly copies, I am afraid, and not very good ones, except the Krishna over there. A present to Gisela from the Cambodian Government for help-ing them design a family planning program. The original Bernini, as you know, is in Villa Borghese in Rome. Who can copy those marble fingers turning to leaves? Ah, here she is," he said looking up at the sound of foot-steps on the stairs.

A heavy blonde woman appeared on the landing, a broad smile lit up the doctor's bearded face as he leaned hard on the stick to get up.

"Come, my dear, meet Mr Dyson of the BBC. Stationed in Delhi. Here on special assignment to investigate the Dynamite case. Needs liquor permit. Er – er—may I call you Terence?" he said, eyes crinkling with mirth.

"Please call me Terry. All my friends do."

Gisela's teeth gleamed whitely when she smiled, a relief after constant exposure to the nicotine stained mouths in the bazaar. Her clear blue gaze lingered affectionately on her husband's face.

"It's always a special treat to meet someone from England. When he was a little boy, my husband was sent to Eastbourne for private tutoring with friends of the family before going up to Clifton".

Her English was fluent with a slight Teutonic zing.

"Now mostly house-bound, clinic only in the morning. It's my damned knee you see, this one here," Cyrus said tapping it with his pipe. "How about a chotta peg eh, while I write the prescription? Tell you what, why don't you stay for dinner, we'll open a bottle of Chivas Regal I've been saving since Christmas. The real thing, not the desi variety you get with a prescription. Can't stand the stuff. Smells like horse piss."

"Now now, Cy, don't be naughty," his wife said. "It's not as bad as my husband thinks. But that's beside the point. We'd be delighted if you could stay and take pot-luck with us. Only carrot soup and boiled vegetables for us, but our cook Subhadra can make a nice omelet for you with onions and tomatoes. Our daughter Juniper's favorite. She is busy rehearsing for the annual concert at the Convent where she teaches drawing."

Back in his hotel room that night, drink in hand, Terry sat for a long time staring at the bougainvillea bush awash in lamplight. Odd to feel underbred in this provincial Indian backwater, the doctor couple seemed so much at ease with themselves, at one with their urbane past.

The evening's events blinked by like a slide-show; the daughter of the house pulling into the porch as Terry was about to leave, a brief introduction, her offer to run him up to the hotel, his half-hearted remonstrance shot down by the bearded Doctor, the subsequent telephone call to Pat about possible leads to the Dynamite Case requiring another week's snooping around Umeednagar.

During that fifteen-minute ride, he had blithely promised to serve as chief guest and judge the girls' singing and recitation, followed by prize distribution. What was he thinking? The concert was scheduled exactly a week from that evening.

****

After all his battles had been fought and won and the land rid of foes, the Sultan of medieval Umeednagar had laid out a sturdy citadel. The inner township had puckered around the fort with its merlons and battlements. From four archways ran straight roads for a mile and a half, terminating at massive gates at the circular perimeter wall. Five hundred years on, interior bricked up against fleets of homing pigeons, it now served as a roundabout, reining in the chaos of peak-hour traffic.

In 1976 Umeednagar was an odd blend of old and new; spinster-prim, full of festering grudges and bloated self-importance; but beneath it all was an eagerness to catch up with the world beyond. Industrial smoke shafts were moving from drawing boards to meadows on the outskirts spawning shanties with bricks pilfered from the crumbling city wall.

In its heyday it was a bustling town run by a mandarin court, its whisper-close balconies sagging precariously over caparisoned elephants picking their way through winding lanes with jostling pedestrians.

Terry was struck by courteous gestures blossoming in the midst of squalor as the doctors' car inched its way towards the clinic.

In that throng were horse-drawn tongas with floral parquetry on the outside and red upholstery inside. Noisy motorized rickshaws owned the roads now, the tongas lending a bit of dash to marriage processions. Brass bands in plush livery clogged the narrow streets beating out *Come September* at a jaunty clip.

Finally, the car turned into a driveway at the end of which stood a redbrick bungalow. The ground floor was divided into four large rooms set around a sunken courtyard with a fountain. Wooden grills separated Cy's surgery from the compounder's dispensary. Built in the previous century by a musical prince for his favorite courtesan, the place was an oasis of peace at the far end of a bustling bazaar.

After the lurching drive through crowded streets it was a pleasant shock to enter a spacious building with nurses in spotless uniforms gliding across polished floors. Seraphic in their white tunics the doctors seemed to be thoroughly at home amidst twisted bodies, broken teeth and eyes bulging with distress. This was their world.

In Cy's surgery bandages were removed, wounds dressed, throats peered into and stethoscope applied with a sapper's attention to hawking chests.

Gisela's operating room stood at the end of a jasmine-covered walkway where according to the Matron a C-section was in progress.

On the stage at the Convent of Jesus and Mary, girls in pigtails sing 'Mr Gallagher and Mr Pym.' Eyes like a ruminating child's, Mother Superior sitting next to Terry beams and whispers something adulatory about Juno, ravishing in a primrose chiffon sari. The elocution prize goes to 'All the World's a Stage,' rendered by a buxom lass.

Stage one: The Sorabji bungalow silhouetted in the background, Juno and Terry stroll hand in hand in the rose garden.

Stage two: Juno's studio in the loft. On the easel is her latest cobalt blue canvas with thin yellow squiggles running vertically. "Monsoon breaking over nearby Vindhya Hills. Rubato art," she says, "you know, jejune but synaesthetic. Seeing music in color, Scarlatti in reverse."

Stage three: At the Mahatma's ashram retreat in Ahmadabad a vermilion sun sinks at the bend in the river. Daughter of a British admiral, Madeleine Slade, whom the great man called Mira Behn, used to wear white cotton saris spun on the iconic wooden wheel; Juno's sari of lavender silk skims her body. Mira Behn subsisted on low calorie vegetarian meals and even cleaned lavatories as required of Gandhi's disciples.

Stage four: Hoary step-well on the outskirts of Modhera town, rainforest of pliant bodies leaping out of stone, undulating like sub-aqueous plant-life. From the inner freezes, a saucy dancer dares Terry to enter her bazaar of carved limbs. Morning sun, held up briefly at the archway suddenly floods the inner sanctum with incandescence.

'They have their exits and their entrances...'

Stage five: Shikara honeymoon on Dal Lake in Srinagar, then London.

Stage six : 'happiness is egg-shaped,' says a sign on a passing double-decker.

Stage seven: No topiary artifice in Capability Brown's Wimbledon Park. His creation fills with children's trills; under wispy clouds, ducks recede like cable cars on the lake, Juno tucks loose strands under her blue beret, chestnut trees fling their leaves sideways like tresses in the wind.

Terry's lifelong struggle with the British class system so far waged in public places, erupted indoor like a stray incendiary. It wasn't just a question of 'trust deficit' at first sight with Mam letting her 'salt 'n vinegar' tongue unfurl at the slightest froufrou of Juno's jet-set posturing. To Mam's neighbors her son's wife for all her la-di-da manner was just a glorified wog, and to Juno who had known only grave-toned British Council types in Delhi, her mother-in-law was a dirty family secret best kept under wraps.

Fortunately Mam had absolutely no intention of giving up her 'allotment' where she grew tomatoes and other seasonal vegetables and moving to London. "I haven't yet gone dusty in the attic," she snorted.

Life in the years preceding the arrival of Sissi had all the trappings of marital bliss, interspersed with a few low intensity 'kiss 'n make-up' altercations. Weekday mornings Terry drove Juno in his rattlety-bang Morris Minor to the Gloucester Road Underground before heading for White City. She had managed to worm her way into the Slade School of Art as a 'casual student' with her enticing talk of making a drawing from a simple outline of a banyan leaf or a cowherd 'silhouetted on the lea.'

Terry thought the tutor for admissions was charmed by the archaism of 'lea' coming out of Juno's colonial mouth rather than her drawing samples.

Pat Aspel had managed to secure him a desk job at the Television Center, initially on work-placement and then full time, sub-editing international news. Terry also prepared research notes to be used later in the evening by program presenters. By the time he drove home it was quite dark, leaving enough time for Juno after her Underground commute to have dinner ready. It was mostly cold cuts, roast and greens, rounded off with caramel custard. Modest fare, but eating together made it sumptuous. Those were the days when coming home from the self-reflexive News Room was a relief.

Percival Simpson read news with a cut-glass accent and bellicose stare. His voice seemed to emerge from a miniature recorder lodged in his larynx. Other newsreaders and producers were polite in a structured sort of way; they smiled without engaging their eyes. They laughed among themselves, their voices dipping to a murmur as soon as Terry walked into the room. They checked their appearance in each others' approving eyes.

Dispensing with words, they made it clear entry into their sphere was determined by apostolic succession. What kept them standing in buffeting winds of change was a deep insularity, the sort of blindness that had impelled the likes of Anthony Eden to play Bulldog Drummond during the Suez crisis.

Terry felt like a war-hardened veteran returned to university to finish his degree. He wanted to fit in but on his own terms. He had rubbed shoulders with real men huddled by gutted walls under collapsed roofs from where the empire had padded away like an old caparisoned elephant, people with grit picking themselves up to fashion a tentative half-world in which to rebuild their lives with dignity.

The only exception among the Olympians was Helen Cavendish, the main presenter of 6 o'clock news who beamed absentmindedly at Terry and often stopped by his desk before going on air to check how to pronounce unfamiliar foreign names. She had been born to a doting Raj couple in Calcutta during the War and had fond childhood memories of ice-cream parties at Firpo's before being sent to school in England. She was a big girl, with a bold Twenties bob-cut, who wooed the camera by squinching her hazel eyes into a half-smile during pauses or canting her head to let auburn bangs layered on both sides frame her full round face.

Percival stared at the camera like a stuffed tiger-head; coming from his mouth Qatar sounded like 'Cutter' and 'Chilé as 'Chili.' He would pause at the door expecting a chorus of good mornings and was miffed when heads remained lowered on pounding typewriters. He had tried to make Terry feel like an interloper at their first meeting.

"Just off the train from Huddersfield are we?"

"Not quite, 'we' have been potty training the natives in the colonies."

Simpson's smooth countenance blanched as if hit by a rotten egg. Banter he could understand, an eye for an eye had not been part of his upbringing.

One day Terry overheard him being deliberately rude to John Shimmin the cameraman.

"I thought you Cornish Pirates had a natural bent for numbers and went into banking or the stock exchange."

John's accent had a slight lilt but he was something of a perfectionist; he wanted newsreaders to keep their faces turned to the camera till the final fade out. He was too busy rolling his equipment off to the storeroom and didn't retaliate but Terry said, "Don't you worry, lad, that geezer gets off two stops after Barking."

Among researchers and technical staff there was an endearing camaraderie and generally everyone was ready to show the ropes to a newcomer. Blokes like Percival never had to dirty their manicured hands in collieries; their mums were probably presented at court and didn't have to warm the beds of drunken lodgers to make both ends meet.

On weekends in Salford, laid-off men in overalls wandered listlessly up and down the streets with spanners sticking out of their pockets or squatted on their doorsteps with sullen unshaven faces when one by one manufacturing units pulled down their shutters in the Sixties till only one was left standing. For the price of a hot meal their daughters went out with anyone with ready cash.

Even so Terry was a little ashamed of himself; breaking a butterfly upon a wheel was not his preferred choice when dealing with cussedness in colleagues. Underneath his smart MGS blazer his dormant working-class genes could suddenly flare up at the slightest hint of a snub. Simpson, who had probably never heard an explosive sound beyond the popping of a Dom Pérignon in a well-appointed drawing room, equated knowledge of the world with accent.

The presenter spoke condescendingly about India in a Daily Mailish tone; the political aspirations of the Irish were a personal affront to him. He had no doubt the Raj had been the best thing to have happened to the colonies and the natives who didn't appreciate it were ungrateful upstarts.

Returning to the semi-bucolic Wimbledon was a relief after a day spent in the company of these walking forts of arrogance, but Juno had no inkling of what Terry had to endure, her work at the Slade had opened up a new vein of creativity. She had never had much training in Life Class and was learning to trace the human form under the legendary Hank Stallybrass, who always had time to comment on her sketches.

Juno had presented Terry a watercolor of *One-legged herons in Lake Umeed*, a sequence of washes executed with individual brush strokes. The sky was bright and sunny at the time she made the sketch, yet in the finished work it was light blue and the herons had darkened dramatically.

Terry could see how delicate the color transition was from light to dark, lending the five contemplative herons a feathery texture. But her precocious talent would remain unfledged for lack of application.

Once Terry found himself in Bloomsbury during lunch break, students spilled out on to Gower Street and hurried towards Euston Road. The Slade was eerily quiet, the walls on either side of the corridor were crowded with plaster forms staring straight ahead. Terry felt like an intruder even though no one paid the slightest attention to him. A door slammed and a pair of high-heels went tick-tocking up the stairs. It was like a moment in Alfred Hitchcock when a strangled form is laid gently down the floor by a pair of black gloves.

Terry's gregarious Mam couldn't be in the same room with anyone without speaking.

"Oo, we had some jolly times in Oldham when I was a little girl. My old man was only a churchwarden but he was no skinflint. Breakfast wasn't just wet nellies but Mary & Elizabeth Sardines, and Dundee Marmalade. Tea, mind you, had to be Jackson's of Piccadilly."

Mam was put out by her daughter-in-law's studied silence. She had that slightly bewildered look of a child awakened from sleep.

At first she made difficult adjustments, treated Juno like a Wedgwood set too posh for her routine brew. But who better than a daughter-in-law to share long pent-up stories tracing her lad's journey from the two-up-and-two-down terraces to the BBC in London. She presumed in Juno a matching eagerness to be briefed about her husband's childhood escapades.

Her brother Tom comes in. The pair sits by the fire whispering, he gives her a hug before leaving. Afterwards Mam who's pregnant with Terry opens her husband's crumpled letter, reads it and carefully puts it back in the Bible.

That evening, the lodger Mr Dennis Venables given to declaiming 'Once more unto the breach dear friends, once more; Or close the wall up with our English dead!'

Stops halfway up the stairs and announces drunkenly, "The 2nd Royals with the whole bloody lot surrendered Singapore to Hirohito's army."

His words touch a raw nerve, Mam comes out breathing fire.

"You are a fine one to talk about our lads out there fightin' in forrin lands, you dirty skiver, when all you do is sit on your backside whingin' all afternoon and roll round to the local ever' evenin. Eeh, what a place the world is.'"

The lodger is so taken aback by the fusillade from Mam's fiery tongue that he clambers up to his room with as much speed as his wobbly legs can muster

But she couldn't justify the strong words hurled at the lodger. The War ends without her bloke limping back into her arms with a bandaged head as in Movietone News.

She meets every man from his outfit on the incoming trains at Manchester Central. No one can tell her where her Johnny has disappeared to. Some say the tough life in the POW camp drove him bonkers. The hospital ship bringing back wounded troops from the East had docked at Marseilles. Some had seen Johnny going down the gangplank at Port Said in the company of the Eurasian nurse who had befriended him on board.

One day Mam takes three-year-old Terry to the dyestuff factory. Huge vats of liquid aniline stand in a row. Holding little Terry aloft her friend Elsie asks Mam what color she wants her first-born to be. Mam shrieks, snatches him from Elsie.

The staircase sagged over Terry's tiny cot in the living room. On cold winter nights it creaked as Mam tiptoed up to the Lodger's room. Whispers and giggles, rhythmic chug and squeak of the fourposter and she pussy-footed down gathering her candlewick nightgown. Terry pretended to be sound asleep, but hot tears rolled down his cheeks; she stopped, leaned over to wipe his face with a napkin, hugged him before tucking the blanket in. Terry kept his face averted.

Next day when Terry came home with a bloody nose she bathed his face with warm water and brought him a cup of hot chocolate and biscuit. No questions asked. She knew the older boys ruffled her son's sandy hair and shouted 'eh Terry lad when's your Dad comin' home then? Your real Dad.'

For a fortnight the staircase didn't creak at night.

Old Venables had a dog-eared copy of the complete works of Shakespeare in flaking green buckram covers with engravings printed on marbled end papers and the novels of Dickens with sketches by Cruikshank and Phiz from which, perched on his desk by the window, he read aloud, stopping to drag on his pipe, spraying saliva all over little Terry's upturned face. When he got to his favorite bits, Venables's eyes dilated over the sputtering bowl; then strange powerful words quavering with passion hit the lad's ears as he hunched below the desk in that smoke-filled room. At eleven, no stranger to want and squalor, Terry arrived at Manchester Grammar with an ear already trained to catch the faintest tremors in the depths of the Bard's verse.

Mam was determined to send him to university just like Mrs Himmelman's Saul with his head always in a fat book even when minding the bakery in her absence. Working barefoot on the slippery floors of the beam, bleaching plant till well into her forties, Mam never bought a loaf of Mother's Pride on tick, coaxed rent from the lodger on Fridays before he squandered it at the local, and worked as Shabbat Goy for Jewish neighbors on Saturdays. With a little charring on the side, she paid on the nail for butter and sugar, baked mince pies after church on Sunday to be sold at Mrs Himmelman's, scrimped and saved enough to pay Mr Smithers to tutor her son in Maths, History and English. The lad won a Direct Grant from the Local Authority and secured a seat at MGS.

"That's Manchester Grammar School for you," Mam says to the wall.

Terry comes in at the end of her monologue. His wife is nowhere to be seen. He half carries Mam to bed and waits for Juno. She returns with something wrapped in a steamy greasy newspaper.

"Look,' she says "I got you some fish and chips from the shop round the corner."

✳✳✳✳ ✳✳✳✳

(ii)

Barricaded in her bungalow Gisela lies awake, listening. No more the low rumble of cars coming up the driveway through rows of giant banyans, only the sputter and scrunch of an auto-rickshaw at the threshold.

The lost world of parents leaks into our memory. Their backward glance gives us an extra pair of eyes; we see ourselves dozing under tartan blankets; sound of a gently rocking fiacre clip-clopping down cobbled lanes to the Wurstelprate, in a swaddling cloth, a plaited loaf with branded crust leans in the hamper.

Papili's circle of friends had singing bones passed from one generation to the next, each of them a link that led back to that past when the Viennese moment was born, Lipizzaners streaming from the Riding School. Bred to move with grace from cradle to grave, Papili could pick a thoroughbred townmate at a glance from a crowd of gawking tourists strolling down the Graben.

Papili at the piano — eyes closed — evening shadows lured in by the second movement of Beethoven's Pathetique. No one moved when his eyes had that elusive 'elsewhere' look.

Papili was a romantic at heart, unlike my pragmatic Cyrus, born halfway across the world. Both men in my life believed gentility was inherited, could not be acquired no matter how much money you had.

'The Paris of India,' Cy called his Umeednagar. "It's the spirit of the place that counts," he said surveying the domes and spires from the balcony. His hometown was off-limits to caveats.

When the midnight Mail deposited Gisela at its ivy-covered ochre and cream station all those years back, she could feel her fidgety heart settle down to a measured beat. Umeed had been just what the doctor ordered for this refugee from a storybook town that loved horses.

The new Umeed is refracted through the old. Bandstands, museums and palaces linger in the fading rhapsodies of pensioners huddled together on a lonely park bench, their thin old voices barely rising over the roar of traffic behind them.

A backfiring auto can release the catch on the casement, tipping you into past nightmares, motorbikes arrogantly revved up by men in black, a crumpled bearded figure in a heap, the crash and tinkle of breaking crystal on the Ring.

She must have dozed off just before dawn. Someone else seems to be in the house. Subhadra and Bahadur miss the creaky top step by habit. Her heart begins to race. Liebling Sissi must have arrived during the night and tiptoed up. Juno could never be so light-footed, incapable of moving from here to there without turning heads.

****

The Ormolu clock ticks companionably. A gift from Perrin, my august mother-in-law.

How should I present her? Stately home elegance grafted on to Parsi merchant-prince life-style.

"Call me Perrin, all my friends do," after the first welcoming peck on each cheek. Holding me with both hands like a proud owner of a Renaissance masterpiece, she said, "We must forget all this nonsense about son's wife always wrong, mother always right. Never stopped wanting a little girl of my own after Cy was born, but Khodayji said, that's it, no more trade in babies, store closed. Now here you are. How many women can say, 'my daughter is a London-trained doctor?' We must present a common front against all men, my Cy not excluded. Dear boy, heart of gold but in there somewhere still a bit of a Bawaji. Been abroad far too long for me to do anything about it. Managing Jimmy his Dad, left me quite packed-up, but it was all worth it. He was Dewan you know, prime minister of Umeed, but no Government sponsored project for women's education or a new art and craft center was too large or for my input. Unofficially of course. We didn't want tongues wagging, you understand, especially at the Club.

"It's Perrin Sorabji who runs the show old boy, she the de facto Dewan' and that sort of balderdash."

Any doubts I might have had about my mother-in-law being 'the power behind the throne' so to speak, were laid to rest when War broke out in Europe and the Resident, Mr Talbot, imposed travel restrictions on non-British foreigners living in the State of Umeednagar. If his writ had prevailed I would have been bundled off along with Sister Schultz of the Convent of Jesus and Mary to the Internment Camp in Madras. But Mr Duckworth, who held the Sorabjis in high esteem, intervened.

Terry is a throw-back to the time when the Empire drew from its top drawer men like old Mr Duckworth; lonely, scholarly Englishmen who served as tutors to under-age princelings and stayed on to steer them through the muddy waters of imperial diplomacy, long after their charges came of age.

Deep-set hazel eyes, tiny tapering nose in a florid face, fringed with wispy graying sideburns, John Stewart Duckworth came straight out of Dickens via Cambridge in 1875 as a young man of twenty-four to tutor the twelve-year-old crown prince. A quick alert smile diffusing a wistful gaze when meeting you on some state occasion, his sort were firmly committed to justice and fair-play, unlike your typical Residency sahib in a white tropical suit, sweaty head stuck in a sola topi, or regimental 'koi hai' in khaki shorts, swagger stick and gimlet eye, commands dropping from mouth like spent cartridges.

In London my life with Cy had been frugal but relaxed, faces of colleagues and patients at Hammersmith Hospital wreathed in smiles as soon as they saw us in the morning. As an intern I was run off my feet but friends and strangers alike corrected my occasional idiomatic lapses apologetically.

In Umeed I found myself suddenly metamorphosed from the most sought-after dinner guest to 'enemy alien' as soon as War broke out in Europe. German citizens were immediately put under house arrest and marked for transport to internment camps. The word 'transport' had not yet begun to reek of packed cattle cars.

My Jewish-Austrian lineage did not cut any ice with Mr Talbot who was incapable of seeing beyond his aquiline nose. Mrs Talbot was a constant source of embarrassment to the Old Her Highness who soon after she came to Umeed as a young bride was sent to Switzerland to attend a finishing school on Lake Lucerne and spoke fluent German and French.

I was invited to the Palace for every state dinner to the chagrin of the Burra Mem. Her Highness quietly observed,

"Mrs Talbot would make a fine housekeeper for some burgher in Dorset."

Perrin had an album full of photographs of Sir Jamshet being honored by the Viceroy. She selected two from the collection and sent them to Delhi with a covering letter which simply said, "Shall a daughter-in-law of Sir Jamshet be subjected to the indignity of imprisonment on a mere technicality? I request Your Excellency to halt the proceedings for her house arrest since as my son's wife she is automatically domiciled in the State of Umeednagar."

Four months after arriving in Umeed, I was still something of a curiosity, being fussed over by servants at home and Cy's friends and royal patrons who threw lavish parties in my honor in their moonlit gardens. Anointed as the new mistress of the household by my own mother-in-law, I was still finding my feet, one ear cocked to the wireless, hoping against hope that somehow Papili and Mutti would be able to cross over the Tyrol to Italy with Rudi. But with Hitler in Poland the trickle of news coming out of Europe dried up.

Umeed had a leafiness stretching all the way from the palace gardens to its outskirts. At the start of the hot weather Perrin packed her bags and headed for Matheran where she owned a villa complete with a Goan cook, his wife and three children who ran errands for her.

****

(iii)

Next morning Juno and Terry leave for London. Mam stands in the doorway, a lonely stooped figure shivering in her old candlewick dressing gown. Her nocturnal visits to the room upstairs have faded from her memory. Terry gives her a V sign; it brings a wan toothless smile. The train pulls swiftly out of Piccadilly Station, hurtles past a blur of terrace houses, a red and blue neon sign still flickering over an off-license, a figure wrapped against the cold at a news agent's, flash of an Odeon marquee, then the sun breaks through the clouds and spills all over Cheadle Hulme.

Back then every morning Terry put on his school uniform freshly pressed by Mam, walked the mile and a half to Piccadilly and caught Bus No 41 to MGS in Fallowfield. On his way he could see behind The Whitworth Gallery large stretches of bombed out Moss Side earmarked for demolition. A solitary spire rose sheer above houses with broken windows and tipsy walls waiting for the wrecking ball.

Once on a bus to Old Trafford he saw a church set ablaze in the distance. Someone on the bus said a famous director from London was shooting a documentary about Manchester rising from its ashes.

Terry grew up thinking cities all over the world looked like blocks of Swiss cheese, with gaping holes. Well into his cub-reporting days for the *Evening News* in London there were large sections of Manchester sealed off for demolition. These empty spaces deepened the sense of dereliction with harsh columns of light crashing through gaping skylights of disused warehouses.

As the train picks up speed, working women in dun-colored coats hurrying down the steps of gritstone houses to catch double-deckers are soon eclipsed by a storm of defunct industrial chimney shafts. At least that hasn't changed much. Legs pulled in, head resting on one arm Juno dozes by the window like a young girl going home from her boarding school. She's had enough of narrow rain-swept streets and sluggish traffic under a gray louring sky.

The girls Terry had known in his childhood and youth had heavy bosoms and giggled fit to die.

Every Christmas he used to earn a few quid clocking eight hours a day at the main Post Office in the City Center just off Piccadilly Bus Station. Sorting out letters and greeting cards next to him was this large bucktoothed lass Maggie. Good old Maggie, built like a brick shithouse and dressed in tweeds she would have made a smashing Widow Twanky. They stood side by side in front of pigeonholes, reading names of cities and chucking the envelopes into relevant boxes; and it was Inverness that did it.

While Terry puzzled over unfamiliar place names, Maggie would go, Nottingham, Bradford, Glasgow, Aberdeen and Inverness. Inverness brought her to Terry but Glamorgan tilted him towards her. She would come up, wiggling her bosom, smelling of bangers and mash. She had adopted him right from the start, and they'd ended up eating Christmas pudding in her bed on New Year's Eve. Hair gathered in a ponytail, rolls of fat hanging loose, it was Leda and the scrawny Swan.

The summer before the start of Michaelmas Term at Goldsmiths in London, Terry did a two-month stint at Mam's beam-bleaching plant. When the lads on his team sang 'Four n' twenty Virgins came down from Inverness,' he used to get frightfully nostalgic for Big Mag.

Among them were two Nigerians, Patrick, an Igbo, and a Yoruba called Abdel. Long used to living next door to immigrants from Eastern Europe, working-class Salford was welcoming of the few African students to whom the doors of the Polytechnic had been opened.

While their folks at home were slashing each other's throats, these two, Ickle meets Pickle, were always full of carnival squawks. The old jovial foreman having retired, a man called Pete Monkhouse was put in charge. Monkey, as he soon came to be known, obviously thought a varsity degree was something you picked up after three years of larking about. With a menacing stride he would suddenly appear at the entrance to the bogs to flush out the Nigerians, who dawdled away hot afternoons exchanging tribal insults.

"Took yer time didn't you?" Monkey would growl as the lads tumbled out, zipping up their flies. "Why must you both go to the loo at the same time?"

"Look, Mr Monkhouse, Sir," Patrick would grin assuming a serious ethnic tone. "Abdel here and I, we be Nigerians, right? Back home in the bush we all get the call of nature at the same time and it is a sacrilege to hold up bowels."

Terry's early brush with proletarian action came when the Nigerians organized a strike at the plant because student workers were not paid full wages although they worked just as hard as the regulars, preparing the bleaching powder, tightening the clamping arms on the warp beams, wheeling up the cross-wound cones, checking the pressure gauges and sweating it out at rows of winches, jiggers and banks.

The following day as Patrick stepped out of the Manager's office, scratched his nose to signal failure of negotiations, and began belting out *Mathew & Son*, no one, except Terry and two girls from the screen-printing section came out chanting *"We've been working all day, all day, all day."*

The others had caved in. There was a dry cough or two, a buzz went around, then died and gormlessly the lads, including Abdel, picked up the tools and cranked the machines into action. While Patrick was talking to the manager, a middle-aged bloke with a silky James Mason voice, Monkey had gone around warning the strikers they'd be let go because there were enough lads from the University waiting in the wings.

"Look man," said Abdel to the crestfallen Patrick, "there wasn't much choice. It was either back to work or back home without a degree. You understand."

Then in the early Seventies, in one frenzied act of spring-cleaning the City of Manchester swabbed off centuries-old layers of soot from public buildings, cathedrals and railway stations. Piccadilly Plaza lay heaving gently, all spruced up and green and the great Cathedral in Deansgate lost its granddad-in-night-cap geniality. With the soot went the war-induced togetherness, genial dart-board camaraderie in pubs and old Music Hall numbers at the piano.

At Goldsmiths Terry had been too busy staying abreast of his class to go snogging in the bushes. One sunny day, leaving his digs in Holborn he walked down to Fleet Street and was astonished by the courteous manner of the doorman who opened the big front door to let him into the offices of the *Evening News*. The whole building roiled with copytakers and subs rushing in and out of the wire-room amidst clacking of machinery. Men in overalls, faces shielded by visors, doubled up on trays sorting typefaces with sooty fingers. Terry's Mancunian blazer (the only one he owned) probably led the doorman to mistake him for a toff come to see the chief sub-editor.

Going down the stairs to the presses in the basement Terry ran into Aiden Whitcomb who had lost a toiling cub to Australian immigration and was looking for a replacement. Next morning five cubs including a girl were let loose on an unsuspecting London. They hung around the Old Bailey or the Bow Street Magistrate's Court, mostly to pick up gossip from office boys dawdling outside chambers. They spiced up hearsay giving it life and color, albeit with some crucial dots missing.

Despite vestiges of a Lanks accent in Terry's speech Whitcomb thought he was better educated than the rest. While his fellow cubs continued to scour the city, tailing and door-stepping 'kiss and tell' types, Terry found himself covering Bertrand Russell's anti-nuke rallies in Trafalgar Square and making educated guesses for the reason of Sylvia Plath's suicide or the murder of Joe Orton by his live-in partner.

He managed to stand up at least one story every day, but his passage from cub to scribe was more by fluke than design.

Aiden was waiting to be hailed as the new Graham Greene and his beat covered Covent Garden, the Royal Albert Hall, the Wigmore Hall and Shaftsbury Avenue. Then one day in June when Terry was busy swotting for his finals, Aiden was found dead in his bedroom, fully dressed, hanging from the ceiling; the crumpled suicide note in his breast pocket was a line from Plath with a burlesque twist.

'Dying is an art like everything else; give three cheers and one cheer more for the hardy Captain of the Pinafore.'

In his desk drawer the police found a wad of rejection slips from publishers. On the latest Aiden had scribbled, 'Anger Mr Whitcomb, that's the ticket, dish out some anger and stick *Brideshead Revisited* where the monkey put the nuts.'

Autumn of 64 — election time, Harold Wilson, pipe dangling from mouth is headed for 10 Downing Street and Sir Alec Douglas Home back to his country estate. At the *Evening News* all hands are on deck, covering different London constituencies but there's no one to go to Echingham, lodged in the rolling downs of Sussex. Aiden is scheduled to interview Sir Simon Derramore early next morning.

The Deputy Editor clears his throat fidgeting with a paper knife.

Was Terry aware of any views Aiden might have had on whether Sir Simon should stand for election or not?

Terry had heard Aiden say, "Yes, I do believe you should take the plunge," before hanging up the phone.

"I think Aiden thought Sir Simon would make an excellent candidate."

"Splendid, I suggest you catch the first train from Charing Cross tomorrow morning. I'll telephone Lady Derramore we are sending you to interview Sir Simon. Come back and file a report for the evening edition."

Terry was taken aback. His hesitation prompted the Deputy Editor to a rallying cry, "Aiden said you showed promise. So off you go and get a comment or two from the old boy and we'll fill in the rest."

Sir Simon had an artistic side and was known locally as the Picasso of the Downs, probably because sketches of the herd on his estate resembled the decapitated cow in *Guernica*.

Lady Derramore, who was waiting in her vintage Silver Ghost at Robertsbridge, drove Terry directly to the atelier behind the manor where a small bald man with a 'seven dwarf' beard stood smiling at the entrance. He led Terry to a settee by the window.

"Tell me, Mr Dyson, can an artist make a good politician?" asked Sir Simon.

For a moment Terry's mind went blank, nervously he tugged at the school tie with the picture of the owl. 'Mustn't let the team down.' Luckily the MGS motto, '*Sapere Aude*,' came to his rescue.

"A true artist, if I may venture an opinion, would have a mind of his own and should make an honest politician."

"Well spoken young sir, now let's go in for lunch."

Sir Simon was dead set against decimalization, called it "invasion more pernicious than the Spanish Armada."

In the warm glow of the huge Tudor fireplace in the main hall of the Castle, with a glass of brandy in hand, Terry drafted his report and was back in London in time for the evening edition.

Within a couple of years of his visit to Sir Simon's castle, Terry found himself in the imploded back alleys of Beirut as assistant to Mike Bartlett, who was making a documentary for the BBC about the plight of Palestinian refugees. In the post-war period, competition for overseas assignments was not exactly fierce. Despite frequent nods to the 'spirit of Dunkirk' Jimmy was loath to 'pack up his old kit-bag and say good bye to his little room again.'

Mike had lost an eye in the jungles of Vietnam and left war reporting to scribes who could think on their feet and react to sudden danger with dispatch. Speaking from the relative safety of a hotel lobby Mike would say, "The annals are filled with stories of courageous reporters getting caught in a cross-fire and perishing in some god-forsaken alley in a city under siege. I am second to none in my admiration for those stout hearts who reported the Battle of Britain from rooftops but as a teenager cooped up every night in a damp air-raid shelter I can stuff that for a game of soldiers."

Terry's main assignment was to transform the chaotic events of the day into graspable copy. For a quarter pound of baklava Terry could ferret out valuable information about which parts of Beirut were likely to be infested with snipers and stay out of range of ongoing mayhem. In a country like Lebanon, the state being weak and two superpowers locked in a proxy war, global tensions could suddenly transform yesterday's happy families into cowering refugees of today, pangs of deprivation running like an interminable sore across faces young and old. It was their hauntings Terry clicked out on his keyboard.

Mike had to rush back to London when he received news that his wife had been seriously injured in a freak accident on M1.

In the Christian parts of Beirut Terry fell in with a group of whey-faced American college dropouts. Most of them were barely out of their teens with a few veterans, their forearms riddled with needle marks. They had to abandon the overland Hippie Trail through Pakistan now considered too dangerous while its Eastern wing was preparing to cut loose. They took a train to Basra and traveled steerage to Bombay on a British owned tub plying between the Persian Gulf and Cochin. Terry shared with them grub, beedis and sometimes an erudite girl called Rita-May from Phoenix, Arizona, who read Hesse, quoted Nietzsche and slipped into Terry's bed on a windless night. As if to atone for it she was up early in the morning, chanted Buddhist hymns, banging cymbals no bigger than a florin while her boy-friend accompanied her on a harmonium the size of a piggy-bank.

While the ship dawdled through the Gulf, stopping to make brief calls at Muscat and Karachi, Terry gathered that the next big conflagration was to occur in the Bay of Bengal with Islamabad mobilizing a well-fed army for a massive ravagement of what was then East Pakistan. At Bombay Terry parted company with the flower children and booked himself a sleeper birth, third class, to Calcutta.

Those days one could live on a quid a day in Calcutta, paying only ten rupees a night for a bed in a tourist hotel on the banks of the Hoogli. With war clouds gathering overhead Terry began sending pitches to the editors of the *Guardian* and the *New Statesman* about his willingness to undertake on-the-spot reporting from Dhaka. At that stage the bloodletting had not yet begun and the West had to wait for another two months to comprehend the enormity of suffering that awaited the hapless population in the Ganges Delta. During his apprenticeship in Beirut Terry had learned to decipher the diacritical marks of severed limbs extruding from the interlaced scrawl of bodies.

After waiting for over a month to hear from the editors he airmailed a copy from Dhaka to the *Sunday Mirror* without any expectation of payment when Pakistan started air-lifting regiment after Punjabi regiment to major cities in their Eastern territory to wipe out local militias engaged in deadly guerrilla operations. Then in a flash, with the US Seventh Fleet steaming towards the Bay of Bengal to assist a NATO ally, Nixon's perfidy stood exposed. Imagine Terry's thrill when he got a six-month contract from the *Sunday Mirror* accompanied by a check for 800 pounds.

In London he discovered that even though the Public School feeder line from which new recruits were drawn by the BBC had been ruptured, its iconic face during a news broadcast invariably belonged to someone who'd barely managed to scrape through Oxbridge with a 'Thora', spoke with a posh accent and blithely accepted the official interpretation of events without questioning. At Goldsmiths it was taken as read that all governments routinely swept uncomfortable truths under the carpet in the name of national security.

"A reporter must be like an archaeologist," Mike Bartlett used to say, "a nosy parker unashamed of looking up a skirt when necessary. Where your academic historian harps on hard facts like Gradgrind and pours over inscriptions on stone, a good reporter sifting through a dig reaches deep into the wastebasket of culture. More often than not he'll find what was discarded was more significant than the script on the tablet. But then even Gradgrind couldn't get away from metaphor, 'Plant nothing else and root out everything else.' "

(iv)

Auschwitz and Belsen were still far-off, confusing echoes in India when the British suddenly packed up and left for home in August 1947. Hauling corpses of Hindu and Muslim passengers, blood-spattered trains groaned into stations across the new boundary dividing India and Pakistan. Men were plucked for slaughter from convoys of refugees trudging along the countryside on foot, children impaled, mothers raped in front of their dazed families. In a land bloated with blood, horrors reverberating across Europe fell on deaf ears.

The Anglo-Indians of the railways and the small Parsi community of Umeed felt orphaned and Perrin went into mourning when the British left. She sat for hours on the veranda waiting to catch the sound of feet marching on the parade ground. She felt widowed for the second time in her life. Cy said she had not looked so distraught at the passing of his father back in 1933.

The Parsis had evolved from business partners of the British to their surrogates, retaining one foot in the Fire Temple while tapping away Sunday evenings with the other at the park where the regimental bagpipes played 'On the bonnie, bonnie banks o' Loch Lomond'.

Perrin had spent her childhood in the cantonment township of Mhow in central India where the piquant Parsi dialect was heard only when relatives from Bombay came down for holidays. What little Perrin had picked up there had got rusty during her time in the rarefied world of viceregal Simla.

"When she married Dad," Cy said, "two of the most Anglophile Parsi families confluenced in a torrent of Englishness, flushing out vestigial traces of our native tongue."

Perrin's ancestors, the Wakharias, had struck an alliance with the early British settlers in India. Trust Perrin to make it spicier with a twist of lime.

One day she said to me, "Look, your people the Jews and we Parsis have enterprise in our blood. You know how our Wakharia ancestor laid the foundation of his business? Kekobad Wakharia saw that the British troops came down with severe dysentery after every up-country battle. Why he asked himself? He made a shrewd guess that the regimental bhisti's oily waterbag with one tiny spout at the lower end meant that the goatskin interior remained unscrubbed. Well, the next thing you know Kekobad invested what seemed to be a fortune in a Portable Water Purification Machine and trundled after the battalions on the march. Before you could say Jack Robinson he'd made the entire progeny of Gunga Din obsolete between Jhansi and Neemach."

"That must have been extremely strenuous work, I mean for one not used to hard labor," I said with growing admiration for Perrin's venturesome forbear.

"It most certainly was. But we Parsis are a sturdy lot, not like the potbellied sethias in the bazaar. Kekobad's son Dinshawji Wakharia was even more resourceful. When the East India Company turned rulers from traders, he saw destiny smiling in pints of beer and barrels of whiskey imported from England for parched troops in Mhow. During the Sepoy Mutiny his son Behramji, who had fled with all his savings to the safety of Deolali, began bidding for labor contracts for the new railway network in the Bombay Presidency stretching from Karachi to Dharwad in the South West. He retired to Mhow after making millions and built Villa Rossette on Simrole Road in Mhow where I was born."

By now my mother-in-law and I were firmly on first name terms.

"Perrin dear, I am curious to know, was it love at first sight between Cy's father and you. Going by your only son's track record I would say it must have taken all your womanly wiles to secure his attention if Sir Jamshet was anything like Cy."

Oddly Perrin seemed to be at a loss for words for a few seconds. Then she went to her dresser and picked up the Ormolu clock with that exquisite bronze Mars and Venus wedding allegory on top.

"Here," she said, "I would like you to have this, it was a present from Jimmy on our engagement. Love came later in our life, after Cy was born, to be exact. Our first meeting was hosted by my father's business partner, Mr Busby, at his villa in Clifton, the magnificent seafront of Karachi. You might say ours was what they call a dynastic alliance but we both had a choice to either reject or accept each other."

By contrast Cy's family seemed to have been a relatively pragmatic lot.

"The Sorabjis had been astute 'vakils' ", said Perrin, "successfully defending profligate maharajas and nabobs in Katiawar and Rajputana who had been put out to pasture by the Viceroy for misrule or by settling disputes out of court between various competing pretenders of doubtful patrimony, whose claims to their — how shall I put it- 'oversexed' progenitors' thrones couldn't be easily proved. You may well ask why? Well my dear, as far as I can tell those days the difference between concubine and queen was still a matter of priestly rather than legal certification. Anyway, when the highest administrative post of Chief Dewan fell vacant in Umeednagar, what do you suppose the dowager Maharani did?" Perrin asked.

"I haven't a clue," I admitted. "You know how Cy is."

"I know, I know, he is too British," said my mother-in-law, "can't bear to talk about himself, let alone blow his own trumpet. But he must follow protocol. This is your family too, for goodness sake, you are not some boxwallah's bibi invited to a garden party. Well, to cut a long story short, the astute Maharani sent for Mr Duckworth. John was quite young then, barely twenty-six I think, brilliant scholar but also a very practical mind. I wasn't there to know what transpired during that meeting. But without batting an eyebrow the English tutor is supposed to have said, 'Your Highness there is only one man in the entire Bombay Presidency who is capable of shouldering such heavy responsibility. His name is Barrister Jamshet Sorabji, he resides in Karachi and is considered by his peers to be the finest legal mind of our time in the entire Presidency'."

Young Perrin and Jamshet set about renovating an old bungalow they bought from an impoverished nobleman. It was called Kunj in keeping with the Umeed tradition of naming houses after groves and gardens. The parched weedy ground canopied by hoary banyans had to be cleared all the way from the trellised porch to the ornate wrought-iron gate, lawns and flowerbeds laid and the wooden sentry box painted olive green. Within three months the Sorabjis were ready to welcome guests to their house warming party.

**** ****

Kunj was a delight to come back to after a grueling day cased up in the clinic.

Two Doric columns held up a triangular gable masking a tiled roof. Drawing closer you saw a rattan card-table and chairs on the left of the fan-shaped veranda and half a dozen wicker chairs on the right flanked by potted Jelly Bean, Laurentii and Sunflower plants. Soft-leafed creepers cascaded down the columns. An arched doorway with a stained glass fanlight led into the main hall spacious enough to play tennis in but for the furniture. Frosted flap doors opening into the adjacent dining-room and light filtering in through slats of blinds on tall French windows made gold trims on bone-china dartle in the semi-darkness between meals. A thickly carpeted staircase ascended gracefully from the back of the hall to the bedrooms.

The life-style of upper-crust Parsis in general eerily reflected English county culture in dress and manner, their Jerusalem was by the Thames, not on the Straits of Hormuz.

They made themselves relevant to the British by putting on display an unthreatening athleticism and masculinity but primarily by accumulating goodwill as honest and upright brokers. According to Perrin only a handful of non-Parsis of princely background and officer-class Anglo-Indians were thought to have achieved similar apotheosis. The priv-ileged Parsis served as a buffer between British and Indian high society, their children rarely allowed to visit classmates in their wooden-grilled mix-breed Eurasian homes in the railway colonies.

Parsis like the Wakharias salvaged ancient artifacts from derelict sanctuar-ies and re-enshrined them in museums, winnowed libraries from seminaries and expelled quacks from hospitals.

When Western classical music entered the Parsi ear, it found its way straight to the heartstrings.

"Once the Vicereine herself commended my performance as Yum Yum at the Gaiety," Perrin said.

By the time of Gandhi's long Salt March, one of Perrin's cousins, a disciple of the great man, straddled culture and politics with a finesse that drew high praise from both sides locked in the conflict.

Perrin's voice trilled with family pride.

"I still remember that evening at the Opera House in Bombay where my cousin Hoshang Wakharia sat in a pool of light at the keyboard during the per-formance of the *Well-tempered Clavier.* At the end when he rose from the stool, there was utter silence, the audience sat mesmerized unable to move, then someone started clapping and there was an explosion of applause, the loudest among those cheering were two European couples. But funnily, our Hoshang was also a staunch Gandhiite and apparently spent months at the Ashram in Ahmadabad spinning cotton, scrubbing the kitchen floor and doing heaven knows what other ghastly things disciples had to do. But at a cotton-spinning competition he beat his fellow disciples by notching up yards and yards of patriotic yarn on that absurd wheel."

As a girl Perrin had traveled frequently and extensively in Europe spending months at a time shopping in London and Paris.

Fishing-fleeters preening in dresses that seemed to be made of curtain material were stunned when the Sorabji couple entered the Club on Empire Day for the Resident's Ball.

"Some of my gowns refitted by our clever darzi for my expanding figure (I was preggers with Cy) still had the elegance of Parisian haute couture beyond the reach of the fleeters who had to make do with what was on offer at White-way Laidlaw Department stores in Bombay and Calcutta. And would you believe it, once I saw Nijinsky dance with Pavlova at Covent Garden."

Perrin could leave the haughtiest colonel's lady speechless by naming the entire cast in the latest D'Oyly Carte at the Savoy. The Dewan and his lady spent their summers in London vacationing with the Umeeds.

"Their Highnesses loved horses and naturally Jimmy and I went with them to the races."

No wonder Perrin was well up on the most fetching hat and gown seen that year at Ascot.

But Perrin was also openly skeptical about Indians taking charge of the Government in Delhi.

She felt vindicated when her prophecy came true and stories of savagery and massacre in the north with thousands of Hindus and Muslims fleeing towards the newly-marked borders began to appear in print and on air.

'Milksops and poltroons who'd never taken an aim at clay pigeons were put in charge by Lord Mountbatten. He should have known they simply didn't have the ability to govern. Taking out processions and shouting slogans was their thing. The Mahatma would begin a fast at the drop of a hat. He must have thought he could bring in real 'bandobast' if he stopped downing his daily pint of goat's milk and sat on a mat twiddling his thumbs."

**** ****

(v)

As Dewan of a princely Indian state with a venerable cultural tradition and artistic heritage of its own, Sir Jamshet often found his wife's highfalutin' Englishness embarrassing. Fearing that his light-skinned lad at Clifton College might turn out to be more British than the British, he decided to do something about it. One summer evening towards the end of his vacation in India, Cy found an article left on his pillow about Dadabhai Naoroji's victory in the British Parliamentary Election.

"His election to Parliament," young Cyrus read, "was assured when the Tory Prime Minister Lord Salisbury assailed Britishers for stooping so low as to vote for a 'black man'. Incidentally Naorojee's skin was fairer than that of his rival. The only thing was he was Indian, being a Parsi of Bombay."

The racial slur tipped Cy's memory to the time when his father had returned from the Palace fuming after an argument over the drain on the State Treasury for hosting the Viceroy's visit.

"I can understand," he said to his secretary who'd brought in his red bag with official documents to peruse at night, "that His Highness is anxious to be seen as loyal to the Emperor as His Highness the Nizam, but egad, we can't compete with Hyderabad. Our territory is not even half their size; our total revenue is smaller by comparison and expenditure on public works projects bigger than that of any other princely state. We have opened libraries and civil hospitals even in the moffusil. That tiger hunt for Lord Chelmsford and his retinue of two hundred would leave us scraping the bottom of our Treasury. And I shudder to think what that necklace for the Vicereine is going to cost. We shall know when we get the bill from Zaveri Bazaar in Bombay."

The article on Naoroji unleashed a storm in Cy's mind and during his last week of vacation in Umeed, Perrin found her son sitting on the veranda and staring at the malis toiling in the garden.

By then Cy had come to think of England as his second home. The affection showered on him by his guardians Col and Mrs Jenkins and their two married daughters had more than made up for his homesickness. Tom Jenkins, who was his senior by six years, had been his cricket coach during summer holidays. Tom was medium-built with a mop of straw-colored hair; while teaching Cy how to lob the deadliest googly he would talk of plunging 'into the troubled Tiber' and being swept off to something larger in life than cricket. At Winchester, the mental effort required in mastering the ablative and genitive cases of Greek and Latin grammar had not blunted his voracious appetite for tales of self-sacrifice served up by the Classics. Brushing off unruly strands with his left hand, his right arm swinging like a scythe at harvest time, he would stride to the wicket with the grim determination of the vastly outnumbered hoplites about to take on the Persian hordes. The ball cut a zigzag path, the air humming with the words penned by Herodotus 2500 years before.

"Go, tell the Spartans, passer-by,

At their bidding here we lie."

Then in the manner befitting a hoplite he turned his back on Cambridge, became a foot soldier for Ramsey McDonald's Labor Party in Battersea on a teacher's modest income. At some point in the mid-Thirties the battle cries from distant Thermopylae began to blend eerily with bombing raids on Republican positions by Franco's troops. Tom took off with the volunteers to go and fight in the Spanish Civil War.

Cy had gone down as usual to spend the Christmas of '36 with his adopted family and walked into an unusually silent house. Coming down for dinner that evening he was greeted with laconic handshakes and hurried pecks on cheeks. It was when Mrs Jenkins asked everybody to join hands and pray for Tom's safe return from Spain that Cy knew his friend had enlisted without telling anybody. That was Tom's way of sparing the heartbreak over his departure. Later a brief note from Portsmouth brought news of Tom's death in the Pyrenees while helping a wounded comrade escape into France.

Mr and Mrs Jenkins had always treated Cy as one of their own yet he had never been held up to the strict standards of human perfection as Tom was. When he came to live with them, the Jenkinses were already in middle-age with their daughters married and Tom in the final year at Winchester. He lacked the blasé adventurism of the *Boy's Own Paper* and seemed more thoughtful and kind in the way he spoke to the polio-stricken son of Mrs Sturbridge their widowed neighbor, carrying him piggyback to the stream for a swim. Tom had always been expected to act like a 'proper man' by his parents, whose love for their son expressed itself in ways that seemed a bit exacting to Cy.

Tom's valor had created in Cy the urge to link his medical training to some larger purpose, to immerse in a distant struggle fraught with danger. While shopping in Bristol he had cheered regiments marching towards the rain-swept harbor singing *It's a Long Way to Tipperary.*

From the relatively safe environs of Clifton College where lessons conflated poetry and patriotism, War had seemed a great adventure and dying for England 'in some corner of a foreign field' as sweet as Harrogate Toffee.

Later during his Residency at Hammersmith Hospital he'd treated men over whom the Great War still hung like a pall. Stories of thousands of lives lost through miscalculations of quixotic generals, townships littered with embittered war widows and bereaved mothers echoed through the wards. Occasionally there were passing references to Indian Regiments who had fought to defend the Empire.

For the rest of his life Cy would look back to his years in England as the happiest in his life but after attending Sir Jamshet's funeral in 1933 when he returned to London to finish his final term, he was a changed man. Gone were the Savile Row suits, the gold cuff links, and the occasional flutter on horses.

Once dozing in his cubicle during a night shift he had a dream in which he saw a white Ancient Mariner beard materialize like ectoplasm from the glass cabinet, followed by a tall Parsi pugree and a figure in the likeness of Naoroji assembled itself before him like a perturbed spirit. The next week finding himself in the Charing Cross Road he walked down to Foyles and asked if they had any books written by Naoroji. After some rummaging among the shelves the assistant had returned empty-handed. With war clouds once more massing over the Channel, England took its dressing from someone in helmet and full body armor instead of a bookish Parsi savant from the colonies.

Already committed to opening a clinic in the old section of Umeed where his father had laid plans for a hospital, Cy grew a beard and spent the rest of his spare time in England boning up on tropical diseases.

**** ***

"This mirrors my soul," Juno said in a shivery voice. They were at the Tate in Millbank. Terry looked at *The Yacht Approaching the Coast* set in whorls of light by Turner.

"This is what I've been waiting for all my life." There were real tears in her eyes.

Terry became adept at humoring her when she got into a self-induced trance implying none but she had special inwardness with certain paintings. Like a muse on wings, hair streaming, she flew a step or two ahead, briefly pausing to reflect on a minuscule but incalculably significant brush-stroke that lifted the artwork out of the ordinary.

Her connoisseurial talent was deployed in turning the world inside out, rearranging it to suit her taste. This she achieved by pretending that life and art shared the same seams and interstices like two sides of a tapestry and it was left to the discerning to lay bare the details, biases, confusions and the ineffable shimmer registered by the artist's fancy.

It had something to do with the precarious doubleness of her background. The offspring of upper class Indo-Europeans were an oddity like the albino; they lacked the kinship network of Anglo-Indians who despite the stigma of miscegenation had a palpable group identity.

"Which suits me fine. I rather like my not belonging to any caste or community. There is too much of that sort of thing in India anyway."

Gisela had other relatives besides Gabby, her cousin in New York, but she never bothered to get in touch with them. It was as if her life before Umeed had been bleached out. Juno's knowledge of Vienna was limited to a few odd bits and pieces picked up from Sister Schultz.

"All those museums and palaces choked with art. God how I tried to make

Mumsy talk about them. I can understand her silence about her parents and how they suffered under the Nazis, but really what's that got to do with Klimt, Schiele and that absurdly colorful (no pun intended) Kokoschka. I mean that bit about him dancing at a party with the life-size dummy of Alma Mahler is a scream. All because she jilted him."

At the Convent everyone had a religion. Even her Grandma drove to the Agiyari with her aunt Armin when she came down from Bombay.

Neither parent went anywhere to pray. At school the Goan Catholic girls would gabble about the Feast of Fatima or St Xavier's Basilica in Panjim. The Anglo girls attended christenings or weddings at the Anglican chapel, Hindu and Muslim girls yapped about Ganesha and Tazia processions and brought her sweets during Diwali and Eid festivals; Juno had nothing to offer them but cake and ice-cream on her birthday.

When she was seven she discovered that her mother's parents had been Jews and her Dad was a Parsi. She was thrilled, she had not one but two religions. Jews had been part of the coastal landscape of India for centuries, living in lush remote villages and towns of Kerala and palm-thatched hamlets in and around Bombay. Their ancestors had landed on the Western Coast of India even before Jesus walked in Bethlehem. In the Sixties, they had begun to migrate to Israel by the planeloads for a better future but also because at long last it was there – after centuries of exile the lost Ark winched up and set down in the Holy Land.

Juno learned to sing *Hanukkah O Hanukkah* and began to plan a garden party on the Parsi festival of Papeti. But she never felt an emotional link either to Jews or Parsis.

There was no puja room at home and the only work of Indian art with any religious significance was that carved Krishna in the hall. Grandma Perrin had an old print of Caravaggio's *Supper at Emmaus* in her office overlooking the rose garden instead of a portrait of Prophet Zarathustra in long white flowing tunic and pugree as at her friend Pessy's home. The Caravaggio had belonged to some Residency widow whose belongings had been auctioned off after she'd died suddenly at a ripe old age. To Perrin the resurrected Christ seemed too well-fed after three days on the cross, only the roast chicken in the plate, grapes in the bowl and the small basket with apples almost teetering at the edge of the table passed muster with her.

One Diwali Juno prevailed upon Grandma Perrin to let her light clay lamps and fire crackers. Later she insisted the family celebrate Navroz, the Parsi New Year on August 20th of that year.

"Frankly, to this day, I don't understand the difference between Papeti and Navroz. All I remember is that Aunt Behroz sent caramelized vermicelli cooked with raisins and a lot of almond slivers. For lunch Subhadra made *pulav* under Grandma's supervision but an emergency at the clinic tied down Mumsy till midnight and that was that."

Having only Perrin to watch over her freed Juno from convention, made her self-reliant but left her nothing but her instincts to see her through a young girl's teenage dilemmas.

In India religious rituals and festivals are meant to siphon off tensions within the family. At Kunj they were received as visitors to be entertained at tea under a banyan in the garden. Juno did not have memories that glowed in the dark like tiny clay lamps at Diwali. Her heart was never set aflutter at the coming of the feast of Fatima, a pang never registered at the immersion of the red-and-gold Ganesha, her ears never tingled to a prayer wafting out of a minaret.

"I could never tell why we couldn't install Ganesha in our dining room. He looked so cute with his baby elephant smile and pot belly. And on Roxana's street, during Muharram there were Tazias green like pistachio-embedded Bombay halwa."

During torrid summer afternoons when Grandma Perrin was away in Matheran Juno ate lunch alone. Nothing in the house moved except the ceiling fan.

"Even as a child I felt that Daddy and Mumsy shared some great secret from which I was excluded. They wanted to spare me the horrors from Mumsy's past but how was I to know that? I agree there is no way of explaining Auschwitz to a small girl, but even when I was all grown-up was there any need for such secrecy?"

At the Slade she had met a young visiting student from the US called Gretchen Bloom whose grandparents had been gassed by the Nazis. Every Thanksgiving her best friend at school went to her Nana's in Maine. When

Gretchen asked her mother where her 'Nana' was, her mother got up and quietly handed her a paperback to read. It was the *Diary of Anne Frank*; Gretchen finished it at one sitting. Then her parents told her that all their elders left behind in Nazi-occupied territories had died in concentration camps like Anne Frank and her sister.

Gretchen's parents had treated her like a grown up and gradually over the next few years she had become aware of racism masquerading as science.

"I realize now that Mumsy wanted to shield me, but large tracts of her inner life remained unknown to me. I know parents often disappear into their rooms and children wonder what they do there. If I had a brother or a sister I would not have felt so lonely."

Occasionally there would be a letter bearing a foreign stamp waiting for Gisela on the tray in the hall. Once Juno steamed open an aerogram but it was in handwritten German. She had a hard time sealing it back.

"The gum left a big stain below the puckered flap."

Once when Perrin was away in Bombay Juno walked into her parents' bedroom. Gisela was crying, her head on Cy's shoulder. He put a finger to his lips and little Juno shuffled out, her nightgown trailing behind her.

Next morning when she got up and came down for breakfast, her parents had already left for the Clinic.

That evening Cy and Juno were alone at dinner.

"Mummy has received some bad news from Vienna," was all he said. "She will tell you when it's time for you to know. No questions now, there's a good girl."

In the evening when her mother returned from the clinic she went straight to her room.

"I wanted to go in and fling myself in her arms but Subhadra said Memsaab had a headache. Next day when I returned from school Mumsy was having a late lunch. Dad did all the talking plying me with a series of questions about school. I must have been around ten then but I was convinced the two of them were ganging up against me. It was like Buddha's parents trying to shield him from knowledge of pain; I was barred from Mumsy's past for so long that I was immunized against it. Dad was so protective of her that it was embarrassing."

Girls at school often said behind Juno's back, "She is not Indian. She doesn't have to marry the man chosen by her parents as we do."

"Which was true enough, with disastrous results. I got pregnant by Pessy's cousin Dara who used to come down for a visit from Bombay. Dara was a fabulous dancer and swore eternal love while he cornered me in the attic of Pessy's bungalow. That summer before the end of school year I missed my period, I told no one save Grandma. But for once the Matriarch panicked, seemed at a loss what course to follow. She took me with her to Bombay ostensibly on a shopping holiday. One night in Matheran her Ghati cook Sakhubai served me my favorite bengan masala. It had the slightly odd smell of an over-cooked kidney. That night I bled profusely, all the towels in the house were drenched with blood. That Ghati woman might have killed me but Grandma Perrin was determined to avoid a scandal in Umeed."

Cy was furious with his mother when a cousin from Bombay spilled the beans a few weeks later. He almost sent her packing back to Bombay but Gisela intervened and Perrin was spared the humiliation of being sent away in disgrace.

**** ****

Terry's mind went back to that first meeting with Gisela. She had seemed more like her husband's shipmate than a stranger in his world.

Not being well versed in local social rituals, Terry had dropped quite a few bricks during his first six months in Delhi. He had to watch his step in the bazaar as well as the club where rigid conventions of Edwardian costume drama still lingered on. To live among strangers when international travel was slow and arduous must have compelled Gisela to make extraordinary personal adjustments. What went on in that medieval Indian town that helped salt down her pain? What was her backstory? Did the glittering tale of a beautiful Jewish maiden rescued by a dashing Indian prince hide a universe riddled with black holes?

By the late Sixties people had realized that far from being part of a larger shipwreck, or 'collateral damage,' the Holocaust was a beached whale that couldn't be rolled back into the ocean. The sea fronts of Normandy and Dunkirk had been cleaned up, graves of the fallen arranged in geometric order, but the Holocaust remained uncleanable. Even those who had lived through the Blitz simply shook their heads in disbelief.

Independent India had drawn a curtain across its own blood-spattered history when the vastly outnumbered British troops, eager to get back home had stood by watching helplessly. Could some of the sub-continental reluctance to engage in far-off European atrocities have rubbed off on Gisela? Did witnessing her poor patients' flinty struggle for survival blunt her pain?

Gisela had greeted Terry with a smile that carried not a hint of secreted sorrow. Scrubbed to a healthy flush, blond hair peppered with gray gathered up in a bun, and not one dolorous crease on her face around which to construct narratives of unimaginable suffering; at their first meeting she had excused herself from the table to phone her clinic in accented but fluent Hindi to make sure the infant plucked that day by Caesarean section was resting quietly.

The Sorabji's dinner table exchange was usually in musical shorthand; Terry listened silently as his hosts weighed the relative merits of the early Bruckner of the *C minor* symphony against Schubert's *D major* composed when the latter was only sixteen.

After dinner following a particularly hard day at the clinic while Cyrus dozed in his stuffed chair, a glass of brandy dangling from his hand, Gisela drifted to the piano by the large window. Coming in after a stroll in the garden with Juno, Terry would stand entranced in the doorway as Gisela played Chopin's melancholy *A Minor Waltz*, caressing the keyboard as though probing for broken bones.

"I was never good enough to play my father's favorite Schubert *Sonata in B-Flat Major* or anything by Scarlatti, although heaven knows I tried. Beethoven's *Moonlight* had barely come within grasp when I moved to England but what little spare time I had went into brushing up my English and it simply slipped through my fingers. Really speaking my talent never rose beyond Schumann's *Kinderszenen.*"

Terry could claim only nodding acquaintance with the Free Trade Hall concerts attended largely under MGS peer pressure. He took Beethoven and Mozart in big gulps as if learning to swim without a system, listening without understanding.

He was beginning to sense that it was the Sorabji setting he'd fallen in love with; Juno was its most graceful embodiment. He was taken even before she appeared on the scene. Kunj and its surroundings were far removed in time and space from his own 'kettle on the hob, geraniums in the window' Salford. The elegance of the Sorabji household, its great radiant form, had unleashed in him a passion to be gathered into its fold. He had both oars in water and the next thing he knew he was honeymooning on Dal Lake in Kashmere. Much later in Wimbledon Park it became clear that unlike her parents Juno was incapable of a sustained and deep engagement with anything other than the current fad.

At the turn of the century entire villages had been transplanted from Eastern Europe to the impoverished Industrial North of England, and every Monday their domestic distress drove Jewish women with discreet bundles to the backyards of pawnbrokers.

The poor Jews lived in odd-numbered and the gentiles opposite in even-numbered houses. The Luftwaffe made no distinction between gentile and Jew; there was weeping on both sides of the street after a bombing raid.

As it happened, Mam was one of the first to cross the twenty feet of space dividing the two communities, while her next door neighbor Mrs Hardcastle, a seventy-year-old battle-axe, stared at her back. She was given to banging her door shut whenever old Mr Finkelstein, who was from Poland and repaired shoes right on your door-step, entered the street stroking his beard muttering, ' *El Rachum, Oy mi nisht gut gevorn.*'

The better-off Jews had corner shops or a bakery like Mrs Hammelman's but it was not unusual to hear of one being gutted when those not allowed buying on tick tossed in a Molotov cocktail during the blackout. All they found from the smoke-filled wreckage were two charred bodies.

The *Guardian* of March 1933 reported that Manchester had been "swept off its feet by a tornado of peroration yelled at the defiant high pitch of a tremendous voice."

That stentorian voice belonged to Oswald Mosley, after whom the city was to name one of its major thoroughfares. Mosley held his Fascist rally at the venerable Free Trade Hall. Later in the Sixties during Terry's youth, Sir John

Barbirolli standing in its well would make beautiful music with his beloved Hallé Orchestra.

War became brutally personal for Mam and her friends during the Christmas Blitz on Sunday, December 22, 1940. All, including Mrs Hammelman and Mrs Hardcastle, huddled in the brick shelter because the Anderson was flooded with water overflowing from the hoses. According to Mam it was teeth-chatteringly cold; in that dim-lit place, world becoming small, she saw Mrs Hardcastle's hand surreptitiously stretched in the dark to receive bread and boiled eggs passed around by Mrs Hammelman. Recalling that evening many years later, Mam would say, "I tell thee lad' I'd seen nowt like it before, an' nowt like it again."

****

(vi)

I know my time has come yet I cannot let go of Rudi — last drop hovering at the tap-end of my days. Sissi shall have him — a keepsake pearl.

Part of my story is also Terry's now. We have Sissi in common. Umeed was her childhood home till age eleven, thanks to Juno's sojourn every three years to an exotic location with a new protégé, 'to help him rise above the humdrum.'

I had not seen with my own eyes my parents, stripped of reason, tottering to survive in a death camp; I had fled before Vienna soiled itself primping up for the Nazis. I had to calibrate the slow waning of life in Mutti's eyes from the memoirs of survivors. There was always a tormenting gap between recorded horrors and the silvery lilt in her voice, the roll of Papili's large amused eyes as he stood in the doorway of the Alpine cabin we rented every summer, watching us play in the snow.

Those early years in Umeed I used to lie awake listening to the night-watch strike the ground in unison with staves, counting each thwack. If the last one trailed off on an even number Rudi would survive the War. Surely it was reasonable to hope the RAF would spare a children's hospital.

Every morning in Umeed our patients waiting in the hallway greeted us with gentle smiles of subtle shyness as we walked to our surgeries past their scrawny brown hands raised in salaam. Perrin's long nose was instantly out of joint when we accepted Her Highness's offer of an old bungalow for our clinic in the oldest section of town instead of setting it up in the cantonment area where we lived. She went away in a huff to Matheran and returned only after Juno was born four years later.

"Didn't I tell you, for all his years in England Cy is a pukka Bawaji," she whispered as she gave me a parting hug. "Sakhawat doesn't mean putting yourself at risk."

If she knew that Cy had my full support in the matter she ignored it.

"Sakhawat is a tradition among Parsis to reach out to the poorest in the community," Cy explained. "That's why you don't see any Parsi beggars. Actually, Mummy is a crypto-Sakhawati herself, although few know it. There is no women's organization in town, Hindu or Muslim, for which she has not written checks. All hush-hush of course, as Dad would have told you. Absolute strangers would come up and pump his hand in gratitude whenever he made official visits to their locality. People simply couldn't imagine that a woman would part with large chunks of her lolly without prior permission of her lord and master. Little did they know. For all her cucumber-sandwich loftiness Mummy is as bourgeois as your average Parsi housewife in matters of sanitation. She thinks the poorer parts of town are by definition unhygienic."

Two childhoods – my daughter's and Sissi's.

Juno's was glimpsed from something like the upper gallery level; by the time I trained my glasses on her the scene had changed. But Sissi I watched cribside as she wheeled her legs, worked her mouth, and pulled at my hair with tiny fists, winching up my German from where it had languished all these years.

> *Kinn wippchen*
> *Rot lippchen*
> *Spitz naeschen*
> *Augebrauchen*
> *Stirnradchen*
> *Ziep, ziep, ziep mein Härchen*

I am no linguist like Sissi, but I do believe baby talk is a mother-tongue bequest.

By age three Sissi was a polyglot in the making. The child's Anglo-Germanic babble was laced with rich Indian sounds. She and Subhadra cooed and trilled at each other in cantonment patois when we were away at the clinic.

But when Sissi Baba was four she would let only her Oma put her to bed. My English had lacked pliancy to tell Juno bedtime stories expressively. In Sissi's nursery I hummed and thrummed in German and recounted from memory Rotkäppchen, that is until I got to the part where the Wolf awaited the little girl after polishing off the grandmother in her cottage. At that moment Sissi dived under the counterpane and hid her face.

The original Grimm Brothers tale was too close to the bone with the wolf devouring the girl's Oma. So I bought a new set of illustrated fairy tales in English and translated them while reading. Now Little Riding Hood had a very practical English father who saw through the wolf's wickedness before the beast could do harm to his girl.

No wonder even after ten years in England Sissi still speaks German when she is in Umeed. This is her real home, here by my side.

Except when stuck mid-sentence for the right English word or phrase I had not allowed my submersed Deutsch to come up for breath since boarding the P&O liner at Southampton. Every single day during our passage to India with murder in my heart I had cut it up into little pieces and pushed it overboard.

Passing through the Suez Canal I was assailed by a bout of nostalgia so strong that I found myself chattering in German with an old doctor going to his post in Malaysia. Closed-cropped square head and steely blue eyes, he would lounge in a deck-chair making snide remarks in German about the English, assuming no one would follow him. The other passengers instinctively avoided him because he had an ugly scar running down his right cheek. He never smiled, mostly stayed in his cabin, showing up only for meals and doggedly refusing to speak any language but German with the mostly Indian waiters from Goa.

One day on my way to the upper deck in search of something to read, I overheard the doctor asking a politely smiling but uncomprehending waiter for directions to the library. Suddenly I heard a German voice, "Entschuldigen Sie mich, eigentlich bin ich auf meinem Weg in die Bibliothek. Es ist auf dem oberen Deck. Ich werde glücklich sein, Ihnen zu zeigen, wo es ist."

Those words simply slipped out of my mouth, so starved was I for German. So was the doctor. We must have stood there chatting for twenty minutes until the waiter coughed politely and asked permission to leave. Luckily the Herr Doctor did not know our professional background, otherwise he would have simply attached himself to us and made the remainder of the voyage an ordeal. After leading him to the library I picked up a book hurriedly and ran down the stairs and into our cabin.

Sissi's gurgling laughter dissolved the icy floes of time and broken bits of my lost tongue came waddling up in a quacking row. I was back in Vienna with Rudi singing,

Alle meine Entchen

Schwimmen auf dem See

Köpfchen in das Wasser,

Schwänzchen in die Höh.

Sometimes a sort of silent hysteria seized me as a train approached Umeednagar station and I felt a stranger's probing gaze settle on my face. My European skin cringed and my mind flew back to that day at the Westbahnhof when Mutti reached out to tuck a rowdy lock under my gray beret, snagging a pair of unblinking eyes hooded by a black Gestapo hat.

I had often seen such resentment on the face of the Burra Mem when Cyrus greeted her courteously at a party. If she had spoken in her own voice no one would have noticed how common she was. It was excruciating to hear her affect a Mayfair accent to chime with Cy's crisp public school diction.

Perrin persuaded me to translate for the Burra Sahib transcripts of Hitler's rants coming over the wireless. The Burra, who had only a smattering of German, had a look of utter disbelief on his face while going over the translation. He would read it slowly line by line and linger over a particular passage full of unbridled diatribe. His eyes would dilate and he would stare at me a bit longer than official propriety allowed as if I were pulling his leg. He would shake his head, grab his sola by the rim and walk away stiffly. As a young man he had served in upcountry native fiefdoms barely touched by British law, but nothing in his experience of dealing with maniacal petty Indian rulers had prepared him for the madness in the German Chancellor's speeches.

The Residency crowd in princely states behaved as though the Raj would go on forever. They viewed Gandhi's movement as something their compatriots in the directly governed British territory had to contend with. It was Calcutta, Bombay, Madras and Delhi where incendiary nationalism had a foot in the door of the Whites Only Club, not in Mysore, Jaipore and Umeed with their polo playing rajas.

The cacophony released in the air by each new speech in distant Nuremberg made it impossible to make sense of the events on the ground. Gabby's letters from England and later from the United States were the only source of information about Vienna. Both Papili and Mutti had been deported to Auschwitz just before Uncle Franz moved to America with his family. That much I had gathered from Gabby's last letter from Vienna. Nothing more.

Long after closing time I hung around the clinic, dreading going home in case there was a message sealing the fate of my parents. Gabby's correspondence had dwindled to a brief occasional message about her life at Hunter College in New York and her part-time job as a sales girl at Bloomingdale's.

Halfway into the war the defection to the Japanese of rebellious Indian soldiers and the escape to Germany of the nationalist leader Subhash Chandra Bose from British custody undermined Allied propaganda against the Nazis. In certain quarters Hitler was openly being projected as a potential liberator of India from alien rule. Almost against my better judgment I began to hope that official media might be inflating Nazi brutality to justify British imperial agenda.

The incredulous look in the round blue eyes of the Resident Mr Talbot prompted me to make sure I had not inadvertently made Hitler sound even more inflammatory than he really was. But the frenzy in his speeches bubbled over like a geyser. There simply wasn't any other way to sweeten the words steeped in blood.

It was a time of blackout at night with Japanese bombs falling on the outskirts of Calcutta; the Arabian Sea slowed down bad news coming across from Europe. The clinic became my daytime sanctuary. Not until the War ended in Europe did I have further news about Papili and Mutti.

Alone in the darkened office I began playing a private game of chance, rigging it in favor of a severely dehydrated prematurely born baby placed in the incubator; a Russian Roulette of sorts with foreknowledge as to which of the six chambers in the revolver was loaded with a blank. If the little thing beat the odds Mutti and Papili would come out of Auschwitz impaired but alive.

In the worst-case scenario I had Papili facing a Bavarian peasant-turned-camp-guard speaking in a thick drawl. The Nazi would resent Papili's Weimar polish. He had once told me how it had upset him to find his cultivated tone provoke derisive laughter among German officers on the Western front during his days with the Ambulance Corps. So I steeled myself to a rifle butt smashing into Papili's face, a black boot with a shiny tip drawn back to land a kick at his slumped form. I stopped short of conjuring up anything more dire than my father reeling under the blow, mouth bleeding but somehow still alive. That was the utmost of his hurt I could hold without slashing my wrist with a surgical knife.

Occasionally I insulated myself from reports of atrocities in death camps by allowing myself a less stressful reverie in which Mutti's cello, simulating the human voice in Auschwitz, opened Beethoven's *A major Sonata* and dissolved into pure sound at the end, My parents' first choice at the sham concert rigged up for a Red Cross visit would surely be the much-loved Rachmaninoff *G minor for Cello and Piano*. I'd first heard that desolating melody on returning home after a trip with my Botany class to a farm outside Vienna where they grew dwarf Russian almonds. Wandering alone with the sun in my eyes to the edge of the farm I had accidentally sunk my foot in a collapsed anthill. There were tractor tire marks through which wound a train of ants conveying grain held in tiny mouths to a new home. My eyes were drawn to a nearby sign

> *Dies ist unsere Heimat, das ist, wo wir nach schuften auf dem Gebiet, wie Sie Ruhe kommen. Bitte nicht pflügen uns hinunter.*
> *Ihr Freund,*
> *Ameis*

At Auschwitz the patriotic Commandant scuttled the Russian in favor of the German.

**** ****

(vii)

Even when promoted to Deputy News Editor Terry had to stay focused, not shift his gaze beyond useful facts, admit no suppositional what-ifs in making the day's events relevant to the average working man or woman turning on the telly in the evening with 'an automatic hand.' Had he not as a married man traded the randomness of freelancing for the security of employment he might have become a regular columnist at an intellectually livelier organ like the *New Statesman.*

Voices were being raised against the BBC's double standards in exposing the stifling of dissent in Britain's ex-colonies while turning a blind eye to the police excesses against the IRA. Recently every parenthetical clause in Terry's report on the confrontation between the Afro-Caribbean marchers led by Darkus Howe from Deptford to Hyde Park had to be removed, leaving the impression of near-normalcy on the streets of London.

In the former colonies of the Empire the BBC was applauded for its crusade against corruption in high places or government unpreparedness to rush aid to flood victims, but all dark shadows had to be airbrushed out of the shining face of Maggie Thatcher's England before it was beamed on the screen.

MGS with its emphasis on Greek and Latin classics had washed Terry's troubled childhood in Salford out of his language but not his memory. Back then his favorite teacher favored grand narratives and encouraged his pupils to hunt for that miraculous connection between on-going conflicts and historical antecedents. It made the writing of the weekly essay more than mere homework. The History Master had an ear for ancient collisions and shipwrecks echoing through events unfolding in the contemporary world. Sometimes he would deploy well-worn plots like those of the detective story, medieval saga or even the western to set up an unfolding disaster. Anthony Eden's bungling over the Suez Canal would reverberate to the gullible Mark Antony left shame-faced at Actium by Cleopatra, the sacking of Carthage by the Romans became emblematic of the brutal repression of the Algerians by French Colonial administration and the assassination of President Kennedy, a price paid by a modern day Prometheus for daring to ease the human condition.

Terry's mentor Mike Bartlett scoffed at any attempt to embroider history into myth and probed the little details, the fading smudges in the margin, the jagged edges that made it difficult to tell a new construction site from an old ruin. In Terry's journal-entries crumpled bits and stubs jostled with the most eye-catching debris lying on the outer perimeters of disaster but only the latter made it to the reports that went on air. Now and then a historical parallel from Higginbotham's lessons or a figure covered in rotting weeds rose from old Venables' mildewed volumes and offered to unveil the secret that led to the recent smash-up.

Terry's closeness to Richard Craven the News Editor was a matter of concern for those with a pedigree as was his North Country background and left-wing discourse. A rumor wafting through the Television Center branded him a mole planted by the KGB for recruiting colleagues deemed to be comrade material. Fortunately from the Manager Director down to the youngest sub-editor everyone shrugged off all such rumors.

Dick Craven, who had actually been a member of the Communist Party in his Cambridge days, lived with his wife in a quiet side street in Highgate. Often after work Terry walked down with Dick to a nearby pub. One evening he thought he saw a figure in a trench coat and trilby detach itself from the shadows and tail his friend to the Underground. But Terry was taken aback when the editor warned him not to let his cloak-and-dagger impulse run amuck.

"It seems to me you overcompensate for your humble background by always pumping up a hunch into conspiracy. The last War knocked down most barriers, a few remain, but they are bound to fall sooner or later. Let's not raise new ones is all I am saying, there's a good chap."

Terry felt his talent remained under-utilized in his job. After five years at the

Television Center he longed to go where the rumble of a fractured world noisily reassembling itself could be heard. Mike Bartlett, who was back in London after finishing a searing documentary about the plight of labor reservists of Lesotho in segregationist South Africa, thought Terry had enough field experience to make a transition from script-writer to documentary maker. He helped him write a proposal for an investigative project about the Jonestown Massacre in Guyana where close to a thousand mostly black women and children had been massacred.

One evening Terry told Juno he was thinking of relinquishing his position to make a documentary based on his own script. Juno was very supportive but she would not let him sell the car. Her jewelry box was crammed to the brim and she sold a diamond-studded necklace given to her by Grandma Perrin.

That remote outpost in Guyana marked a turning point in Terry's career; he began to shape a script around a thing with a rake risen from the underworld scarfing down inhabitants of a doomed city. But Reverend Jones's settlement was more like Camus' Oran with a firm beachhead in actual history rather than mythical Thebes planted with dragon's teeth.

The main premise of Terry's pitch to the editor was that somewhere along the line, America's McCarthy-era paranoia about Communism had mutated like a virus and lodged in the Caligula figure of Rev Jones.

He began with a tentative analogy between Jonestown and the skull-festooned compound at the Inner Station in Conrad's Congo; African-Americans re-enslaved, a thousand dead bodies piled up on top of each other, a resident chimpanzee policing disobedient children, the Green Beret and the Black Watch on the prowl in the nearby forest and a Kurtz-like evil watching from the brush.

A heady mix.

A week later when Dick personally handed him a three-month contract to finish the documentary he couldn't hide his surprise.

The Eighties opened their innings with Juno dashing off to Paris with her painting class, 'just to breathe in the air Monet inhaled' while Terry headed in the opposite direction to get to the bottom of that two-year-old mass suicide in the Caribbean.

After boarding the train at Victoria Station Juno turned around at the door and said, "Do look up my aunt Gabby in New York. Her address is in my desk diary. Mumsy's only living relative in the whole wide world. I never met her, but when I was a little girl, every year in April — it must have been during Passover — we received an airmail shipment of torts, strudels, cheeses and cookies from New York. There were these awful stories of famine in India in newspapers all over the world. Aunt Gabby must have thought we were all starving."

Dust had not quite settled on Jonestown; its surface seemed covered in octagonal cracks of the kind that every now and then raise the ghost of life-sustaining damp on a distant planet.

Terry found himself in charge of a project slightly beyond his pale. Along with Harry Knickerbockers the Stringer and his wife Becky who operated the sound equipment, he flew to Miami where they clambered on to a small plane with 12 passengers and one crew. Even in 1980 an aircraft with a propeller was 'a pain in the butt to board' for Harry with his TK47 Camera, batteries, chargers, cables and tapes. Becky carried a collapsible fish-pole mounted with a mike designed by her husband.

Two years on, nothing much remained at the site, the soil once blood-soaked was squelchy and overgrown with grass; the wilderness had just rolled back in. While Becky and Harry were out scouting for dramatic sites and interviewing eyewitnesses, Terry tried to pick up signals of silent collisions taking place underground, out of sight of officials and pundits armed with hypotheses and theories. Sometimes he asked Harry to record with an external mike distant sounds like the cawing of scavengers or heavy feet marching in the forest. At night under a mosquito net his Olivetti clicked while crickets chirped outside and a script was born that captured something vital fracturing beyond the boom operator's mike. The foreshortened Salford vowels with the unreleased 't' in the voice-over were most recognizably Terry's.

Post-disaster reporting, Terry's stock-in-trade was fraught with unexpected challenges. On the other hand a seething, unfolding calamity required nerves of steel. Terry couldn't forget the horror of watching a frenzied mob of armed vigilantes in what was to become Bangladesh drag out three pro-Pakistani Biharis and butcher them like pigs in the streets of Dhaka. For weeks he couldn't retain food in his stomach.

Walking through carnage, letting the camera move like Homer's blind gaze, was supposed to yield handsome returns. The hope remained that, however footsore, if you trudged through the potter's field you were likely to spot the overlooked, something odd discarded because it didn't fit.

Becky, good sport, nodded her head but the stringer was not convinced.

"Shucks," he snorted setting down his 16mm on its tripod, "there's nothing here to shoot, old buddy. All I can see is empty shacks and whadyamacallit in the center that looks like an oil drum by that warehouse. I've already shot that fucking tractor from several angles."

Was that bumpy ride from Katima in a hired jeep along the broken dirt road worth it after all? What would Mike have done?

In Georgetown the Guyanese authorities were tight-lipped about a massacre on a genocidal scale on the front-doorstep of their obscure country. Pontius Pilot-1ish shrugs, a few snickers about Americans doing things their way but nothing to explain a massive perversion of Utopian ideals that in the initial stages of the movement had fascinated even the First Lady.

How had men and women of distinction been taken in by this Rasputin in saintly robes?

There was absolutely no awkwardness in Mrs Carter's manner or voice when during a visit to the White House Terry asked if she thought Jones had been a potential Gandhi suddenly gone round the bend?

She smiled.

"Well look, in those early days Mr Jones had all the moves and passion of the young Gandhi in his South African commune. Who knows at what point in their career folks begin to have delusions they are Jesus Christ. I must admit I didn't see what was coming, and I was not the only one to make that mistake."

The final edited version the BBC aired lasted barely forty-five minutes. Terry's script separated the plausible from the conjectural, cutting to comments of early enthusiasts like California Governor Jerry Brown recalling the idyllic commune followed by stark current images of the desolate landscape. He asked Harry to point his camera at various locations in the camp from where dead bodies had been carted off. What the viewers heard was a quiet voice directing their gaze to a grassy knoll followed by a still image borrowed from the archives of children's twisted bodies. The contrast between the bland overgrown wilderness and the recalled horror, the palimpsest effect, the past site dense with corpses and the same run over by wilderness had a harsh logic that stunned the viewers. By establishing the present tense of the documentary and the viewer alike Terry had tried to recover the receding horror of the past from archival photographs permeating them with a sense of 'eventness', of unspeakable things happening before their very eyes. Terry's voice asked his audience to visualize a father slitting his child's throat to stop it writhing, before raising the cup with a mixture of cyanide and Kool-Aid to his own lips.

One thing stood out in stark contrast to Gandhi's South African farm. The Guyanese retreat had been structured like a boot camp, the disciples were made to subsist on a diet of gruel and beans, but, as Terry noted, 'The Master's own refrigerator was stocked with butter and milk. At his Temple Rev Jones had supped with high-calorie horror.'

**** ****

Looking down from the plane at the New York skyline Terry sighed.

"I have to see somebody in the city next week. A sort of Holocaust survivor, a cousin of my mother-in-law's."

Harry, who had been dozing, opened one eye.

"Listen bud, there are no Holocaust survivors. There are only leftovers. Survivors are able to make choices to beat the odds. The Jews in Europe had zero choice. Some escaped getting killed because the Nazis ran out of poison gas. What's more there is just one Holocaust story, there is no other narrative embedded or otherwise. No alternative ending either as in fancy modernist fiction. Five million Jews but only one goddamn linear plot with just the one ending. When it was actually happening people in power said, 'Look there's a war on. We can't be bothered now. We'll visit your story when we are done with Hitler.' Newspapers owned by Jews tucked it away inside their vast story-making machines. The Allies flew over Auschwitz and blew up a strategic target because they had their own heroic war-story to tell. Holly-wood wasn't interested in Anne Frank until she hit the headlines, made money on Broadway. Cecil B. DeMille, a Jew who became rich putting biblical epics on celluloid, pissed on Otto Preminger for making *Ship of Fools*. Heck, the Holocaust was no box-office material like *Casablanca*. No teary-eyed Swedish blonde making goo-goo eyes at a boozy American gambler running a back-lot gin-joint pretending to be North Africa."

Strictly speaking Gabby (née Rumplemayor) Wasserman didn't qualify as a survivor since she and her parents had been sponsored by a cousin living in America before the Allies declared War against Germany. But behind that age-defying Lower Manhattan woman of sixty-five trailed a schoolgirl with a haunted look of one reprieved from a firing squad.

During Terry's first visit she kept adjusting a glossy brown wig with trembling fingers.

His cryptic method of questioning useful in conflict zones like Beirut and Dhaka produced a fidgety silence; while Terry explained the purpose of his visit Gabby lowered her gaze with a shrug sank into the sofa and never looked up. He heard a fly buzz around her clenched mouth and quietly let himself out. He had desecrated a burial ground.

Between his first and second visit to Gabby's he had a revelation. A flash of common sense during a chance pause while the First Lady signed some papers saved him from getting bounced from the White House for his 'how could you have missed all the red flags' tenor of questioning. To be seen as a judicious inquirer eager to learn seemed to be the right tack when dealing with the cultivated Mrs Carter as was playing an Englishman out of his depth in America with Governor Jerry Brown and his cohorts in California. Gradually the mist faded and the Jekyll & Hyde Jones stood exposed like a figure on a peeled-off decal sticker.

Ten minutes into his second visit to Gabby's apartment reached by creaking steps under scuffed red carpeting, a compliment on her pluck and determination in fending for herself in her old age brought a sweet smile to her lips. A framed photograph of the Sorabji couple on a sofa with Juno and Terry flanking them in their posh bungalow proved to be a magi-calibre gift. A tearful Gabby hugged and kissed him on both cheeks and made him sit down by her side. Slowly over the course of tea and knish Gisela's Vienna emerged from her cousin's rambling account, echoing lost footsteps and silenced voices.

Gabby had taught German and French for nearly forty years at a local high school until a stroke made her housebound. She'd lost sensation in her left foot but daily physical therapy had restored partial mobility. Before moving to Houston, Texas, her lawyer son had tried unsuccessfully 'to off-load' her in some fancy 'mausoleum' for retirees called Rainbow Retreat with quality health-care at the press of a button, a full view of the Hudson from the bedroom window to see the sun go down behind the hills, plus all the latest gizmos a well-endowed facility of this kind could provide to coddled parents of doting well-heeled children.

"Saul and his wife Barbara pleaded and pleaded but I said 'Thank you but, no thank you.' 'Retreat' my foot. Just a fancy word for ghetto. Had enough of that in the old country. With my pension and social security I don't need to be beholden to Saul or anyone else. I can go to the neighborhood convenience store and take in a movie all by myself. In the evening when I am feeling good I walk slowly all the way to Sarah Roosevelt Park where couples bring their little ones to play. Just watching them run around is better medicine for me than anything they dish out over there on the Hudson."

Living among Holocaust survivors in New York Gabby had kept her ghosts at bay, confronting them mostly in the company of fellow refugees and other support groups, sharing their sorrows, learning to walk on broken legs.

Brunch once in two weeks at Katz's Delicatessen with a young niece, a 30-inch TV and a phone with unlimited calling to keep in touch with friends scattered across various retirement homes in and around the Catskills, Gabby 'had it all.'

"Some of my friends in old people's homes would give their left arm to be back in New York."

Gabby and Gisela had lived two different lives but both had found relief in work with children.

Gabby fetched an album from the little shelf behind the sofa. Sepia photo-graphs including one of twelve-year-old light–eyed Gisela in lederhosen, sun bouncing off thick Brunhilde braids, young Gabby in a dirndl leaning against the doorway of an Alpine cabin.

During Gisela's first year in Medical School in Vienna gormless Aryan professors let Nazi thugs storm the biology lab and thrash Jewish students. The following year with support from her Mutti's old Uncle Balthazar married into a prosperous Jewish family of bookbinders, Gisela transferred to London. Childless Uncle Balthazar, a dentist with a surgery in Basingstoke, was pleased to have his sister's brilliant daughter come to live with him in England.

Their maid Hilde was of peasant stock from Linz but Gustav Hartmann insisted on her joining them at the dinner table. She was a roly-poly frau with an apron that was barely broad enough to go around her.

When slightly tipsy Herr Hartmann or Papili — Gisela's father was everybody's Papili — would dance with Hilde, yodel and jolly her along in her dialect to Mutti's bourgeois horror. Hilde was more like an elderly aunt to the entire family and when Rudi was sent to Steinhoff she had been very cross and wouldn't speak to anyone for days. Mutti who had also cried that day explained to Hilde that Rudi would return after being cured. He had almost scalded the maid the previous week by knocking a deep pan full of boiling milk on to her lap. Even while writhing in agony Hilde had not uttered a single word of reproof and blamed her own clumsiness for the mishap.

Papili had sensed that Rudi had flown into an uncontrollable rage and had to be treated. He had met Dr Freud only once when the great man had come into the shop to pick up a travel guide to Rome.

"I did not get to read Freud till I was a sophomore at Hunter College," Gabby recalled. "He said 'in some happy corners of the world some lives may go gently by, unknowing of aggression or constraint'."

But Papili clung desperately to what even Freud considered a utopian dream. The post-Anschluss Steinhoff managed by Nazi doctors would not discharge Rudi. Under the old rules all treatment including psychiatric care had been the City's responsibility irrespective of the patient's race. Now Jews were not only ineligible for free hospitalization but had to remit a sizable amount for past treatment.

"No certificate of discharge meant no tax clearance papers from the Rathaus," said Gabby "therefore no exit visa for the family. The only possible mode of escape was an eight-hour trek to Italy, negotiating dangerous twists and turns down steep Dolomite ridges. Mutti refused to leave without Rudi."

Papili sold *Le Monde* and the *Manchester Guardian* to French and British expatriates living in Vienna. But glass windows daubed with 'Juden' and no customers coming in, Papili's bookstore had no market value. The week following Papili's arrest for treason, young Gabby had watched from a bakery the eviscerated form of Gisela's mother being escorted by two SS men to the waiting van.

The rest of Gabby's narrative encapsulated the harrowing experience of all the Jews who were trapped in Nazi-occupied territories. One day Papili collapsed while digging graves for a mass burial, was dispatched with a single bullet to the head and rolled into the pit he had been digging. Gabby's family survived, eating only once a day, dodging marauding gangs who snatched bread from an old woman's hand.

"Somehow life goes on at normal pace even during a siege," said Gabby. "Cooking ranges are fired, babies bathed and put to sleep, people trade, barter, make love, bury their dead while the enslaved population lives under constant threat of extermination. Attila at Rome, Hitler at Leningrad."

Gabby and her parents had scrambled aboard the last refugee ship sailing to America.

She had invited Gisela several times in the past to visit her in New York. Once she offered to send her an air-ticket for an all-expenses paid visit.

"You know what she wrote. I still need time to reflect on what happened to all of us back then. What was there to reflect? It was butchery, pure and simple, not some bacteria wriggling under her microscope."

Terry saw the gentle face of his mother-in-law as she slowly peeled off her surgical cap and blue scrub in her clinic. It must have taken an extraordinary effort of will to keep her hand steady in the operating room with Vienna on her mind.

✳✳✳✳ ✳✳✳✳

The day before Terry flew back to London Gabby's niece Leslie Singer drove them to a Mexican restaurant.

It seemed to be Gabby's favorite haunt because they were greeted warmly by the chef himself and seated in a cozy warm place. Manuel the chef also owned the restaurant and his wife dressed in a long indigo skirt and mauve blouse outfit with lace trimming took their orders. Gabby's eyes followed her as the Mexican woman went in and out of the kitchen.

Leslie was quietly attentive to her aunt, ordering a smooth and silky flan topped with caramel before Gabby who had a sweet tooth could say 'I really shouldn't.'

Terry was particularly curious about Papili's preference for the *Manchester Guardian*. Aspiring journalists on the editorial board of MGS's *New Mancunian* dreamed of stepping into the shoes of stalwarts like Norman Shrapnel, Taya Zinkin and the man of many legends Sir Neville Cardus who could move with the grace of a majestic swan from a Hallé Concert the night before to Old Trafford next morning to catch England play Australia. Once armed with a sheaf of his writing samples Terry had marched to the *Guardian* building in Deansgate to offer his services as a budding columnist but had cold feet at the entrance and turned back. He asked Gabby why the English in Vienna read the *Guardian* and not the *Times* or *Daily Mail?*

"Papili provided many other resources for what today you would call 'cultural exchange,' " Gabby replied. "He had a copy of the *Guardian* delivered to Freud's apartment at 19 Bergasse."

It seems before he became famous Freud had spent some time in Manchester where one of his cousins lived and worked. But more importantly the *Manchester Guardian* was the only European paper that continued to publish reports of atrocities against the Jews even after Hitler was elected Chancellor of Germany. That was Papili's undoing. Two months after the Anschluss the Gestapo raided Marcus Aurelius, seized the unsold copies of the paper and arrested him.

"Papili was no scholar," Gabby said. "He had just enough intellectual curiosity to be excited by new ideas without the stamina to extend its reach through an in-depth study. After reading a literary review in *Neue Freie Presse* he could hold forth on Schnitzler who'd anticipated in fiction Freud's theory of the 'libido.' In the process of browsing Papili had absorbed so much Goethe that he could floor the most erudite scholar by recalling in detail a passage from *Faust*.

His love of books was passionate enough to impress the lay reader though not perhaps a specialist. Most of his thoughts came from editorials and by-lines but his opinions were expressed with the aid of a classic text. I remember he was fond of quoting Hamlet, *'Ich bin ein alter Römer, nicht ein Däne'.*"

"My aunt really likes you," Leslie whispered, "with others she is never really comfortable talking about her past. I believe it's because you are married to her niece."

Back in the flat Leslie set about making coffee, Gabby closed her eyes. As she talked her voice gained a stronger Germanic resonance.

"I haven't talked about Vienna but you are family. Going hungry became a habit, as seeing those whom we loved and respected stripped of human dignity did not. It still hurts to think of those bewildered eyes of Papili the morning after *Kristallnacht.* He had spotted among the attackers two grown-up sons of his own assistants Bettlemann and Schlick."

Gabby's father had found Papili on the pavement across the street cowering beneath the caved-in wooden frames of his bookstore *Marcus Aurelius.* Splinters from the broken windows lay gleaming in the flames. He was finally persuaded to spend the night at Gabby's place. Gisela's Mutti had already preceded him to avoid getting mauled or killed by the rampaging drunk mob.

Gabby's father had been shrewd enough to realize that it was all over for Jews in Europe.

"The Nazis are here to stay, they are not a passing blizzard but the start of a new Ice Age. It's time to pack our bags once again and move. It's our destiny anyway. Those who do not see the writing on the wall must be both blind and deaf. Didn't you hear the sound of madness, the *Sieg Heils,* when the Nazi goons strutted through our streets as though they owned them; I saw two of my colleagues, dedicated musicians, in the crowd pushing and jostling to catch a glimpse of those thugs marching down the Graben. There was joy and relief in the eyes of Herr Mueller, our next-door neighbor, as if he had been waiting for this moment all his life. And our greengrocer Oscar Hesse of 'the graveyard face,' was waving his hat in the air, a stupid grin plastered on his face. I tell you I had a slight fever that evening but kept springing up from bed as though someone had emptied a bucket of cold water on my head."

There were practically no books in Papili's bookstore with specific Jewish reference except the novels of Stefan Zweig. Even though *Marcus Aurelius* tucked away in Ruprechtsviertel was completely engrossed in a world of its own, on *Kristallnacht* it went up in flames like any other Jewish establishment in Vienna.

The streets were deserted on November 9th, there were very few people on the tram. Wild screams and fire burning in the distance, gangs marching down the streets, drunkenly singing the *Horst Wessel* lied. Next morning when some sort of precarious order was restored and Papili reached the cobbled street, he couldn't recognize his shop. Black soot hung on the olive-green doorframes.

When a customer asked him why his shop was named after a Roman Emperor he always replied 'because Aurelius was just.' There were many writers and philosophers whose works Papili knew but Marcus Aurelius was at the top of his list.

He would say, "It is not the output that makes for greatness in a writer, it's the quality of his thought."

Papili's oak-paneled small but cozy office was behind a glass partition. He and Mutti sat at their separate desks, he staring through his magnifying glass at a rare volume sent by Signor Tursi from Rome and she bent over her typewriter, like characters in a Maeterlinck play not knowing that disaster had already befallen them.

"Papili loved children as much as books," Gabby said. "As a teenager I would sit browsing between shelves for hours staring at the illustrations of Empress Elizabeth on a visit to her dairy farm."

The Nuremberg laws crippled Jewish business in Vienna and Gabby often saw Papili sitting all alone in the store with his head resting on his desk. It was a wrenching sight. He couldn't pay his loyal assistants Bruno Bettlemann and Hermann Schlick, but they came in every day, dusted the books, rearranged them neatly on the shelves, made coffee hoping that soon the Nazi storm would blow over.

"Poor Papili, financial ruin and the uncertainty about his family's future drove him to make the ultimate sacrifice." Gabby was barely audible, her voice had dropped to a whisper, "In desperation he put *Marcus Aurelius* on the market to raise money for Rudi's discharge from hospital. Gaining entry into the US with a mentally ill young son was next to impossible. Time was of the essence if you wanted to cross into Italy before the borders closed."

**** ****

BOOK II

(i)

The old Umeed had started as a hamlet under a clump of banyans and continued to scrabble up by fits and starts along the Alka river. The King had built a clock-tower but the toil-bent poor hardly ever looked up.

Monsoon made a slow lingering exit, lying doggo in clothes and doorknobs till late September, lurking unseen in ancient banyans only to reappear and shower you splashingly when the wind blew; everything you touched started leaking, and gurgling. Leaving behind a watery, swollen world, its fading patter lasted almost till October.

Right from the start Gisela and Cy knew that to cure the poor was only a part of their job, it was even more important to hammer in that malaria and typhoid were not forms of penalty incurred by them for defaulting on a votive offering to some godling but maladies bred in nearby sewers or stale sweets bought from shops listing over open drains. The reservoir from princely times, which provided safe water, was stretched to its limit with temporary settlements mushrooming around factories fringing the old fortification.

One morning as soon as the Sorabjis settled in their offices they were surprised to see a group of patients in tatterdemalion clothes standing in their respective doorways. A man with tobacco-stained teeth stepped forward and handed Cy a creased piece of paper on which were scrawled the following lines.

Your honor, it is our painful duty to bring to your notice the fact that the Matron Mrs Savitabehn belongs to the unclean Bhangi caste. We cannot let her touch our bodies and therefore request you most respectfully to dismiss her and appoint a suitable person.

Before Cy could finish reading the flap door swung open and Gisela came in with a carbon copy of the note.

"For Goodness sake what is the meaning of this?"

Cy asked the men to leave his office immediately. He opened his flask and poured Gisela a glass of water. She drank it slowly in small gulps and put the glass on the coaster depicting two trunk-entwined elephants from Umeed's courtly sport of battering pachyderms. In a voice still quavering with emotion Gisela recounted what had been essentially a re-enactment of the just concluded tableau in Cy's office. One by one her patients had filed in perhaps goaded by their men, slightly lurching forward like a chorus of old women in Greek Tragedy.

"I know how ridiculous this must seem to you; I am in a state of shock," Cy said taking Gisela's hand and pressing it gently. "I've been away too long to remember this ugly face of India. Let's close down the clinic for the day, go home and take stock of the situation. These idiotic people need to be taught a lesson."

"I don't think closing down the clinic even for a day would be the right solution," Gisela said. "It would be an admission that we took heed of this outrageous behavior. And it would only annoy dear Savita. No, we must nip this thing in the bud. I am sorry I reacted so strongly to the note. I should have just thrown it in the wastebasket. No, no there's only one way to deal with it. We'll ignore it and start examining other patients – there are still plenty of them out in the waiting rooms. We'll just act as though the incident never happened. And if the men and women who brought the note to us come back for treatment we'll ask Mr Kazmi to tell them we won't treat them if they misbehave again."

Cy relaxed. Of course Gisela was right. That was the only way to convey to the misguided lot how vainglorious and grotesque their high caste posturing was. The Sorabjis had chosen Savita from a pool of nine other applicants. With her immaculate training at the oldest and most prestigious Nursing School in Bombay, her starched outfit and scrupulously maintained standards of hygiene, those women in rags and men in unwashed clothes were not good enough to lick her sandals.

Throughout that comic opera the Matron had maintained a dignified silence. Under her no-nonsense style of supervising, the wards soon settled down to a brisk and cheerful routine. The matron had won many battles against caste prejudice in her village near Bombay. There were times in her early life when she could not fill jerry cans at the only water pump till well-fed high caste women who wiped their runny noses with loose ends of their expensive saris had helped themselves to their daily quota and gone home. As a brilliant girl child of a low-caste family she had learned to make do with a single dress, washing and drying it every night ready to wear for school next day. She had to sit alone on a rickety bench at the back. Slowly she gained a reputation as the brightest in her class and when her father secured a job in a textile mill in Parel, she enrolled in a nursing school in Bombay headed by Miss Fergusson, a Scottish lady who had served in a field hospital during the Great War.

One day, disregarding the I-told-you-so glances of the petitioners who'd demanded her ouster, Savita rounded up all the nurses, filled buckets with hot water and led them out into the street. Armed with brooms and mops they started sweeping off fly-encrusted cow-dung whorls and picking up the litter. People watched in horror at this bold salute to the Matron's night-soil moving ancestors, but were soon shamed into assisting in the clean-up operation she had initiated on their street.

The Sorabjis soon found themselves working well beyond their respective specializations. Cy did not claim more than a generalist's knowledge of pediatrics yet the poor flocked to their clinic with sick children. At times dad or mum seemed to be in a greater need of treatment for afflictions ranging from the common cold to tuberculosis than did the child with distended belly or snotty green nose. Elsewhere in town children continued to die of tetanus because instruments were not sterilized in Government-run hospitals. There was always an unappeased god or a vengeful ghost of a dead mother to share the blame.

Those early years in Umeed every moment of respite was heavy on Gisela's eyes till a new patient claimed her attention. By then the Nazi mind had revealed its basic structure as mousetrap with its lethal tripping device. Only by Cy's comforting side her appetite for life remained robust. He argued that she too would have perished had she not got out of Vienna before it was too late. But Gisela couldn't even bear to look at her daughter who was born with Mutti's almond-shaped green eyes.

Every other year the paneled bedroom walls of the Sorabji bungalow were treated with linseed oil, giving off a snug nutmeg smell that mingled with the incoming breeze. Gisela's eyes would snap open at the crest of a nightmare to find Cy sitting up watching over her. But for that faint soporific smell coming off the wall she could have been back in her small bedroom in Vienna, Papili pressing a cool compress to her fever-wracked forehead. She had this sensation of being gathered into a vast, forbidden tenderness. It turned off the pressure valve that kept her suspended between life and death choices at the clinic and put the mother in her on the surface. In that moment, the sap of life flowing free, she felt her time on earth being reset.

Gisela tried to make up for surrendering her daughter's childhood to her grandmother but it was too late. Juno never warmed to her, was too willful to understand the massive history of European Jewry. She felt in no way connected to the fate of her mother's people, took greater interest in the voluptuous Vienna of Klimt than in the way its Jews were booted out into exile.

For thirty years Gisela toiled by her husband's side to make his dream come true, and for years after his passing kept the clinic going. Now she is done, has no more to give. Sometimes at night, alone in her bungalow, she hears Cy's crisp public school voice exhorting her,

"We must press on, dear girl, regardless."

But she cannot keep the 'show on the road,' India is no longer the country she had come to as a young doctor with her husband.

**** ****

One evening Terry finds a swanky Bentley parked outside their house on Revelstoke Road in Wimbledon Park. Sounds of laughter in the kitchen, wife doubled up on the floor, a light-skinned subcontinental type, napkin shaped like Nehru cap, doing an immigrant with exaggerated Indian accent. "Blimey guv'na'," he cries, switching effortlessly to stage cockney, "If it ain't the Man from Aunty, 'ow are you mate?"

"This is Shekhar." Juno's tone is that of a curator unveiling the *Blue Boy* by Gainsborough at a traveling exhibition. "He was the school chum of the Kashmir Prince, in *Death on Dal Lake* at the Duke of York's?"

"Wonly a minor role, sorr," a Bollywood South Indian head-waggle has her in stitches. Then he is off again segueing to a Music Hall comic turn, walking sideways, waving an imaginary hat, chanting,

'All round town it's the same

With every pop, pop, pop goes up my fame

I'm the darling of the barmaids

Champagne Charlie is my name.'

Occasionally Shekhar's mummery flags; a consonant slurs; a vowel is fudged in a flare-up of Indian clackety-clack. Color-blind performances are still not common. Shekhar blames typecasting for his stalled career.

The flip side of his self-mockery is a hatred of things British. Asks for a packet of *Benson & Hedges* at the corner store in Peter Sellersish pidgin, then watches them squirm under Queen's English.

Shaky sends Juno into hysterics, especially when he moves like a mechanized Teddy bear, assembled with parts that do not always engage each other. Terry's partiality to 'fish n' chips', Lanky accent, rooting for Manchester United are fair game. Terry's coming home early one evening unmasks his backhanded mimicry.

For Juno it's harmless play-acting, for the moribund actor it's political.

One Sunday Juno and Shaky cook chicken masala but it is too hot for Terry. Sitting side by side on a sofa facing him, both begin to make fun of English food.

"All great civilizations", Shaky observes "produced great cuisine, the Chinese, the Indians, the French and even the Mexicans but the English have nothing to offer except roast beef and fish 'n chips. Why's that?"

"Yes, why's that Terry?" Juno asks.

Between Juno and Shaky there are looks, a private joke flickers.

"It's because we've been too busy building a great empire and teaching you wogs good manners," Terry replies, as though he were breezily engaging in a cross-chat with old friends.

"You mean grabbing our lands and lording over us," Shaky quips trying hard not to betray emotion.

"Why not? If your so-called great civilization had its bum hanging out the window."

Shaky seems nonplussed by this eruption of pugnacity in Terry. A high-pitched giggle from Juno gives the first round to her husband.

"Well, what would you say to that?" Juno nudges Shekhar hoping to ignite fireworks.

But the actor gets up saying he has 'to see a man about a dog,' slips into the toilet and soon makes for the front door with his tail between his legs.

After seeing him off Juno returns and sits down by Terry.

"Naughty boy, you were very mean to Shaky. He is so fragile."

"Fragile my foot. The man's given to puffery, all talk and no trousers."

"Terry, what's got into you? Where's the gentle charming man I married? I must confess this new you frightens me a bit."

"There's nothing new about it. It's called plain-speaking where I come from. I am all for some jolly back-chat but when he gets downright offensive, giving himself airs, talking as though butter won't melt in his mouth."

"Is he put out," Juno says brushing her lips against his cheek. "Darling, Shaky is just a friend, nothing more. He was very disappointed when Dino Shafeek got the role of the Bangladeshi in *It Ain't Half Hot Mum*. Shaky was turned down because he was too light-skinned for an average Bangladeshi. No wonder the poor dear feels victimized by forces of darkness. But with you gone all day, I couldn't possibly do all the shopping and laundry without him. Petrol costs are going up but he never refuses me a lift for my scheduled check-ups at the hospital now that I am pregnant."

"That's all very well but why does he have to play Laurence Olivier off stage as well?" Terry asks. "Why can't he be himself for a few seconds? I am sure he'd land a suitable part if he loosened up and stopped acting within acting all the time."

The next few weeks Terry remained too busy to carry on a sustained campaign to wean Juno away from Shaky, whose dog-like devotion flattered her at a time when approaching motherhood constricted her movements and she was unable to stand at an easel for long hours. She was also trying to prevent her figure from ballooning but without much success.

At the end of a tiring day at TVC when Terry sat down for dinner, she gave vent to her feeling of being trapped in Wimbledon Park. Terry's mind was on the latest confrontation between the IRA and the Loyalists-backed police action in Ulster. Maggie Thatcher's paranoia about lefties subverting the BBC into an anti-Government cartel had finally created a rift within its ranks. Battle lines were being drawn between those who cherished their freedom of expression and those who bent over backwards not to be seen as fellow-travelers.

At such a crucial moment in his career, with the distinct possibility of getting fired, his wife's litany of real and imaginary grievances ejected him from the table without finishing his supper.

Before pregnancy put paid to her long leisurely excursions, Juno loved window-shopping in Knightsbridge and Regent Street. An aristocratic man or woman in Umeed did not visit hairdressers, tailors and cobblers. A tailor arrived at the bungalow with his measuring tapes and a pencil stub tucked behind an ear. Haberdashers brought in bolts of cloth; laundry was collected and delivered at home by dhobis. You rarely walked down the bazaar, jewelers and diamond merchants called at the bungalows with their latest acquisitions.

Although Juno broke with tradition and went shopping by herself in Umeed her presence was noticed and her car recognized as one belonging to the house of Sorabji. She could not move in Umeed without creating waves.

Her anonymity amidst crowds spilling out of the Underground, jostling with shoppers at Harrods, striking up conversation with a knowledgeable stranger at the National Gallery, having someone flick open a lighter as soon as she held up a cigarette to her mouth, in short to draw admiring looks from absolute strangers rather than be treated as an artifact adorning a pre-eminent house was very seductive. Terry was free over weekends to drive her to the green-grocers and butchers in and around Wimbledon in his small car, but for the rest of the week she needed Shaky and his roomy vehicle for jaunts into town to relieve her boredom.

Terry spent most of his time buried in the bowels of the Television Center while Juno explored London in the company of Shekhar. The bond between them was growing; despite her European pallor and his Mayfair posturing, a door never opened without dilation of their facial muscles, coordinated flutter of eyes, a temple-dance togetherness against crumbling ruins, a thin line of smoke curling over a burning ghat.

The Swinging Seventies were over and Thatcher was dividing England into haves and have-nots but Juno didn't mind or care. Politics bored her. The 'haves' found her interesting. Her looks set her apart from frumpy house-wives in Wimbledon Park. In Umeed the men she knew were friends of the family, in London there were young attractive faculty at the Slade and prom-ising fellow artists with whom she could have long conversations in the pubs around Bloomsbury.

Spreading wings was what she did best. Being trapped in a bourgeois marriage was proving to be suffocating. She had already stopped wearing her wedding ring.

At the annual Christmas Party his colleagues who had some inkling of Terry's drab North Country background were startled to see an exotic woman standing by his side. Terry was considered something of a dark horse for squiring such a sensational beauty. Those who saw Juno for the first time always pictured her in a Riviera-like setting hurtling in a convertible down twisting roads carved through mountain passes, silken locks blown back by gusts from the Mediterranean.

Her hair fell in soft waves around her oval face; her near myopic eyes gave the impression of unwavering concentration as she listened. She was a good listener to those whom she had decided to take under her wing, so to speak. Artists in the making were particularly vulnerable to that calm emerald-flecked gaze which dramatically boosted their self-image.

During the early stages of pregnancy Juno expanded moderately; except for a slight puff beneath the chin her face did not thicken, maternity gowns fell slinkily around her in tantalizing folds. Her skin shimmered and her blue-green gaze deepened as she reached pre-partum stasis. Standing next to a budding artist in a portrait gallery she could easily pass for his muse.

Initially his tenacity for self-assertion helped Shekhar land a few minor roles but his gifts lay in superficial mimicry. He was essentially a schoolboy doing an impression of the absent teacher; his talent wasn't deep enough for major roles. Juno thought dapper Shekhar eminently suitable to play Nehru in David Attenborough's *Gandhi* but the casting director told her, when audition-ing for the plum part her friend had sounded like a linguaphone record rather than an actor delivering lines. Terry was convinced that his rival for Juno's affections was a man whose soul was sensitive without being enthusiastic, it was too languid to thrill out of self-consciousness into passionate life; it went on fluttering in the swampy ground where it was hatched, thinking of wings, not flying.

Eventually Shekhar was picked up to play an Anglo-Sinhalese, mixed-breed manager of a coffee plantation who tries to pass himself off as a full-blooded Englishman in a film to be shot on location in Sri Lanka but time and again his performance lacked conviction and the director ticked him off for not memorizing his lines.

While Terry was in famine-ravaged Ethiopia in 1980, Juno took Shekhar with her to Umeed. After spending barely a month with her new baby girl, she flew to Colombo where he was location shooting.

By the time Juno returned to London after a hurried visit to Umeed to see her six-month old baby girl, Shekhar was already hooked on cocaine.

**** ****

Perrin was only an occasional Parsi, mainly in the kitchen but most of the time she was vice-reine in a tiara. Like a snickety governess grooming a princess she closely monitored Juno's speech and deportment. Juno's ayah, Mrs Fernandez, came highly recommended from Residency circles — she had looked after the Sanders twins. She was interviewed for the post by Perrin herself and selected on the basis of the excellent reference furnished by Mrs Sanders the Surgeon's wife who named her 'the best ayah in Hindostan'. But that didn't cut much ice with Lady Perrin Sorabji, Mrs Fernandez's accent was flawed, like most other ayahs of the time she said 'bebby' instead of 'baby.' That absent diphthong did her in. The poor woman could dress the child and attend to all her toiletries but she was not permitted to read to her. That task was undertaken by the doting grandmother herself.

By the time I returned home Juno was already fast asleep and I was off to the clinic before she was up. Then one Sunday in May Juno Baba uttered a perfectly formed sentence. That hot summer evening while we sat on the terrace trying to catch the breeze, the little girl being led to her bedroom by Ayah Fernandez stopped in the doorway touched her forehead with the back of her hand and said, "Oh dear, I shall simply fade away in this heat."

Cy was amused by his daughter's impeccable mimicry of Grandma Perrin and swooped her up laughing loudly. I was too taken aback to find it amusing. Later that night I had a dream in which little Juno stood smiling in a pool of light, taking a bow with the artful smile of a seasoned diva when suddenly a red curtain began to descend massively, burying her in its plush folds.

Juno Baba's impression of Perrin giving instructions to the syce in pidgin Hindi was pitch perfect.

"Toom baccha ko ghore per seedha bithao, baccha ka back abhi banka hai.' (See that the child sits upright in the saddle, she should not bend forward.)

The clinic permitted me little time for any intervention; I saw from the corner of my eye the mock-adult girl with her taking ways grow into a willful teenager, flashing winsome babyish charm to demolish adult lines of defense.

No toy train imported from England, an engine painted silver gray with red carriages on tracks running along nursery floors, or a doll with deep blue eyes and blond curls straight from Paris was too expensive for Lady Sorabji's adored grandchild.

Old copies of *Aucktimus*, the magazine of her boarding school in Simla, were dusted off and granddaughter regaled with stories of escapades during pony rides to Jakko, eluding the matron. Perrin described in great detail the spread at the viceregal tea to which the Principal of Auckland House, 'dear Miss Pratt', escorted only those girls who had mastered the art of curtsying to the Vicereine.

At the Convent of Jesus and Mary, Juno was a lonely child because Perrin would not allow her to associate with 'half-breed' Anglo-Indian or Goan Catholic girls of 'paunwala' (baker) pedigree, although some of them were very bright and had nice manners. Juno's only other companions were the two shy little princesses with similar restrictions on their movement despite the Old Her Highness's enlightened views on the emancipation of women.

Juno adored Mother Schultz who was appointed Principal at the Convent after the War. Our daughter would say 'I can't believe all Germans are evil' just to provoke me into saying something disagreeable about the nun. The Principal and Sister Clement who taught French were oddly kind, and somewhat foolish. I did not actually spurn them but had little time or inclination to befriend them. They resented my growing friendship with the Old Her Highness.

Along with Perrin, those two became surrogate mothers to Juno and encouraged her in her silly games, flattered her and turned her head, filling it with ideas of Europe's superiority over India. They subtly corrupted her and watched over her possessively till Juno got arrested at that self-regarding, now-girl, now-woman stage.

Everybody's life was a backdrop to her own. Towards the end of her life Perrin realized that her granddaughter was too skittish for her age and social class. She snorted and fumed when Juno brought home scruffy-looking beedi-chewing class-mates in paint-splattered dungarees who sprawled over her antique mahogany furniture. They spoke no English but were said to be trail-blazing painters and sculptors from the College of Fine Arts. Perrin found it difficult to keep up with them while they lounged and joked in bazaar Hindi well beyond her grasp. Some of them never even washed and left such a stink behind that Perrin locked herself up in her bedroom upstairs while Subhadra and Bahadur opened all the windows and sprayed antiseptic detergents. Fortunately Perrin didn't live to see Juno marry feckless Chanda Sahib, a promising polo-playing cousin of the royals gone to pot who soon drove himself to death in a ditch.

Juno's lack of conventional sentiment, the drifting, rootless rage, the fascination with sensation all stemmed from being brainwashed into thinking that she was special, a norm unto herself.

Perrin merely did what a woman of her generation and upbringing thought fit. It has taken me all this while to understand that in my mother-in-law's Edwardian fantasies there were elements of Papili's and Mutti's stubborn fealty to the Vienna of the mind. How far removed was the life Perrin and her kind from that of my poor women patients!

Madam Sorabji soon realized that I wasn't going to be her ally against all those who challenged her. At first she took pains to project herself as an ultra-modern woman well versed in western music and art to her Viennese daughter-in-law but gradually, when I began to spend what she considered an inordinate amount of time at the clinic, instead of accompanying her to the bandstand in the Park on Sunday where the brass band played old worn-out Raj-era tunes, or organizing whist drives at the Club, she began to withdraw into an Olympian silence.

Most mid-level British wives of that period had been heavy-bosomed middle-class Mems whose sole purpose in life was to provide their hard-working spouses with heirs to be schooled in England. With her childhood monitored by bossy-boots governesses and Miss Pratt of Auckland House, Perrin had taken upon her the task of dispensing British haute couture in Umeed. In addition she spoke French with a Parisian accent and recited Baudelaire and Verlaine, making the English housewives feel uneducated. She was on first-name terms with the wife of the Governor of Bombay and English ladies of her entourage who had been blessed with advantages similar to hers.

My English improved rapidly in her company. I learned to say 'box of matches' instead of 'match-box' and 'rich' instead of 'wealthy' when talking about a well-to-do person. Since I could barely bring myself to speak German till my late Sixties, Goethe and Rilke never figured in my small talk as Keats and Tennyson did in hers.

She kept the priests or dasturs at the Fire Temple at bay and made a hefty donation every year for never bringing up her absence from prayers. When invited to distribute prizes to girls she let it be known with a pitying smile how far the nuns had to go in improving the educational standards at the convent. The Goan Catholic and Belgian nuns deferred to her in matters concerning the correct pronunciation of names of past Residents who had donated money for various prizes. Perrin gleefully corrected them when they stumbled upon family names that were pronounced differently from the way they were spelled such as Affleck for Auchinleck, Mannering for Mainwaring, and Marchbanks for Marjoribanks.

Such was Perrin's Umeed, a studio-mock up of Cheltenham and Bath, of grand theatrics and hollow pageantry.

But beyond that mimic imperium was the real city the Old Highness and his English tutor had constructed, a place of many simple joys, with hints of heart-breaks at the passing of great seasonal rituals such as the adoration of trees and rivers. It was that Umeed I fell in love with.

In those early days I used to watch the smiling tanned faces of patients and wonder if I could ever be accepted as one of them.

Umeed and Wien — was there congruence, an elective affinity? From palaces to colleges, courts of law and parks with bandstands, the ideal polis every old Indian princely city being modeled on was London. Seamsters in makeshift cardboard boxes called themselves Savile Row Tailors, a barber with a mirror and a chair was Mayfair Hair Salon and tea and snack shop the Ritz or Claridges. Vienna had not even scratched the surface of Umeed before I arrived.

In princely Umeed power became as graceful as in Franz Josef's capital, with just a touch of flamboyance on state occasions.

Evenings in Vienna's Kohlmarkt, footsteps of late shoppers faded softly, well-oiled wrought-iron gates of big houses opened with a decorous swish to let in riders. The pavement echoed in Bergasse with the slow ruminating steps of Herr Doktor Professor Freud and his wife as they set out for the garden across the canal.

I imagined Umeed to be a scaled-down version of Wien, not the narcissistic imperial capital with its baroque splendor on display, but the town fallen silent after the glittering Staatsoper gentry had gone home, a lonely fiacre slowly disappearing down an avenue for a well-earned rest, and along a side street with drawn blinds the faint sound of 'a violin giving itself to someone' — all touched by the same idea of unflaunting urbanity.

In Umeed the clip-clop of horse and carriage fading into the night had the same sound of friendly farewell as in the Vienna of my childhood. It too had grown old like a veteran actor who has taken good care of his aging body. City of royals, all its vital signs intact, not loud or bristling, a buggy here, a motorcar with a canvas hood there, nosing through the bazaar, blowing a muffled guttural horn.

Umeed was much smaller than Wien, and certainly dustier - yet this city of my exile had all the right instincts for elegance with a fleet of hosing vans tamping down dust in the afternoon. With seven magnificent palaces, it was comfortable with its heritage, the past being constantly modified to serve the present.

The dome and clock towers, museums, observatories and libraries revealed the ruler's plan to open his subjects' eyes to other possibilities, an attempt to explain in local terms how the larger world lived. He built a palatial building of sculpted marble to house a vegetable market; the enormous Romanesque domes of the College of Arts and Sciences offered his people a stake in his vision of the city. The royal processions of the Old Highness's times, which used to fetch village women in colorful saris and men in red and green turbans to cheer the cavalry regiments and infantry battalions dressed in uniforms with splashes of red and gold, petered out during the war years. I had arrived in Umeed during its twilight years when it lay quietly breathing its last under a vast umbrella of banyan leaves.

That green cover has disappeared and during summer the sun comes at it
like a wrecking-ball. Watching tongue-tied as yet another town declines into
a crypt, its public parks taking on aspects of untamed wilderness I feel as if
once again I am being shown the door. But there is nowhere to go.

****

*I hope, at this distance in time, I can separate my Vienna from Papili's without any awk-
wardness. In essence, what for me was walking the plank Papili saw as navigating the menacing rapids of history by an improvised raft. For him anti-Semitism was something that
happened to those who clung to old ways, the black hat, the beard and the long jacket. His
reaction to Miriam Strobin's older brother being attacked by Nazi goons on the ramp of
Vienna University was to join the exodus from the Café Central to Café Herrenhoff and
bury his head in the pages of Neue Freie Presse.*

He'd enrolled me at great personal expense in the progressive girls' Gymnasium founded by Eugenie Schwarzwald because Otto Rommel taught
literature there and Oskar Kokoschka drawing and painting. But already
there was resentment in Vienna because Schwarzwald students who were
predominantly Jewish began to claim a disproportionately large number of
seats at the Faculty of Medicine. Slowly for our generation anti-Semitism
ceased to be an academic issue and became a bread-and-butter one affect-
ing our future careers.

For Papili Vienna was *Heimat*, plain and simple. My going to London to
study medicine was akin to a misguided Athenian youth traveling to Sparta in
search of knowledge.

*If I had Sissi's skill to make an effective power-point presentation I would not choose
the most talked-about episodes from Vienna before the War. I would not linger too long
laboring the obvious; Nazi Germany pre-empting Chancellor Schuschnigg's attempt to hold
a referendum on a free and independent Austria or Hitler, with the Hofburg as back-drop
preening himself before cheering crowds. Rather, I'd direct the laser beam at the sneers that
greeted Jewish shoppers in the Naschmarkt even before the Anschluss. I would let it wander
across to Papili's bookstore Marcus Aurelius and let it settle on some hardliners among his
regulars whose expression changed from scholarly curiosity to indignation when they spotted
the works of Thomas Mann and Joseph Roth. One such browser finally betrayed him, had*

him deported to Auschwitz. History bottoms up reflected more clearly what was to come.

More German than the Germans by the grace of Goethe and Schiller, Papili's tirade against Zionism grew even more strident as he retreated further into his Socialist Utopia. *Marcus Aurelius* was located almost within the Innere Stadt, was patronized by the white-gloved elite who moved through the aisles wrapped in silence. His cousin Moisher ran a hardware store in Ottakring, jostled by workers in greasy overalls.

The more Vienna began to cozy up to the Aryan brigade the more Papili withdrew into his fantasy Kultur. Without pausing to reflect on what was happening, he vented his frustration in a language of echoes and reverberations.

I could see that Papili was withdrawing into a chimeric Vienna of his youth and it frightened me. It was no longer a case of cultural preferences but a calculated head-in-the-sand shrinking from truth; he traveled to Rome along with Mutti on 26th July 1933, the day after the Nazi-sponsored assassination of Chancellor Dollfuss. Papili's long time friend and fellow bibliophile Signor Tursi who ran one of the oldest bookstores in Rome, was 80 and his family laid out a birthday party straight out of the Satyricon — one of Papili's favorite books.

Clowning for each other is a madness for which there is no asylum.

****

<h1 style="text-align:center">(iii)</h1>

The first flyover snuck into Umeed during the Emergency, spanning a railway crossing where a branch line train used to back up peak hour traffic for half a mile in either direction. Commuters on scooters and drivers of sputtering auto-rickshaws revved their engines up the new ramps with cheery toots and horns. Over the next few years, flyovers proliferated with workmen-like cunning, casting dark shadows over bright places, advancing their snouts through snarling jungles of stalemated traffic.

'Kalké Log', yesterday's people, their palaces and parks straitjacketed in concrete sleeves, took their constitutional in the foul air below, overturning litter with silver-topped canes in the hope of finding lost trinkets of self-respect. Mostly, these 'former folk' preferred to eke out their final days in the few remaining slivers of open spaces that had eluded the builders' cranes.

At first the new builders of Umeed with their soft pampered bodies covered in muslin, foreheads daubed with red caste marks, gold chains dangling from padded necks looked like members of an esoteric cult; men of few words but skilled practitioners in moving massive bulldozers and giant cranes across vast building sites as if they were no more than hieratic dragons on a deck of cards.

Pavanlal, the doyen among builders, had the droopy look of an owl that suddenly perks up and whirls its neck almost ninety degrees without straining it. He seemed to conduct his business in a trance-like state. One could argue that his silence implied lack of an English education; the sly look in his eye belied such assumption. He let his lackeys do all the talking while he lolled on bolsters chewing tobacco and betel, ejecting with dead accuracy red jet-streams into a pan-dan or spittoon without bending forward. Sidekicks came and touched his feet but he never blinked nor spoke. Even as a recently bereaved father he'd received with a shrug the news of his infant daughter's death due to hepatitis.

Pessy had come to fetch Gisela and Cy to the dying child's bedside. As an English-speaking lad who ran with the builder pack, Pessy didn't quite fit the profile of your average upright Parsi who held sacrosanct the Zoroastrian rift between the good and bad eggs of Ormuzd and Ahriman. He saw his induction in the developers' cabal as a way out of genteel poverty into which his father's honest Parsi practices had landed the family.

Pessy looked at the pinched face of his mother Behroz, the gaunt form in a threadbare brocaded sari of his unmarried sister Homai, and decided to throw in his lot with the winning side, elevating palm-greasing to an art form. His fetching ways and polished speech opened doors of palaces and villas where old feudal lords and their dowagers drowned their sorrow in chotta pegs over the loss of privilege in the crass, dog-eat-dog world of independent India. One by one they signed away their mango orchards and farmlands to grasping tribes of developers.

By the time the Sorabjis reached the child's bedside it was all over. Staring balefully at his wife for making a mountain out of a molehill over the loss of a mere girl-child, Pavanlal stood in the doorway talking to young Dr Trivedi, the pediatrician who'd been treating her. But as soon as his wife began to curse him for not consulting the foreign-trained doctors sooner to save her child, he turned his back, walked stiffly to his scooter parked outside and roared away to his new building site. Dr Trivedi mumbled an apology on his behalf while the bereaved mother shed silent tears.

The young doctor could not determine the cause of the child's death. Cy lingered, asking questions that seemed almost irrelevant to Dr Trivedi. Gisela and Cy immediately suspected that the child might have drunk some contaminated water regularly over a period of time. In death the girl was extremely pale, her eyeballs like wilted marigolds. Dr Trivedi had correctly diagnosed hepatitis but had not been able to trace it to its source. The bedroom where she had died was quite clean, there was nothing to suggest that the child might have caught the infection from some source other than water. Cy asked permission to go into the kitchen and look around. He found a utensil filled with watery milk.

Between sobs the poor woman said a shepherd delivered the milk every morning. Gradually all the pieces of the puzzle fell into place. As Dr Trivedi stood open-mouthed, Cy told him that the unpasteurized milk consumed over several months could have damaged the child's liver.

Dr Trivedi asked the mother why she did not feed her girl milk produced under hygienic conditions by the local dairy that had been in business since 1935. Beside herself with grief, the woman began to beat her chest and curse her husband.

It wasn't as if at the start of his building enterprise Pavanlal could not afford to buy pasteurized milk bottled by the Umeed Dairy Corporation. But any extra expense for the sake of a baby girl seemed unwarranted to him. He claimed to have grown to healthy manhood on milk delivered by the farmer. "What was good for me and my brothers is good enough for my daughter," he had retorted.

In a sorrowing working woman dressed in the same threadbare sari every day the pain of a lost child gets sedimented as soon as she hoists a pile of bricks onto her head to carry it up the ladder at a construction site. But Pavanlal's wife in her sari of floral silk had no training in churning pain into toil.

With no support group to heal with, she grieved alone in her childless empty house while Pavanlal who'd started as a junior partner in the construction business went on to become a top honcho in the building trade and was eventually elected to the board of governors of the thriving Umeed Dairy Corporation.

Women construction workers in magenta saris sang in chorus to ease the heavy loads that strained their bones to breaking point. As the new buildings soared skywards dwarfing the sheltering banyans, their keening grew faint and free of resentment, a whispering dirge rustling through the green core of grief.

When a ten-month-old child from a roadside hammock swinging by a smoky, makeshift cooking range, smell of tar lacing the gruel in the pot came down with gastroenteritis and stopped breathing, they brought it to the Sorabji Clinic. The pulse was still there but low and erratic. Cy would administer fluids intravenously and the child would move and begin to breath again. Fellow women workers hailed 'Savior Sorabji' and sang a song of hope that one day the same miracle might visit their wombs.

In the early days of limited diagnostic tools, eyes of the spent mother boring into her, Gisela stood still till that familiar bad-tempered squeal escaped the tiny mouth. Then she felt herself to be a part of that circle of singing women in magenta saris.

**** ****

Rubbish, no one can say that I, Pavanlal do not love my wife. What's more, I was also fond of my dead girl, in my own way. Not feeding dairy milk was not a deliberate act of thrift, it was family tradition. Rest assured I am my own man and can give as good as I take.

How was I to know that the milk would kill the girl? I don't understand all this bacteria-shacteria stuff. If the kid was snatched away it was Balaji's wish. I have absolute faith in Balaji and make a pilgrimage to Mehdipur in Rajastan every year by bus since there is no direct train from Umeednagar to the holy shrine. When the girl was taken ill I pledged a donation of ten thousand rupees to Balaji, plus a new pitamber of yellow silk for the lord himself. Balaji has been our family deity since my great grandfather's time and even after my own father migrated to Devasthan to set up a grocery shop in the main bazaar the Lord has been guarding our house. I am sure the mace wielding Lord who single-handedly flew to Lanka carrying in his arm a mountainside crammed with medicinal trees as it says in the Ramayana, will provide us with another child, only let it be a boy this time, O Lord, so that our line shall continue.

I simply couldn't hang around when Sundari my wife was scolding me right in front of the foreign doctors. I was angry, and why not? Don't I buy her a new gold necklace or diamond-studded bracelet every Diwali?

The doctors must have got the impression that I am some sort of a country bugger, which I am most certainly not, ask that Parsi gentleman Pestan Sanjanwala. Just because I cannot speak 'gotpit' English like them doesn't mean I am old-fashioned

I had to drop out of high school when my Bapuji died suddenly after our grocery business took a hit. You see our warehouse where our groundnut oil was stored pending the expected price hike during Diwali burnt down. The bazaar gossip alleged that Bapuji set the fire to collect insurance but as the police report confirmed there was no evidence. How can storing what is yours be a crime? The papers call it hoarding and use ugly words like 'black market' to condemn it. But don't maharajas and nawabs sell their gold ornaments only when the market is right for them?

The insurance agency paid up but I knew there was not much profit to be made in the grocery business. The new housing projects were infinitely more lucrative now in our developing country, and specially after Narasimha Rao took charge in Delhi and freed businesses from socialist restrictions.

I had no one to help me finish education. But did I sit down on a fat takia farting all day and doing nothing? No, I apprenticed myself to Rajabhaiya who had started developing housing estates. It was back-breaking work but from Rajabhaiya I learned every trick of the trade, started on a small scale building houses for friends and relatives till I had enough expertise to work from a blueprint. I made trips to Surat and Ahmadabad, Indore and Jaipore to see how they were putting up multi-storied structures as in New York and Chicago. And that too by buying land cheaply.

All my bungalows have the latest plumbing, fixtures and gardens with chowkidars. Gated communities the papers call my housing projects. So who the hell are Sorabji and his kind to look down their long Parsi noses and say I am a junglee?

Now Pessy, who is a Parsi Bawaji himself, understands business. He is not like Dr Sorabji with his nose in the air who if he had his way would keep Umeednagar looking like Fatehpur Sikri, all empty monuments inhabited only by monkeys.

Please don't get the wrong notion that I dislike monkeys. How could I when our Balaji himself appeared on earth during Ramraj in the avatar of a monkey? We cannot keep Umeednagar looking like a dusty old town in Bundelkhand, all old stone and grass. And what good are those locked up palaces now that we are an independent country?

People say it was I, Pavanlal, who gave Pessy his first lesson for success in the building business. I won't deny it, though I must say he had what it takes to be a good builder. You have to be shrewd as a fox and know what justifies some action misjudged as sinful in the first instance by those who lack an acute business sense. Such a bold business tactic almost always produces the greatest good for the largest number of people. Just look around you. All those families who used to rot in narrow, smelly cow-dung-strewn streets with no ventilation now live in smart little row houses along open clean roads.

But first the young Parsi had to be taught a few lessons in raising capital. In the old country the dacoits unfairly accused my Bapuji of charging high interest rates to farmers who needed cash for their daughters' weddings, kidnapped my uncle and threatened to kill him if a ransom of two lakh was not paid for his release. Bapuji paid up and got his brother released but he decided to move his family to Umeednagar. To make up for the money lost in securing my uncle's release, Bapuji had to sell his part of the farmland and our house to raise enough capital for his new business venture.

Without capital you can't even buy a large copper lota to fill with enough water to clean your behind. Now like a good businessman I freely give credit to our Parsi folk where credit is due. For instance they always arrive on time for appointments. They picked up some good habits from the British sahibs and like them they keep checking the time on their wristwatch every five minutes, and if a train or bus is late they look as if the sky was about to come crashing down around them. We Hindus believe this world is all Maya, we never worry about being late. But in business it pays to be punctual. The trouble is in trying to be like the British sahibs the Parsis also adopted some odd customs from them, gave up our age-old practice of cleaning our behinds after a session in the latrine with good clean water. We never touch our dirty flesh till we have flushed it with at least three lotas filled to the brim. I said Pessy yaar, god knows how you bawajis manage with little scraps of paper to wipe yourself.

First rule in business is having enough capital to start business. Today they call it venture capital. Fancy name. But we Baniyas have known from the time of the Mahabharata that you simply cannot gamble away every bit of your fortune like the eldest Pandava brother. If you are foolish enough to do that the other party will simply strip your wife naked in public. In business there is no Krishna Bhaiya to keep supplying yards and yards of saris to save you from disgrace. That is the great lesson Lord Krishna teaches us. Don't gamble away your wife's last sari.

There's simply no substitute for capital if you want to be in any business. You have to have enough of it to absorb the occasional loss when the market dives suddenly like an urchin in a creek for no apparent reason. I myself had to sell all the silverware and the priceless plate of solid gold on which food was served to the gods in our puja room to make a down payment on the piece of land to construct my first housing society. You have to have guts to take risks when necessary; every builder in Devasthan knows that. Now this Bawaji Pessy came whining to me one day asking for a loan to purchase land from Maharaja Sahib's cousin Thakur Jashwant Singh who needed money for his daughter's dowry. Pessy was penniless and lending him four lakh was a business risk I wasn't prepared to take, so I said listen Pestan, I hear your father has this fancy crockery in the Museum. After all they are just cups and saucers and some tea-pots and such, what good are they sitting in the Museum? I mean what is the use of those cups and saucers if you cannot drink masala chai in them? Now, you tell me that some people would be willing to pay a fortune for them. Why they would do that is their business. I have long since given up trying to under-stand some of the strange habits you Bawajis picked up from the British. As my father would have said 'one man's pajama is another man's dhoti.'

Yaar Pestan I said, why not get rid of the crockery if as you say it would fetch three to four lakh. Those cups are no good to anyone just sitting in the cabinet. What happens if some attendant drops them to the floor while cleaning them?

I could see Pessy's eyes opening wide as he kept nodding his head. He mumbled something about how his old man would be very upset since it was family heirloom. So let him be I said. I don't want to be rude but if you won't mind my saying so, your father is a sentimental fool. We are Indians for God's sake; all these crockery-shrokery fads were brought here by the British. If you like I will get my men to help you pack them carefully in crates and ship them to Bombay by truck so that they won't break on the way. I'll also take care of the police if your silly old man files a complaint for removing them from the

Museum. Besides the new Curator of the Museum is personally known to me and I'll tell him not to make any fuss.

Now every time I meet Pessy he presses my hand and says, Pavanbhai you are my Guru, you showed me the right path to Nirvana.

Look, Maharaja Hanutsing wrested Umeednagar from the Muslims before the British came here, Maharaja Raghuvir Singh built all those palaces which were maintained spick and span during the long reign of the Maharaval Dynasty. They were great visionaries but they were warriors first.

We builders are the great warriors of the new India. We must move with the times. That's progress no? Look at all those cities in Gujarat and Mumbai; most of them now look like New York and Chicago. That's progress. I want Umeednagar to be the premier city in Devasthan. So why this hullaballoo people make about the new buildings I put up everywhere? They should congratulate me. My buildings attract businessmen from Mumbai. They are all fed up with the 'dharnas' organized by the Sons of the Soil. Here there is no such problem. Business is the only religion of our Great State of Devasthan. We have provided shelter to all those industries driven out of Calcutta by the Naxalite rabble. Our people had migrated to Calcutta during British rule. We made great fortunes because the Bengali Babus with their noses in books didn't know how to double or quadruple money.

We made money and then opened new factories. But those sister-fucking communists started killing our managers and inciting our workers to burn down our properties. Those Bengali Babus have no business acumen like us. So our Chief Minister invited captains of industry in Calcutta to Devasthan, gave them land to build factories and now we are counted among the most progressive states in India. I am not boasting, even foreign economists say so. So please, no more talk of how Pavanlal is making money on the backs of workers. Use your sense.

I provide employment to two thousand workers. They live on footpaths I know but at least their women and children have food to eat. And when their kids grow up and are strong enough to carry bricks I employ them also. Show me one business in Umeednagar which employs such a big work force. I assure you time is not far when they will say our Pavanlal is the new Maharaja of Umeednagar risen from the masses. I want to see my city on the screen as location with Amitabh Bachchan and Shah Rukh Khan speeding along our flyovers chasing thugs just like in Mumbai.

My aurat is miffed at the moment, the death of our daughter has hit her hard but soon it will pass. Come Diwali I'll buy her a Banarasi Sari and a diamond and pearl necklace. She'd look good in that, I can tell you. Under her sari she's shaped like a court dancer and gets me all hot under my dhoti at night. But I am patient.

Once she allows me to grab her I'll make up for her loss with double interest. And this time it will be a boy, take it from me. Swami Sadanada has taught me a sure-fire asana not included even in the *Kama Sutra*. It has a success rate of one hundred percent. It had better be. The dog-sired charged me three thousand rupees for just one lesson with his pockmarked concubine for partner. And I have been drinking this foul powder he sold me that smells like a detergent. And that didn't come cheap either. What's more I have to take it with goat's milk, which I hate. The things we have to do just to lie with our own aurat will try the patience of Lord Brahma himself.

**** ****

(iv)

As a child I didn't know what went on in a synagogue. There were quite a few of them in and around Leopoldstat where Mutti's younger brother Uncle David lived, and every time we passed one Papili would look up and nod cordially to someone in the throng of worshippers coming out of the building but we never went in. Most of the congregants were immigrants in black coats, beards, and hats recently arrived from Silesia, Moravia, and other western reaches of the crumbling Hapsburg Empire.

Once in Vienna, they walked gingerly, mindful of Franz Josef's posthumous imperial monocle trained on them for any signs of loutish behavior. Leaving behind their abrupt bucolic bustle in rural Hungary, Greece, or Moravia, within a year of their coming to Wien they adapted to the City's polished manner, lowered their voices, shedding rustic tones and gestures. I remember Papili looking at them with compassion as if they were unfortunate beings from an earlier stage of civilization, secure in their parochial certainties that were frowned upon by urbane Vienna.

At best I grew up in a state of religious confusion because during Rosh Hashanah our friends and relatives came visiting to wish us happy New Year and during Christmas we gathered around the Christmas tree and sang O Tannenbaum.

Often when Mutti's Aunt Frieda and Uncle Hans went home after dinner at our flat, Papili told Jewish jokes. In fact he had a whole repertoire of funny anecdotes about Prussians, Americans, Englishmen and Jews, all amusing because they reflected a typical Viennese perspective. While jokes about foreigners tended to be about their national characteristics, the stiff upper-lipped Englishman, the hyperbolic Texan, the passionate Italian and so on, the funniest were about the Jewish schonorrer with chutzpah, or the persistent match-making 'Shadchan' and the irrepressible wifely baleboosteh.

And there were always the irreverent exchanges between a priest and a rabbi. Eyes closed, head thrown back he was the loudest to laugh at his own jokes. But there was no malice in him, his readiness to laugh at his own people was the real measure of his urbanity, and it extended to other aspects of life. He refused to have Rudi circumcised. The family was spared any possible tension over the question of bar mitzvah. He often said that it was in the final year of his gymnasium that he'd lost faith in God.

Repeated evacuations and temporary halts in various hideouts in the countryside had preceded Mutti's grandparents' passage from the Eastern reaches of the retreating Empire which gradually contracted to a point where military parades and ballroom dances were the only reminders of the Hapsburgs after the Great War.

Papili's grandfather's arrival in Vienna had coincided with the demolition of old walls which excluded Jews and the widening of avenues where they could set up shops and businesses under the benevolent eye of Emperor Franz Josef.

Sometimes I wondered how much of Papili's man-about-town posture reflected blindness or indifference to the plight of those who lived in the substandard housing flats of Leopoldstadt barely keeping body and soul together and how much of it was to reassure me that I must not get distracted from my studies and lose my concentration. He was a bookseller with utter faith in the wisdom reposing between the covers of classics, forgetting that they portrayed the world as it should be rather than the way it is. He clutched at straws that reinforced the notion of the perfectibility of human kind, and believed that once everyone discovered how people shared their destiny with each other, their eyes would snap open and race will disappear from their consciousness.

There had been marriages in his family with homegrown girls from Judenplatz and with the accumulation of social and economic prestige an elevation to a fine apartment on Swedenplatz. His great grandparents' midnight escape from a burning shtetl or penny-pinching misery in a Galician suburb were things of the past, tucked away in footlockers in the attic, only to be opened to remind a straying cousin or a flashy aunt of past sacrifices, while the rest of the family set out to conquer the future with a new tribe of doctors, professors and engineers, some completely assimilated through career-enhancing conversions to Christianity. Uncle Franz Rumplemayor, Papili's first cousin, named after the Emperor by a grateful family, was a baptized Catholic and played the cello for the Vienna Philharmonic.

Mutti didn't have a job but she was not just a housewife; she managed the accounts at the bookstore, signing and posting checks and overseeing the packing of books to be posted.

One corner of Mutti's heart still swayed to the old Moravian strains of *Mayim Mayim* and *Od Yishama* even after she married Papili. As a girl she used to sing those songs at the weddings of her older cousins. Mutti's people had left behind the land of those songs but their choices in life were still dictated by the core rhythms of their past. Skilled artisans by trade, for them Goethe and Kant were academic subjects to be studied at university, that is if any of them made it that far; for Papili they were part of his inner furniture, his eyes and ears. His bookstore was his synagogue and Parthenon rolled into one.

Sunday evenings when Uncle Yakob, Mutti's older brother, who taught Physics at my Gymnasium, came for dinner, the discussion around the table got heated. Uncle Yakob doggedly insisted that sooner or later our salvation lay in following Herzl to Palestine. Papili would shudder and shout, "Never. It would be like going into exile, a national version of Leopoldstadt."

How can one will a homeland into existence, prescribe pride and passion for deserts and palm trees left behind two thousand years ago by one's remote ancestors? How could you ignore the chest swelling with pride as soon as you stepped out of your apartment and saw Tram number 1 sliding past the Staatsoper, the Hofburg Palace, the Rathaus and the large chunk of space filled by the dome of Karlskirche?

Unlike the men in caftans and their women in shawls, he had not breathed the incense, the smell that lingered on, a longing that was reinforced by memories of eviction from the shtetl, a memory that sustained Mutti's grandparents in their Viennese exile.

Papili's past was an equivocal, hit-and-miss affair, littered with historical blind alleys and unwarranted embellishments. But the drums beating in far-off Nuremberg were getting louder and I found myself avoiding going to the bookstore where Papili and his cronies continued to live in a fantasy, even when impending catastrophes stalked the pages of his favorite Schnitzler. His myopia was at least partially caused by pouring over learned volumes and he needed to come crashing down from his step ladder as he reached out to retrieve the first edition of Goethe's Faust in his immaculately-catalogued rare books section.

That crash came in the form of a dark betrayal when the very day after the *Anschluss* the fearless poet Werfel, who had squired Alma Mahler, and Max Brod, the disseminator of Kafka's notorious 'midnight knock upon the door', refrained from intervening in the arrest of their friends who ran the Café Herrenhoff.

When Jews were being hounded out of Eastern Europe Papili's father was distinguishing himself fighting for Austria against Prussia and in the Great War on the Western Front Papili had been awarded a medal for driving his ambulance into the line of fire and jumping into trenches to evacuate wounded soldiers to hospital.

Papili's buddies from the army made him complacent to the point where he hardly noticed that new barricades were going up all around and that one day he would be marching with a beleaguered crowd of refugees clutching his bundle. My father failed to appreciate the danger he and his pals were in as they sat discussing horses and their trainers at the Spanish Riding School, tossing around terms like 'renvers' and 'croup-in' not to mention Pesade and Mézair.

With his light-blue eyes, blonde moustache and straight carriage Papili looked so German that he never experienced serious discrimination. He did honestly believe there was no need in modern times to flaunt ethnic garb, the funny round hat and caftan, to wear an unwieldy beard and sideburns. He was not anti-Semitic but thought rocking while reading the Torah inelegant. If he preferred *Heilige Nacht* to the song *Hanuka o Hanuka* it was because it had a soothing effect on him. He didn't realize that the Nazis would consider his ties with Austria unreal, his lederhosen the mere costume of an imposture. No matter how hard he tried to disguise himself as an Austrian the Nazis saw him in caftan and beard.

For Uncle Yakob and his cousins, Palestine was a safe haven after years of indignity. Their suffering had rekindled a deep nostalgia for the desert and palm trees of the scriptures; far from being an affliction, Palestine had become a refuge.

Papili spoke a more cultivated German than most Viennese. Even in those early days following Anschluss, the deeply ingrained provincialism made the Nazi rank-and-file chafe and fume when confronted with Papili's elegance. This was obvious from the harsh, sullen stare of the new receptionist at Steinhof who gave us permission to visit the Children's Ward where our Rudi was being treated.

Nearly 70 percent of Viennese had been expected to vote for Independent Austria at the plebiscite of March 13th. Papili felt massively betrayed when Vienna revealed its snarling face at the finishing line after running the race for freedom. He was no fan of Chancellor Schuschnigg, but the man who dressed like a Ruritanian grandee had stood up to the ranting Hitler at Berchtesgaden and set a date for the plebiscite that would secure Austria's freedom from Germany. When Uncle Yakob and Aunt Zipora visited our flat on the eve of the referendum Papili recited from memory a passage from a Grillparzer poem,

'Sie werden nicht bekommen Sie, die grün Ufer des Donau'

But the sudden collapse into slavery of the aristocrat and the menial standing side-by-side cheering the Nazis was like a scorpion sting. The refined understated discourse of Vienna was now replaced by the barks of the Gestapo swaggering down the Ring, and shoptalk in the cafés was drowned by slogans, *diktats* and decrees. Suddenly all faces were blanched with fear. Harsh Gestapo laughter emanated from bars like the flap of wings heard by a scurrying thing.

The clean, neo-classical facades standing companionably on the Ring, not vying to outshine other buildings, were strong reminders of a lost harmony. So much solid beauty, such abundance of splendor had accumulated here that the red-and-black Nazi drapes hanging from the pedimented windows looked garish and vulgar.

When I returned to Vienna in May 1938, two months since the Anschluss, the city had changed beyond recognition. Papili tried to brush aside the pain and humiliation of having to scrub the streets and swab off the pro-Plebiscite slogans from his store windows enforced with rifle butts by the Nazis, but even he could not shrug off as aberration Viennese women hailing German soldiers with ecstatic shrieks or dismiss as high-spirited pranks the tearing off of earrings from Jewish housewives by schoolboys in uniforms. Dark circles around his eyes and Mutti's fixed stare told of some rank evil spreading its foul-smelling wings over their lives.

****

(v)

The rise and fall of a civilization is difficult to summarize in one single phrase but sometimes the ruins of one unique structure come to signify the sum total of a city's decline. The Athenian Parthenon and the Library at Alexandria were thought to symbolize the essence of ancient Greece and Ptolmaic Egypt. Terry could see why Gisela and Cy considered the neglect of the Royal Umeed Museum by the so-called city fathers an act of vandalism. The state government had its thumb on the throat of Jahangir Sanjanwala the curator; gone were the days when under princely munificence it had acquired the reputation as the finest of its kind in the country. Cy saw the throttling of his friend's Museum as the first act prefiguring the demise of old Umeed but the city fathers of the Municipal Corporation eager to secure financial solvency hailed it as progress.

Cy was slowly withdrawing into a private world of music and books. Looking out at the changing cityscape from his balcony he would say, "Rome and her rats are at the point of battle."

The late monsoon had left the Museum all covered in moss and lichen, walls cracked and crumbling while bevies of tiny schoolgirls in pigtails led by giggling teachers rushed through hall after hall in the Eastern Gallery open to children. Twittering like sparrows they were bustled across the floor so their teachers could report to the principal a successful educational tour. Children scampered through galleries where various kinds of stuffed birds and animals stared at them with dark glistening eyes. They slowed down by the glass cabinet containing the Egyptian mummy, and the skeleton of the wayward whale. Once Terry came across a solitary older man in private communion with a medieval Persian carpet.

In princely times the Museum had been the heartbeat of Umeed. Through its vaulted corridors walked beautiful ghosts reciting hymns to great masterpieces. Jehangir Sanjanwala had been their last great high priest who had kept it running at full capacity sometimes spending his own money to mend a leaky roof or shore up a tilting pediment.

They say 'a man is known by the company he keeps'; having spent day and night communing with painted figures and reclining statues, Jehangir had gradually lost contact with the real world. Fine layers of dust gathered in the crook of a bronze god's arm or a tiny spider silently spinning its silver thread in the far corner of a painted meadow could send him into towering rage quelled only after he'd splutteringly administered a dressing down to an indolent attendant.

Terry had too much respect for the old man to put him in a fishbowl but the borders between culture and economics were getting increasingly porous and Terry couldn't help typecasting some of Cy's friends; the ex-Curator took center stage.

Terry found the old English habit of stereotyping Indians personally repugnant yet he was constantly startled by the way some members of the Umeednagar Club evoked a bygone era in England. Osman Chacha the retired Forest Superintendent sounded Pickwickian when expressing his outrage with a great deal of huffing and harrumphing over an elected officials' moral turpitude. Col Mehra was not exactly the blimp lampooned by John Osborne and the Angry Generation in the England of the Sixties, but ordering the bearers to fetch him a drink his commanding tone echoed parade ground maneuvers.

There was definitely a time lag here and some of the same social upheavals that had rocked England between the wars were replaying in Umeed; the dissolution of old hierarchies was reducing to caricatures those whose life was shaped by colonial education.

When citizens of an old town live simultaneously in two different time zones, shared moral codes of yesterday get hollowed out to serve as today's rubbish bins. Pavanlal Lakhanpal was no Alexander; but he was seen by an influential section of Umeednagar society as the man of the moment. Those who regarded him as a blot on the escutcheon of Umeed had to watch helplessly as one by one he conquered great swathes of the city by reducing public officials to satraps and chattels. The Commissioner of Umeednagar Corporation, a government appointee of the elite Indian Administrative Service was said to be in the builder's pocket.

By now Terry had learned to close his eyes and reflect on things dug up; shards of potted news, votive offerings to false gods, embroidery torn from the fabric of truth or a bygone godfather's bloodstained dagger. At best they offered only a rough approximation to what might have gone wrong. At every impromptu construction where history and gossip intersect there is much floundering and flying off at a tangent. As he watched Umeednagar remake itself, what came out in the wash was quite different from what went in.

Driven out of its old mansion, the sadly decaying fugitive spirit of old Umeed found asylum in the slightly comic figure of the ex-Curator. But the old man on an inspection tour, charging down empty corridors of his Museum, whipping out a magnifying glass to train it on a fine film of dust settled on an ivory figurine's neck, was more Jacques Clouseau than Sherlock Holmes as portrayed by Basil Rathbone. Dreamy eyes protruding through whiskers, Uncle Jehangir, as Juno called him, was like a character from Chekov where all is over for him even before the opening scene begins. He has been set up by his past. Terry was overcome by a wistfulness that accompanies the sound of the breaking string at the end of *The Cherry Orchard*.

Although her college friends considered him an old stick in the mud for deriding their efforts inspired by Picasso and Braque it was Jehangir's voice that somehow kept Juno's brush from wandering beyond the range of probability, lending her work that sense of life pulsating through.

His Groucho style wisecracks always had his friends at the club in stitches. Any comment on his tardiness elicited an instant retort. The adage 'an early bird catches the worm,' was met with 'the worm must have been early too.'

Apart from a modest pension Jehangir had no other means of keeping the wolf from the door. He had spent his time amassing artifacts for the Museum, an august structure in Jacobean-Tudor style rising from the public park with a central tower flanked by green gables. A dark shadowy presence seemed to hover behind tall opaque upper level windows of its two sprawling wings.

Designed by an English architect in 1875 its turrets and belvederes cast discreet shadows over the equestrian statue of a past Maharaja guarding a Roman fountain in the garden below.

A couple of original works by Johann Zoffany, one very probable Constable and a whole series of Dutch winter landscapes, meadows with distant views of canals, and rolling Tuscan tableland, hill-top towns by half-forgotten painters such as Nicolaes Molenaer and Jan Ravesteyn covered the walls under gilded ceilings.

In another room were landscapes reflecting an Anglo-Indian passion for the picturesque, ruined temples smothered in decorous embrace by climbing creepers, crumbling palaces that recalled Roman ruins rather than the umbrella-topped, multi-tiered rajmahals and hawamahals of the bygone era. The third room contained a rich series of paintings by Raja Ravi Verma whose Rubens-esque women, alabaster skin draped in brocaded saris, luxuriant dark tresses snaking past the midriff, canoodled with swans or fed berries to fawns. On the walls of yet another hall, framed by two dimensional pavilions and zarokhas, delicately tinted and miniaturized kings and doe-eyed consorts from Umeed's Mughal and Rajput dynasties struck mannered poses signifying the underlying unity of human and divine love. In an alcove facing the winding marble staircase stood an ersatz David by Michelangelo.

"Our friend Jehangir is still the de facto curator," Cy told Terry. "The chappy appointed by the Government to the position seems to be a rank amateur. Jehangir tells me the fellow simply malingers on a sofa doing practically nothing. He sits there, like a shaggy dog, lapping cups of tea and gossiping with friends while Jehangir conducts the day-to- day business. I gather the new man was a history professor somewhere in the mofussil. But," Cy added with a meaningful look, "he happens to be the first cousin of the Home Minister's wife."

Laughing at the baffled expression on his son-in-law's face Cy said, "What I am trying to tell you politely is that's how appointments are made these days. Naturally the new man is expected to know nothing more than what's good for him. Old Jehangir tries to teach him how to run the show but the chump is not interested. At least that's the impression I get. Jehangir is probably afraid to say more; he has the satisfaction of still working at his old job."

By now both Cy and Gisella were laughing together at the recollection.

"One day," said Gisela, "the Home Minister's wife paid a surprise visit to the Museum to see how her cousin or nephew was getting on. She had heard that there was an Egyptian mummy somewhere lying in a glass cabinet. Wasn't it a present from the Khedive of Egypt, Cy?"

"Yes, you are absolutely right. The old His Highness and the Khedive who suffered from gout often took the waters at Baden-Baden at the same time every year."

"While being escorted to the mummy's chamber, the Minister's chaste wife strayed into the West Wing and stumbled upon the copies of Manet's *Olympia* and Goya's *La maja desnuda*. The woman let off a shriek that scattered the flocks of pigeons mating under the eves. What happened next was straight out of a Feydeau farce."

Gisella was unable to contain her laughter and Cy had to step in.

"Well, it was like this. Mrs Home Minister crashed into Michelangelo's David and fainted at the sight of his idealized manhood. The outraged modesty of his wife galvanized the Home Minister into action; the West Wing was closed down indefinitely. Six old attendants who had guarded the priceless artwork for over three decades were laid off."

In the ruined lives of those hapless men Jehangir heard the lid closing on him. The loss of his priceless china merely drove the final nail into it, so to speak.

*** ***

According to Cy before Jehangir shifted his ancestral china from Surat, art touts in Bombay had offered him five hundred thousand rupees for his collection. Jehangir had reacted as though bitten by a scorpion; righteous indignation dredging up the scatological street patois of his Parsi childhood in Surat he shouted, "Bugger off, go take a running jump in Dhobi Talav, sala, mother-defiling haramkhor you think I am a bloody fool? May your rotten member be chewed to pieces by a pack of rabid mongrels. Every alley cat in every town from Bombay to Delhi knows the Sanjanwala China is comparable only to the Kohinoor."

Sir Thomas Roe had presented the first dinner set in the 17th Century to Shapurji Sanjanwala of Surat. Jehangir had lent his collection to the Museum for wider exposure as the then Curator Dr Herder who was from the Netherlands had counseled. It had taken Pessy just five minutes of thuggery to shake down the new clueless curator and take possession of the china. The wretch told Jehangir he had no reason to doubt his son and heir was merely carrying out his father's wishes.

All the priceless cups, tureens, ewers, tea-pots, creamers, bowls of the most delicate artistry, Wedgewood, Staffordshire, Limoges, Dresden, Fabergé eggs, French enamel snuff boxes with mother of pearl inlay, Lalique wine glasses, you name it, assembled by a succession of Sanjanwalas stretching back to the time of their founding father who had assisted John Company secure the trade charter for the first British factory from the Mughal Emperor, in short all of Jehangir's pretty ones were plucked from the cabinets in one fell swoop and shipped off to the auctioneers in Bombay. Even the cabinets were disposed of, leaving a searing emptiness against the wall.

Under Jehangir's caressing fingers the stars, flowers, sprigs and soft blossoms that blushed below the gilded rims of plates used to come alive. A strangled cry escaped the old man's throat before his thin body crumpled and hit the floor. It finally sank in that his beloved collection was on its way to London, its final destination. Without waiting for his lunch he rushed out on foot to the nearby police station to lodge a complaint against the curator. The police officer Mr Khan instantly recognized Jehangir as one of the dying breed; he had aunts and uncles in Bhopal and Luckhnow whose wan faces wore that same haunted look. He had witnessed once proud matriarchs cringe before loutish peasants-turned-ministers in state cabinets. He had sympathy for the hapless and knew how to humor them.

Mr Khan who as it happened was also on Pessy's payroll sent Jehangir home after pretending to take down the complaint. He tore it off as soon as the old man left. Later on he would receive an envelope full of large currency notes from Pessy.

His china had defined Jehangir's entire life; it had sustained him through his darkest period when his first-born had died suddenly leaving Behroz permanently damaged. Without his treasure he felt naked, reduced to the face-lessness of a beggar at street corner. The remaining three years of his life were spent staring vacantly at the dance of pale-veined leaves projected on the sitting room wall by a sun-drenched peepal tree outside the window.

The disposal of his father's china was the beginning of Pessy's career as big-time builder. He had lost Juno, his childhood sweetheart once again, this time to a dull-as-dishwater Englishman who said 'boos' instead of bus. Then one day he found his beloved sister Homai sobbing disconsolately in her bed-room. She handed him a crumpled letter from her fiancé with the dire mes-sage that their marriage had to be postponed indefinitely since he'd lost a lot of money on the Bombay stock exchange.

Pessy had a knack of getting under the aged skins of impoverished Thak-urs who had been friends of his father. Their large holdings were in danger of being grabbed by tenant farmers after the land-ceiling act made ownership of more than fifty acres illegal. Pessy began to prey upon old Umeed families who were vulnerable to Mrs Gandhi's much-touted stratagem for banishing poverty from India by forcing indolent gentry into the ranks of the homeless.

Once in a while Cy managed to get away from the clinic to spend time with Jehangir at home. That sad lost man had stopped attending the club where he was an ace bridge player. One morning when Behroz went into their bedroom to wake him up, he was delirious lying in his own vomit. Cy rushed to his bedside and tried to revive him but it was too late. He had swallowed a fatal dose of arsenic.

Pessy's florid face registered no remorse the day his father killed himself. Next morning he found his mother in the kitchen getting his dad's break-fast ready. Her mind had already started wandering, she was utterly inco-herent. Sometimes Gisela found her sitting alone on her veranda smiling to herself because Homai's long engagement to Rustum was on again. She would be married now that her brother had managed to raise the money for the wedding as well as for buying a flat in Bombay for the couple. The Parsis were traditionally a non-dowry community but having lived for cen-turies in close proximity to upper caste Hindus they had developed their own system of blandishments to coax into matrimony a reluctant Parsi fiancé who hummed and hawed pleading lack of funds as the reason for dragging his feet while his intended grew old and withered away under the stigma of spinsterhood.

Pessy who was now head of the family had to make a choice between letting spiders build Miss Havisham webs around his sister or douse her in rosewater at a traditional Parsi wedding ceremony. Her fiancé Rustum would one day inherit the century-old Pastry & Bun shop in Girgaum, Bombay.

Out of the hefty profit Pessy made from the auction of Jehangir's china, rupees one crore secured a flat for Homai in the Dadar Parsi Colony in Bombay and the rest induced the Mamlatdar of Umeed to render a vast tract of prime farm land non-agricultural so that Pessy could start constructing his first housing colony.

A dazed-looking Behroz wandered through her daughter's wedding reception. Only when Gisela and Cy came and sat down with her did she look up with tearful eyes and mumbled something. Gisela could see that the loss of her husband had fatally impaired her already tottering reason.

The small but well-knit Parsi community of Umeed held Pessy responsible for his dad's death but what could they do? Most of them were old, their children had left for the big world of Bombay; some had migrated to the United States during the Indian exodus of the Sixties. Pessy was on a roll and while he regretted the passing of his dad the smile on Homai's face awaiting her first child was compensation enough.

The absence of her husband turned Behroz to seek him in the smoke snaking out of incense burners of those who claimed to have a hotline to all the dear departed of Umeed. Behroz talked to Jehangir at the séances conducted by a one-eyed crone. Gisela was too busy to keep track of all those animals that kept dying with alarming frequency in Behroz's spiritual chatter and didn't realize that something was seriously amiss.

But finally things came to a head and the macabre account of Behroz's covenant with the old 'Bhootani' came out in bits and pieces.

One evening Gisela returned home to find Cy waiting for her, looking distracted.

"I'm afraid I have to report something quite dreadful. Our Subhadra's

Kirpal told me just now that he was returning from school when he caught sight of Behroz walking towards the forest with an old woman by her side. It seems he followed them to a shack behind that gutted dak-bungalow. He saw through a crack in the window Behroz sitting on a wooden box facing the Bhootani. Kirpal is absolutely certain there was a small creature wrapped in a bundle lying between them. He hurried back to fetch Pessy. Together they heard moaning and when Pessy forced open the door the scene was exactly the one described by Kirpal but the moaning creature turned out to be a small boy. Behroz turned to Pessy saying 'Look, there's your Dad, let us take him home.' According to Kirpal poor Pessy was struck all of a heap. I'm afraid it's bats in the belfry for our Behrozmai."

At home when her trance wore off, Behroz told Pessy that the little boy was the reincarnation of Jehangir. The child remembered the old flat in the Parsi neighborhood of Tardeo, Bombay where she and young Jehanir had lived before moving to Umeed. The urchin could even recall their dog Tipu, who had been run over by an overloaded lorry.

**** ****

Terry never had enough time to get acquainted with Sissi properly. Cy had kept him updated about his daughter's progress at school. The little girl after crying for Mummy seemed to be quite happy being looked after by the master and mistress of Kunj with their large retinue of servants.

"She really enjoys riding the little white pony we bought for her. Don't worry we've also engaged an experienced syce who reins in the animal to make sure she doesn't slide off. In her jodhpurs, red tunic and blue cap she is like a fairy princes. I have never seen Gisela look so radiant, loudly cheering Sissi Baba as she rides around the nearby parade ground in late afternoon. She comes back from the clinic by four and after a quick cup of tea *Oma* and *Enke-lin* are off to the parade ground where Bijli and her syce wait for them. If for some reason Gisela is held back I am roped in to accompany the child to the ground. As you might imagine, I am simply too happy to oblige. I don't mind telling you that my old heart is in my mouth every time Bijli gets frisky. The syce has to keep pace with both rider and pony till the poor man is frothing at his mouth like a colt. Piano lessons after dinner with her *Oma* till bedtime rounds off the little angel's hectic schedule."

Sissi filled such a profound void in the lives of the two aging doctors, that Terry had no heart to separate her from them.

He used to rush home to read the latest news about his daughter.

"Every day is filled with fresh surprises at Sissi's gift for learning languages. Barely five little Sissi Baba can enunciate difficult words in English and also in Hindi. Her grandchild has also released Gisela's walled-in German and our Kunj now echoes with the sound of lieder which pleases me immensely."

The distilled sweetness of lyrics set to music by Brahms, Schumann and Schubert had been conserved like vintage wine in Gisela's heart. During the first ten years of her life in Umeed Sissi grew up speaking English and German with equal facility and later playing Buttercup in the performance of *HMS Pinafore* at Ashenden in Kent her soprano would reflect the same purity of diction as when rendering Schubert's lieder.

Terry had the joint custody of his daughter and thought he would bring her over to England when she no longer needed help getting into her school uniform. Already at five Sissi would knit her brow, brush aside her soft brown curls and instruct Subhadra in Hindi how to tie her shoelaces.

After doing her best for mothers and their babies Gisela hurried home in the late afternoon through respectful rows of husbands mumbling apostrophes of gratitude for writing off their fees. Outside the clinic stray cows masticated, working their jaws vigorously as though badmouthing their deadbeat owners who drove them out to forage for food. She couldn't provide the children of patients with all the gifts she was able to shower on Sissi, but even after the handsome stipend from the Palace dwindled to a trickle and sections of Umeed were blanketed by vast sweeping flyovers, jewels and diamonds inherited by her from Perrin kept the milk-bottles filled to the brim for the children in the clinic.

By the time she began attending the Convent of Jesus & Mary Sissi could effortlessly switch from German to English depending upon which of her grandparents she was talking to. Going down the veranda steps on her way to school she waved to Subhadra's son Kirpal who walked with her to the gate where the school bus picked her up every weekday morning. A brief ten-min-ute walk took Kirpal to the Methodist English High School. The boy was compact of body with brown eyes, which disappeared behind shining high cheekbones every time he smiled. In the evening he hurried back from school and was at the gate on time to meet Sissi's school bus.

The Gurkhas lived in a little redbrick outhouse beyond the rose garden. By now little Sissi was fluent in Hindi, the language her classmates spoke at home. In her navy blue frock, white pleated skirt and white canvas shoes she seemed so well settled at Kunj that Terry's resentment at Juno leaving their child with two extremely busy grandparents evaporated.

Cy loved children and it showed the moment they walked into Kunj hiding behind their parents come to drop them off for Sissi's birthday party. He lifted them and placed them gently on the long sofa. Sissi's friends were afraid of Cy's beard but he tried to engage them in conversation that ranged from the most recent performance of the Umeed Cricket Eleven to the latest Holly-wood hits like *My Fair Lady*. Sissi was a little surprised when going home after watching *The Sound of Music* on the big screen her Oma suddenly swooped her into her arms and held her close till they reached home.

✶✶✶ ✶✶✶

(vi)

Gabby's letter brought news of Papili's arrest on charges of sedition. I cried the whole day. If it hadn't been for Cy's constant vigilance I would have killed myself. Both Subhadra and Bahadur shadowed me all the time never letting me out of sight. Cy rushed back every day at four from the other end of town where a grand old bungalow was being refitted for a brand new clinic.

The building had been completed but the current His Highness, the Old Her Highness' only son had decided to sit out the war on his Irish estate and deputed his portly uncle to inaugurate it on December 1st, 1940. It was Sir Jamshet's dream coming to fruition and yet Cy could not rejoice because of the state I was in. He kept saying that the Gestapo would soon release Papili. His friend Malcolm Atherton of the Home Office in London had asked the British Legation in Vienna to intervene. They had reported that Papili was in reasonable health and was awaiting his trial. The news was terse but not without a silver lining. Only in unguarded moments did my inner anguish pruned the smile I had forced out playing the thrilled wife and business partner for Cy's sake.

I was all over the grounds of the Clinic literally running from food tents to the dais festooned with roses, chrysanthemums and marigolds, trying to keep in place the pallav of my embroidered sari of Kanjivaram silk, shot through with every shade of green and yellow. My friend and mentor the Old Her Highness had taught me to wear the sari by molding my angular alien physique to Indian women's comeliness. Standing by His Highness's squat Uncle, hunched like a boulder with arms, and the current Dewansahib, whose paunch hummocked through his brocaded achkan, my husband looked more the prince. In a cream-colored long ceremonial tunic, his unruly curls brushed back, my

Cy was the cynosure of all eyes as he rose to thank the Old Her Highness who had accompanied us to the city to throw open the Clinic. For two months preceding the inauguration Cy did not have a moment's rest, rushing up and down the walkway that divided the two wings of the refurbished bungalow.

There was no forethought or planning that brought me to this remote corner of the world except Cy's love. Umeed wasn't a retreat any more, it was home. I wasn't a seeker looking for an Indian Guru. Cy was the most un-gu-ruish figure despite the beard. Nor did I go native as Gabby suspected. The Danube never silted up in my consciousness; it continued to flow quietly in little eddies and pirouettes as if powered by some unknown force. No matter how hard I tried there was no escape from it.

Together Cy and I trained the new nursing staff to prepare patients for delivery, dress wounds, alleviate labor pains, stem bleeding, give enemas, do tracheotomies, bring down fevers, handle convulsions, and lay out the dead. We helped them build absolute confidence, developing self-sufficiency, which was really the detachment that marks selflessness. There working by Cy's side I really fell in love with my new life with its multiple aromas, colors, textures which were millennia away from Vienna, with its trams clanking past the tur-rets of Prince Eugene's Upper Belvedere, the receding avenues of poplars, the strings trembling under the double chin of the substantial first violinist at the Musikverein.

The gap between treating and helping the hungry poor was slight. Doc-toring was founded on an obligation, an imperative to save life. If you had asked me then where I found such high courage to work in that part of town, I would have answered, 'It was a gift from my husband who made me aware there were deeper shades of misery and deprivation in Umeed than I had imagined; grime-filled nails, broken teeth, breath smelling of hooch and sometimes only one eye staring at you from a fragmented face, wife hunched on the bed hoping for a miracle.' I developed an affinity with brown-skinned women, their hands callused by direct contact with open cooking fires.

There was a whole world beyond the grasp of my German. The British had tried to pack the myriad castes and creeds into what they called 'bandobast', a portmanteau term that stood simultaneously for 'order', 'truncheon charge' 'dawn to dusk curfew,' 'penal code,' 'district magistrate,' and so on. But the 'fissiparous' tendencies beyond the orderly cantonment kept spinning out of control.

Now I rarely step outside my new bedroom downstairs with its bland walls. Kunj feels light with all its heavy furniture auctioned off. Ushakant the antique dealer raised rupees seven lakh from it. Did he cheat me as my colleague Dr Trivedi says? Of course he did. But money was needed to keep the clinic running with a monthly stipend for the good doctor himself.

I didn't say anything when the antique dealer handed me the check. I smiled and waved it triumphantly at Schiele's Rainerbub up on the wall. I am too weak to go down to my 'dark room' as Cy called it, so I had Bahadur bring it up to my bedroom.

When going up the red Riesenrad gondola with Rudi I often wished it would keep rising higher till we could see Franz Joseph's Ringstrasse opening like a fan with ribs stretching from base to tips, allowing Vienna to peer archly over its rim like an accomplished Geisha.

In the twisted adult bodies of the mature Schiele there seemed to be an early apprehension of the deformity that lay beneath the glitter of the Hapsburg Capital. That afternoon when we returned from Steinhof we found our maid Hilde sprawled on the floor holding the Rainerbub in both hands and unable to get up. Obviously the stool on which she had propped herself up while dusting it had tilted. The old woman began to sob as soon as she saw us, holding the cracked frame to her bosom. Cy gently pulled her up and declared that none of her bones had been broken. Papili promised to get it framed again but Hilde was inconsolable. Slowly as her hiccups subsided she told us how she always thought the eyes in the painting and the breaking smile on the boy's lips reminded her of 'mein armes Baby Rudi.'

Her attachment to my little brother was legendary. Hilde pushing his pram and later threading her way through shoppers, as little Rudi took tiny steps by her side clutching her forefinger had been a long familiar sight on the Fleischmarkt.

It was a magical moment when I realized why the picture I had glanced at only occasionally had become such a part of our inner life. Hilde's dimming vision had opened before me a private, self-contained world where the boy in the painting and our Rudi became one.

The likeness was not striking but both boys looked out at the world with the same eloquent eyes, a celebration of childhood's untroubled nature captured in brushstrokes of warm simplicity. From eye level the boy's hands seemed unusually big and expressive like our Rudi's. I remember that even during those fraught and intense sessions when my brother was learning to add and subtract, the made-in-Bavaria pencil dwarfed to a stub between his elongated index finger and knobby thumb I used to think it odd that a six-year-old should have such adult hands. Papili's answer was that all the men on his side of the family had strong Germanic hands of born pianists and cabinetmakers.

Papili carefully removed the canvas and folded it before sliding it in an empty box of tennis balls to make it easier for Cy to pack. The painting was a copy made by one of the customers who had settled an outstanding *Marcus Aurelius* bill with the replica of Egon Schiele's work. While the rest of Vienna swooned over the exotic and luscious women of Klimt and Kokoschka, the young man, an up-and-coming painter, considered Schiele to be his master.

Cy packed it in his suitcase the day we left Vienna. Fortunately our British passports spared us the indignity of having to open our bags for inspection at Innsbruck. The Schiele still burns bright among all the cobwebs and shadows that have invaded our Kunj.

The Vienna of my last visit was a place of forfeited grace, a trained poodle wagging its tail for its new masters. But according to reports in the papers, even after Allied bombardment razed parts of it to rubble, it never looked as desolate as the firebombed Dresden or Berlin after the Russians plowed in. They say it was mostly intact after the blunt sound of goose-stepping jack-boots was heard no more.

They also say people who see ghosts should not be living on haunted streets. I was spared the sight of numbers tattooed on Papili's and Mutti's arms and missed the great harvest of shoes with ghosts of children's feet hovering over them. But Rudi's intense hazel eyes, knitted eyebrows, wet mouth and slight movement of the throat as he munched the Mars Bar I had brought from England are still quite vivid.

Now I have little time to think of Vienna and its fall from grace. I can spare just about enough energy to sift through the tattered remains of my days in Umeed. There were moments in the early years of the clinic when Cy and I restored broken lives and gave them a new lease. The poor lived in a low-slung, dust-in-the mouth state. To be with them in that crouching position, in their kennel-size shacks, was no different from being lowered every day into mining pits without a canary.

Outside the clinic were wheels spilling out on the streets from cycle repair shops, hardware stores full of nails and heavy tools, groceries with pyramids of turmeric and red chilly powder, incense wafting from mosques and temples. Bending over a sickly child, playing the fair-skinned goddess of ransacked hearts was frightening, especially when poor mothers loudly pledged their meager wages on a coconut and brought its fresh pulp to me as votive offering.

****

(vii)

Hearts were heavy around the familiar card table where Jehangir's friends gathered in the evening for a game of bridge. Terry listened to their exchanges, occasionally aiming his camera to snap those faces in repose. They already had the resigned look of passengers boarding with flagging dignity a delayed flight about to vanish in the sky.

A leg injury during the onslaught to free Rangoon from the Japs made Col Mehra limp but he walked erect taking brisk strides. He bristled at Gen Zia's latest attempt to theocratize Pakistan, "It's the thin end of the wedge, mark my words. Mixing religion and politics. Bad show. Leave politics to politicians as the 'Kipper,' I mean Gen Cariappa used to say. Gen Ayub Khan as head of state would have never stooped to playing the mullah. After all he was a Sandhurst man. Breeding tells."

Heated argument over some politically hot topic was settled without name-calling. Indira Gandhi was always the PM and her political adversaries, Mr Narayan and Mr Desai.

The Col regretted the excesses of the Emergency, "There was at least a semblance of bandobast on the streets instead of these protest marches, looting of shops and general mayhem engineered by rabble rousers. Initially the Emergency did instill some sense of purpose in society but Mrs G squandered the opportunity and let her younger lad bulldoze slums and bully industrialists. Made them cough up large donations."

Every once in a while Osman Chacha looked at his ex-bridge partner's empty chair. "Oh how I miss dear Jehangir. Without his winks and whispers from across the table you chaps have me up the creek without a paddle. I need his semaphoring to counter your nefarious tactics."

"And the way Jehangir's face used to light up," said the District Collector, Mr Chaudhary, "followed by wild hoots when you two bandicoots won the rubber gladdened my heart."

They were men of few words, speaking in short bursts when the table talk veered toward their specific interests. Their spouses playing Rummy at the next table talked of the teething problems or mumps of their grandchildren. Drowning their chatter Osman Chacha who'd retired as Superintendent of Forests and Wild Life would suddenly get up from the table, fling his cards down and locking eyes with a tiger-head on the wall vent anger at the poachers.

"I'd have the whole damn lot of them hanged by the neck. That is the only way to augment the dwindling tiger population in Devasthan."

The Collector who'd also served as district magistrate in the mofussil was good at playing the mediator. Catching the eye of the bearer fidgeting behind Osman Chacha he would rise as if adjourning the court and say, "Come gentleman, time to feed the face."

As they sat down one by one he'd lean towards Cy and whisper, "The whole country is going to the dogs. You should see the state the dak bungalows are today. They have reduced them to dharamshalas and musafirkhanas. Where are the Khansamas and Babarchis who served roast chicken or murg masala topping off with caramel custard? Now all they dish out is foul smelling kedgeree and pickled mangoes."

Dr Trivedi, Cardiologist Upadhaya, and Osman Chacha spoke a mixture of Hindi and English like most educated Indians, but Col Mehra started every sentence with an archaic 'I say old chap' in the manner of a retired India hand in Cheltenham, and the Collector drove his point home with lines from Shakespeare or Browning.

If the weight watching Dr Upadhaya declined a second helping of chocolate mousse at dinner the ex-ICS would say, "I do believe any man who doesn't love chocolate lacks some fundamental human faculty and is 'fit for treasons, stratagems, and spoils'."

Cy and his guests were enacting outmoded Edwardian class fantasies of their British boarding schools perched on hill stations like Simla and Darjeeling.

Their chatter was peppered with Latin and Greek expressions like *suo motu,* *ultra vires* and *volenti non fit injuria* frequently used by them in official dispatches in the past.

Terry feared for them, their kind had fueled Music Hall jokes for years. Here was a kind of innocence tragically vulnerable to the jet-set India raging outside.

Col Mehra, tip ends of handlebar waving in the wind, bent by his flower-beds turning the soil with a hand trowel. Sometimes he stood ramrod straight inspecting disciplined rows of rose bushes with a gimlet eye. His roses always won the first prize at the annual flower show. Osman Khan (Osman Chacha to friends) spent a fortune, engaged gardeners with the greenest thumb but the Col's roses always came out on top. He'd been one of the last batches of Indian officers who'd served in Burma under British commanders. The secret of his success as a gardener was attributed to his getting up at dawn and chatting up his roses as though they were young subalterns in training. His conversation with Gisela was full of references to topsoil and subsoil and the proper way to mix peat and manure to produce the right results. Mrs Mehra who taught Home Economics at the Convent considered such references too malodorous for a postprandial chat. Having risen from young lieutenant to colonel her husband knew that conditioning the soil and achieving the desired parity between new flowerbeds was not unlike training a bunch of raw recruits in a Foot Drill. But obviously over the years his alignment commands had lost their magic.

One evening Terry heard him complain to Cy about insubordination in the ranks of his domestic staff, "Ever since I caught Gobinda stealing from me, the same excuses and lies have been trotted out by his successors. You cannot get a decent cook or mali for love or money. Not a blessed soul stops by to admire my roses and now our Meenakshi wants us to move to California. She has managed to get green cards for her Daddy and Mummy. No more flutter-ing the dove cotes, I'm afraid. I've decided to chuck it all."

"Don't take it too much to heart old chap," Cy said. "Must soldier on regardless. I'm sure my wife would be most unhappy if you two left. No more chinwags on matters horticultural. I am sure our Bahadur will find you a pair of honest workers. Good eggs, the Gurkhas. Stand by you till the very end."

"It's no use Cy. But thanks any way. Time to pack the old kit bag and move on. I seem to have lost my compass. You know how it is old man."

****

During Terry's yearly visits to Umeed not all the details of Gisela's Viennese past came out in one long Proustian stream. Listening to Oma's account of her childhood in Vienna, the rides in a fiacre to the Prater Gardens, visits to the Zoo, Sissi would suddenly interrupt her and ask if she'd had a boyfriend when at school. Girl gossip among eight-year-olds at the Convent had decided that the beautiful Sister Josephine had become a nun because she had not been allowed to marry a handsome Muslim youth in Goa. Terry was astonished to see Gisela actually blush. He shushed his daughter and tried to change the subject.

After a brief pause Gisela hugged Sissi and said, "Indeed I doted on our next door neighbors' son Günter. He was a superb carpenter and always entered the room as though gauging the strength of beams and rafters. Head covered in blond curls, baby blue eyes under long eyelashes, he looked like Siegfried trying to locate the singing wood bird. He was much older than I and barely looked at me except to ruffle my hair when he visited us."

Terry could never tell whether Gisela was only twelve when she had been desperately in love with Günter, who made exquisite cabinets with ingeniously concealed secret compartments and accompanied Mutti singing duets from Donizetti, or whether it was just a youthful crush she got over when she went to England and met Cy.

On Sundays after breakfast Cy sat in a stuffed chair by the window of his study overlooking the rose garden reading his copy of the *Lancet*. In his maroon velvet dressing gown he looked like an aging lion occasionally lifting his head to peer with wise kindly eyes when someone knocked at the door. He had a replica of a human torso with an open neck and back section from the cerebellum to the coccyx, including vertebrae. If Sissy wandered in with a question related to homework he would take the opportunity to give her a lesson in human anatomy, "Pay attention to this big walnut like object below the brain carefully," he would tell his tiny granddaughter, moving his pointer up and down. "That's your cerebellum. It directs you to follow the octave commands. This here is your spinal cord. You must always maintain a firm posture while sitting at the piano and not eat oily samosas from the Convent canteen."

Sissi could never understand what eating samosas had to do with her spine but she was an obedient child, gave up samosas and forced down vegemite sandwiches with syrupy tea till Lent during which they served her favorite hot cross buns.

As long as Jehangir was alive builders' touts were not allowed to cross the thresholds of his friends' graceful villas and bungalows in the cantonment even as the rest of Umeed was being run over by heavy earth-moving machinery. He'd lobbied incessantly and finally persuaded the Sorabjis, the Mehras, Osman Chacha and other friends to help him found the Umeed Heritage Society to forestall the razing of old structures by the Barbarians waiting at the Gate with their cranes and bulldozers. Within five years of his passing the cantonment nestling under green foliage vanished and emerged looking like a polyhedron of cement and steel.

"Thank God", Cy said to himself leaning back in his car, "Jehangir isn't here to see this insane muddle."

In the old days once you left behind the crowded bazaar and the old township receded, the road to the cantonment lined with green meadows interspersed with whitewashed bungalows used to be such a welcoming sight. Now the same road seemed to narrow till it disappeared under bumper-to-bumper traffic. The car driven slowly by Mahmud bobbed along like a fishing trawler through an inlet choked with foghorn-mad barges. Shop fronts on both sides festooned with black-on-yellow sale signs, red and blue neon lights on marquees, blow-ups of super models on back-lit frames, contact numbers of travel agencies running the whole length of billboards showing the Eiffel Tower, Westminster Abbey and the Manhattan skyline, closed in menacingly like glacial cliffs in sci-fi movies; a sudden incursion of massively inert reality in a moving world.

Men and women poured in and out of shops in one interminable flux. Every available inch of space pullulated; the casual clutter of a bazaar maximized to a teeming jungle, no individual gesture stood out except when a child in red shoes cut loose from a family and scampered away or a woman cradling a baby adjusted her pallav with a deft flick of her free hand before hoisting herself up on the pinion of her husband's scooter.

Cy, who hardly saw anybody else outside the clinic, tried to hold the group together as Jehangir had done, but his heart wasn't in it.

Then one day, Collector Chaudhary said, "Are you gentlemen aware of the latest project developed at the Corporation in the name of beautification of Umeed? Even as I speak a twenty-foot statue in black marble of godman Bholeram fashioned in Agra is being transported to Umeednagar. Anyone know where they want to plunk it down?"

There was a long pause in the Umeed Heritage Society corner of the club where the old-timers waited with bated breath.

"You might have seen the workers erecting a stone platform in the expanded traffic circle out at the traffic intersection. Well," the Collector looked with commiseration at his friends before delivering the final blow. "They are not building a platform for any art objects, a bronze sitar and a pair of tablas as in the city center, no sir, it is meant for the twenty foot Bholeram who has police cases pending against him for allegedly molesting one of his young disciples. "

Everyone had been feeling a little woozy after three rounds of chotta pegs but woke up with a start.

"Impossible," shouted Col Mehra thumping the table. "We'll never allow it. Why, it would completely block out the statue of Pandit Nehru that has been there for nearly thirty five years."

"Too late to do anything about it," said Dr Upadhaya. "I hear the corporation passed the budget for the godman's statue last summer. We can do nothing about it now."

Cy didn't say anything. What was the point? Umeed now belonged to the so-called city fathers. They could do what they pleased with impunity. Most of the new corporators were devotees of the saint who performed miracles such as producing ash by rubbing his hands together. Resigned to the new reality, he sighed and ordered another round of drinks.

✶✶✶✶ ✶✶✶✶

The following year Cy was named President of the Umeed Heritage Society.

When he refused to accept the position his friends made a compelling case for his selection. "Please understand," Collector Chaudhary pleaded, "We are all outsiders, and Osman Chacha being a Muslim simply wouldn't have the clout to tangle with the ministers in Surajnagar who are chelas of Bholeram. You are the only one with roots in the soil of Umeed. Only you have the prestige and local backing to take on the building mafia, else that scoundrel Pavanlal will simply bulldoze Sir Jamshet's legacy."

It all happened so suddenly that Gisela had no chance to protest. After a stressful day at the clinic the last thing Cy needed was to spend evenings trying to heal the wounds of the city. Jehangir had meticulously researched and evaluated the architectural significance of many of the public and private buildings threatened with demolition, including dilapidated havelis with intricately carved balconies and grand doorways built by medieval merchant princes in the old section of town.

Cy's court battles in defense of ailing structures took him to the state capital with increasing frequency, leaving his elderly patients no choice but to invade Dr Trivedi's corner at the Clinic. The young man told them repeatedly that he was a pediatrician who could treat only their children, but when a man or woman accompanied by a sick child entered his cubicle wheezy with unmistakable signs of chest congestion, the doctor simply had to write a separate prescription for an adult dose. Over the next few years Cy had to divert much time to resuscitating buildings with majestic façades and faltering hearts.

But he continued to stress the importance of 'history taking' when Dr Trivedi came to him for consultation.

"It's easy to throw up your hands and leave the wretches to their fate," Cy cautioned. "We are dealing with minds addled with superstition. Believe you me, there's no substitute for history taking. You must press on, continue to probe."

"But half my time is spent in playing cat-and-mouse with them," the young doctor said. "Why can't they be honest and save my time.? Every day I go home at 7pm. I arrive at 7 am. Twelve hours with five minutes for my tiffin. I get fed up."

"Look, it would be nice if our stethoscopes, microscopes and other gadgets could tell us all we want to know about the sick body. That's why it's necessary to sift through their stories, however full of evasions they may be and not think of it as waste of time."

"But Doctorsahib, if you don't mind my saying so, what history are you talking about? These people are illiterate. They sign away their possessions to pawnbrokers with thumb impressions to buy country liquor. I call it snake juice."

"And that's precisely why we must persist and nail their lies, shame them into cooperating with us. Patience, doctor, patience is the most effective weapon in our armory."

Dr Trivedi smiled wanly and went away looking a little crestfallen.

Later the compounder Mr Kazmi informed Cy that the young doctor had received a lucrative offer from Pessy's building cartel for a senior post in pediatrics in their new clinic choking with the latest medical technology on four times the salary paid by the Sorabjis.

Kazmi had tears in his eyes when he said, "Our Dr Trivedi said no to them. I will not leave Sorabjisahib and Mem Sahib. They are like father and mother to me."

Having grown up in a family where Gandhi was one of the household gods, Trivedi and his down-at-heel patients were destined to swim or sink together.

Mr Kazmi loved his work, the preparation and dispensing of various powders was something he executed with the concentration of a lead violinist. In the light of the dim bulb inside when the corridors darkened in the evenings, the dispensary with its carved mahogany mellowness glowed like a room lighted by stained glass windows.

A visit to the clinic still had the aura of a pilgrimage. Simple folks came to be heard, to have aching limbs touched with a farista's hand. The Sorabjis did acquire some of those silently sliding ghost-like machines but they were set in motion only when the patient's broken story had been stitched together.

Dr Trivedi belonged to a god-fearing family and had an insider's knowledge of fakery, especially of the kind that pedaled little phials of water from a bacteria-ridden holy river as a panacea for all their illnesses. Persuading such patients to dump their false prophets was a challenge for which he was better qualified than Gisela and Cy. Their warnings, however dire, lacked the fire-power of Trivedi's Brahminic jeremiads embellished with Sanskrit maxims. When the Umeed Corporation wanted to put up two water pumps, one for upper-caste shanty dwellers and one for the Untouchables, Dr Trivedi persuaded them to install only one to prevent discrimination based on birth.

The Sorabji Clinic was leading a social revolution that had stalled despite all the efforts made earlier by enlightened princes. In the process Gisela acquired more than a smattering of Hindi that helped her break into the minds of her women where lurked hidden fears and secret social taboos.

**** ****

Why scoundrel? Have I run away with someone's wife like Ravana? The old bevacoofs do not know that the new bearers at the club are my chamchas and report everything going on in their corner. The ullu-ke-pathe wanted to put Dr Upadhaya on the mayor's throne but did they know that it is a job only for those with a lion's courage and a jackal's cunning? I have great respect for Upadayaji, my uncle Rohitji was his patient ten years back. But a gentleman like him would have been eaten alive by those 'shetans' who call themselves corporators. They are 'kutteki aulad' and need to be kept on a tight leash.

I can picture Dr Upadhaya's face when he is summoned to Surajnagar and the CM says, 'Upadhayabhaiya, I am going to need a donation of three crore every month from my friends in Umeednagar and the good Doctor goes 'what for?' The CM looks helplessly at the Deputy CM Lakshmanbhaiyya. Lakshman takes our Upadhayaji out to the balcony and whispers 'the CM needs the money to keep the Dalit leaders and the communist motherfuckers on our side during the budget session. All other mayors of cities in Devasthan make that sort of donation.' The doctorsahib shouts 'But that is a bribe, I won't have any part of it.'

The next thing we know, that highway project that is supposed to link Umeednagar to Bombay for cutting down the travel time for trucks carrying goods to and fro is axed. And who is going to be the loser? All those little people who would get construction work on the highway project and the truck drivers and the merchants who want to send our coal and groundnut oil speedily to Bombay.

Tell me why some of the voters bend down and touch my feet, um? Because they are going to make a lot of money, lakhs and lakhs for letting the Government build the highway through their farmlands. You know what the price of land along the highway route is now, ever since my Shiva got elected as Mayor? Go and ask the farmers who now drive a Toyota Camry and Honda Civic instead of committing suicide when their crops fail. So who is the real rascal now -- me or those who would have snatched food from the mouths of the poor construction workers as well small time farmers who had run up debts for their daughters weddings and were on the verge of committing suicide as in Vidharbha?

'No matter what you do', my father used to say, 'never borrow money without paying it back. That is not only part of being a good Hindu but is also good for business in the long term.' How do you think I've reached this stage now and own a Mercedes Benz? I have had it since 1979 much before PM Rao lifted import restrictions on foreign goods. I had to pay double import duty plus one lakh as bribe to the customs official who cleared it. Now I also own a BMW and got a Toyota Camry for my wife. My son by the grace of Balaji goes to Commerce College. He speaks English like a sahib because I sent him to Mount Abu for schooling. I'll see to it that he gets his B. Comm. next year.

He wanted to be a film star, silly chokra. I also know he smoked and drank with the hostel boys and once I had to pay twenty thousand rupees to the family of construction workers whose baby girl was run over by Munna driving his Kawasaki at seventy miles per hour like an actor going after the goondas in a film. I confiscated it for two months but he went into such depression, wouldn't eat. Finally I let him have it back just to please my Sundari. The stupid woman would not let me touch her, every time I tried she said she had a headache and began to cry.

Look all this talk of how good things were in the old days is really a pile of donkey dung. I admit the Old His Highness was a good king; that is why Bapuji brought our whole family to Devasthan. Bapuji wound up his business and made a quick exit before the dacoits who held moneylenders to ransom ran rampant in the ravines up north. But the Raja in our old desh was a debauch. No beautiful woman was safe from the lech's wandering eye.

With a few exceptions like the Old Umeed Highness most rajas and nawabs only drank, squandered away money on race horses and kept a fleet of Rolls Royces while their subjects sank in potholes during the monsoon or were killed like flies every two or three years by cholera or draft.

The Umeed Heritage Society oldies constantly harp on how the British administration kept order in India, arrested troublemakers, eradicated the thugs and so on. They might have done that in the past but let me tell you they were neither just nor fair. As most people, I remember traveling to Ajmer as a young boy by train from our village with my seventy-year-old Dadaji. He bought first class tickets for both of us but when the train arrived and we managed to open the door to the carriage a British soldier pushed us away and my grandfather's bag came flying out from the running train. And why for? The soldiers had occupied a bogey meant for Indian first class ticket-holders because their Europeans-only bogey was full. Now tell me is there any fairness or justice in it?

I don't go out of my way to court trouble like Ambikaji. You have no doubt heard of her. She is the leader of the local branch of Rashtriya Party. I am a Hindu but I don't go around attacking those whom I dislike. You know what Ambikadidi did last year? Some Bengali Babu who is a Professor in the College of Arts invited that artist Hussein to give a lecture to his students. But Ambikaji roared over radio and TV that if Hussain sets foot in Umeed she would personally throw chappals at him. It seems this fellow Hussain had painted our goddesses Laxmi and Saraswati taking a bath in the Ganges naked from waist downwards. I don't approve of Ambikadidi's methods but can you tell me why Hussain Chacha would do such a thing and hurt our feelings? Have we ever painted the Christian god's mother in the nude or asked how she could have given birth to him without any help from man. And why doesn't Hussain Miyan show his Pygamber Sahib having a cup of chai or smoking cigarettes with his disciples in Mecca?

The Umeed Heritage Society may fret and fume but we are going to go ahead with our plans for developing Umeed into a Singapore or Hong Kong. Now that my boy is Mayor of Umeednagar we will transform it into the New York of India. He is bright and I am hoping to slowly pass on my Construction Company to him. At present he is all taken up with some actor fellow called Hamid Khan. These days all actors are called Khan this or that. In my day it was Raj Kapoor and Dev Anand. People tell me my Munna even looks like this Khan but how can that be? This Khan is a pukka Muslim and we are Hindus through and through.

I made a huge investment in Munna's education so that he could be at ease when talking to Ratan Tata as well as the lowliest of construction workers. And it cost me a pretty penny to get him through college. Every year I had to dish out fifty thousand rupees to get some professor or other to reveal the questions he had set in his accounts paper prior to the exam. What's that? Did you say that's a bribe?

Don't talk to me about bribe-shribe for Balaji's sake. How do you suppose all the children of the doctors in Umeednagar got into Medical College?

Do you mean to say that just because Papaji is a doctor little Munna or Munni is also smart enough to clear the entrance test for the Science Stream? All those doctors are my fast friends. Take it from me; they had to cough up quite a lot of hard-earned cash to get their children through the entrance test. I have it from the doctorsahibs themselves. After all, didn't I get clearance from the Mamlatdarsahib for the purchase of land on which to build their big shining clinics?

Anyone who thinks he is above greasing a few palms to get his kid admitted to one of these fancy schools with riding lessons and dance classes is a bloody hypocrite through and through.

Consider this. Do you think a rickshaw driver or a policeman has the lack of rupees required to put a kid through medical or engineering college? It's logic, my dear sir, logic that makes what you call under-the-table deals the only solution. In Hindi we say 'teri bhi choop or meri bhi choop.' Which means 'keep your big mouth shut and I will do the same with mine.' That's the only way we can make progress. Logic pure and simple. The alternative is stagnation. Capital has to move for the sake of economic, no? If some of it moves into pockets of the mamlatdars and traffic policemen why get so worked up and ruin your blood pressure?

Look, I have had this from the traffic policeman Rampal who was stationed at Char Rasta in front of my bungalow a few years ago. He collected enough from the drivers for truck-overloads to retire to his native town and start a sawing mill. Today they talk about start-up capital. Every now and then I invite the traffic cop in just to provide him some relief from the heat and smoke he has to brave. Do you know how much he makes? I tell you with what he gets by way of monthly salary the Sorabjis and their kind won't be able to buy toilet paper to wipe their aristocratic behinds.

Scratch the soot from exhaust fumes off a policeman's face and you will find a man with a family to feed and keep his superiors happy. Rampal told me that out of every hundred rupees he made while he was stationed at the traffic intersection in the Chowk, nearly fifty went into the top-dog's pocket with twenty five claimed by his Inspector. The cop took home only twenty. But that was enough for him to retire early and do something less exacting. Now I ask you, if he doesn't take notice of my BMW zipping through a red light at top speed when I am in a hurry can you really take issue with that?

It's the same flow of cash that keeps the state government running. But let me stop there. Because now we are talking about good and trusted friends who would sell their grandmother if necessary to help me out if ever I were in trouble with the law.

And all this fuss over old creaky buildings the Heritage Society makes is really getting very tiresome. I mean it isn't as if we are taking down the Taj Mahal? Just look at the state the city palace is in where Maharaja Hanutsing the founder of the Royal clan first lived three hundred years back. It is taken over by spiders, layers of dust in the fountain; all of its precious stone inlay work is gone, scooped away by vagrants. The royal family in their current palace have had to downsize after Indira Gandhi stole their allowances.

The state wants to spend large amounts on housing for the middle class. What's wrong with that? Even Professor Amartya Sen says the middle class is the backbone of our economy. Why should the state waste millions on restoring some 19th century villa built by a bawaji who raked it in selling liquor to the British? Is that fair?

This so-called Heritage Society is a real pain in the hindquarters. Who do they think they are? They are not the only ones who love this city.

I love it dearly, would lay down my life if necessary for it. These chakrams are too hung up on preserving the old. I was very happy when the Hira Mahal Palace became a Five Star Luxury hotel. In fact I negotiated that deal and got a tidy amount for the royals in the bargain with which to do some urgent repairs to the West Wing of the main palace, which is their home.

You know what, the brown sahibs of the Umeed Heritage Society have been all brainwashed by the British. They still follow the British when they should be looking toward Amrika. The British still beat their silly drum and march around the Queen's Palace but we all know they are like a bunch of school kids with a band. I won't be satisfied till people start saying Umeednagar reminds them of New York and Chicago. Because that's where the action is. I mean if someone farts on Wall Street our Sensex index goes into a crazy spin but we don't lose sleep over the dip in London stock figures.

I have said to my friend Pessy that he should knock some sense into those old effigies who run the Umeed Heritage Society. Let us sit down and come to an understanding. We can keep some of those white elephants standing at least for a few more years but let's not get into a fight. I swear by Balaji they won't like my way of fighting. I have great respect for Madam Sorabji and even for the Sahib himself. But really his attempt to deny me membership of the Umeed Club was too silly for words. I had more than the votes needed for my induction, even some of the Umeed Heritage Society members promised their support. Don't ask me how I know it. Let us just say everybody likes an extra something in his old age. Because of me two of them have granddaughters in the New American Academy of Umeednagar and one a grandson in medical college. No arm-twisting was needed to win their support, just a word or two in the right places.

After all we are all Umeed ki Aulad, no? We must stick together.

****

Book III

(i)

To Terry growing up in the post-War England of food scarcity and uprootings, Juno and her men seemed singularly focused on operatic self-fashioning. She had little interest in history; to her Terry's tramping through the jungles of Guyana had seemed like a terrible waste of time.

Born in a country with no history of anti-Semitism there were very few incentives for Juno to feel implicated in the fate of the Jewish people or sing, 'Let my people go.'

Who were her people?

Once in a while when a Parsi cousin's marriage ran aground she felt sorry for her but that was the extent of her interest in family matters.

"I knew it wouldn't last," she would say, "marrying one's cousin is risky, you already know too much about each other. Besides, my cousin Shirin's hubby Adil Jinwala used to make constant passes at me even after he married her."

The multi-decked ship of Indian history had passed Juno by like some impossible enchantment that made her proud by fits and starts but as a daughter of an Anglicised Parsi family and European mother she could never feel a visceral urge to go paddling after it.

"Don't be silly," she had said looking embarrassed when Terry caught her cheering the Indian eleven, during a live broadcast. "It doesn't mean anything. Growing up in Umeed in the Fifties singing 'Jana Gana Mana' the Indian national anthem along with other girls I used to be flushed with patriotic emotion but I'm afraid it didn't last very long. Once I began college and the likes of Nehru and other leaders of stature left the scene, for me India became a Third World country led by little men in big shoes. Like all my friends at the Convent I couldn't wait to get out."

Terry knew they had nothing in common except Sissi. He had little time to accompany her to galleries in London where works of many new artists were on display.

After the lifestyle at Kunj, shopping and hoovering their living space plus the attic left her exhausted. "I feel like a sodden rag," she complained after a trip to the laundromat. Under Shekhar's influence she began to cast herself in the role of an aggrieved housewife and he in turn flattered her and magnified her achievements as a painter.

"Terry expects me to do all the cleaning and washing at home," she complained to Shekhar. "It leaves me very little time to draw. I'm afraid my creativity is drying up while he himself roams the world."

Her childlike exuberances pre-empted adult reproof. In Wimbledon Park her shrieks of delight at Shekhar's infantile pranks rang loud. After Sri Lanka Shekhar could not get any more assignments 'commensurate with his gigantic talent.'

Eventually Juno found herself being squired around town by a high-spirited Argentinean sculptor from Paris whose work had been drawing crowds to the galleries. He told her she reminded him of his sister who had died very young; he could never get over her death because everything he sculpted had been an attempt to recover her spirit in his creations. He was tall and stooped with constant bending down with his chisels and recited poems of Pablo Neruda in a livid cascading Spanish voice.

Shekhar went berserk with jealousy, drank heavily to drown his sorrow at being abandoned in his hour of need and tried to stab Carlos one evening as the Argentinean was leaving his studio in Chelsea hand in hand with Juno. But Don Carlos was agile and disarmed the whimpering Shekhar and sent him home in a taxi without reporting the matter to the police. That act of generosity kindled a bushfire of passion in Juno who at that point needed to attach herself to someone whose talent was solid as a block of Carrara marble. For two years she had lived under a constant threat of the sudden petering out of Shekhar's precarious inspiration. Carlos reignited her creative ambition saying her own work revealed a sensibility of astounding complexity.

Juno had been waiting for just such an assurance to rebut Gisela's strictures about the lack of direction in her life.

"For all her Viennese past shared with Freud Mumsy has no understanding of life beyond her clinic. For all her piano-playing she's deaf to the rhythms that govern the artistic heart," Juno would say without the slightest hint of irony.

Terry could never decide whether the hurt expression that his wife's face wore was a mask or reality. When Terry was hospitalized in Nottingham after an accident on the M1 she had the Argentinean drive her down from London every day for a week. Leaving Carlos out in the lounge, she'd enter the ward alone with a bouquet. She acted the devoted wife so well that Nurse Appleby could not believe that the pair had been living separately for years.

She would turn up dressed in simple dresses of elegant cut and a gray beret, with a pearl necklace around her comely neck, white gloves dangling from delicate pink hands. In the full bloom of her womanhood she looked like someone whose beauty reflected the bliss of enduring matrimony. By the time Terry came to while being rolled out of the surgery where the orthopedic surgeon had performed a minor but delicate procedure on his spine, she had the Midland nurses eating out of her hands.

She so chatted them up, sharing with them real or imaginary anecdotes about her short lived life with Terry in Wimbledon Park, showing them pictures of Sissi in India walking between her grand-parents, that they found Terry's monosyllabic responses typical of the wet-blanket hubby of a preternaturally beautiful woman.

They obviously labored under the impression it was Juno who was the aggrieved party in their marriage.

Terry was no more than your average affectionate and attentive son to Mam but that was enough to make Juno give vent to her imaginary frustrations.

"I am afraid my husband has a Marian complex," she would tell Nurse Appleby. "I am expected to play the obedient corgi to his majestic mother."

As in everything else she was a reckless dilettante when engaging in intellectual matters and recast her life with Terry in Master/Slave terms just because Terry found her chain-smoking troublesome.

Juno took up a job in a Marks & Sparks to make both ends meet. One day she was invited to participate at an exhibition of Indian Artists living in

London. There she met Raymond Chandra, a half-French young painter from Mauritius, with large sad eyes and stubble round his moonface. He began to paint her in the nude, weaving thick luxuriant vegetation around her reclining form. He spoke very little English and Juno decided that his talent was so phenomenal that she would be doing a great service to art by grooming him. She introduced him to artists in London and promoted his work while holding down her day job.

He painted her riding a black stallion; the contrast between the rider's paleness and the animal's gleaming noir tones made it a striking exhibit. On her head he placed an Indian dupatta of blue diaphanous fabric and smeared her forehead with a vermilion mark. Even Terry had to admit that it was an arresting picture. She became pregnant with his child but he forced her to abort it after a bitter fight during which he cut her arm and back with a razor. Still she stood by him and tried to bring him back to art.

She knew how to drop the ones who did not amount to much in their field and only wanted her body. But she desperately clung to those whose promise continued to flower, making them the toast of the salons held by cultivated but heavily-mascaraed women of great fortune and ordinary looks.

Terry's marriage could have survived if she had not mistaken another's image of herself as a true reflection. Terry had courted her for a relatively short span but with the concentrated energy of a Scaramouch, making her feel young and desirable. Once in London he had very little time for that sort of non-stop adulation without which she was like a fish out of water. For the first few months into a new relationship with a budding genius in the grip of explosive creative energy she had the aura of someone who had drifted in with the tide, surfing on a giant seashell. She could never finish her own projects begun with great fanfare; she drew vicarious pleasure from her protégés' widely-acknowledged triumphs.

Pushed to a linguistic logjam Terry once declared her morally polio-stricken, a woman in school uniform. In Wimbledon Park she used to demand that he carry her to bed in his arms. Even at the height of passion she would veer off like an inquisitive child interrupting a bedtime story with tangential queries. Her most willful act was haloed by innocence so angelic that any intended reproof sounded petty. Terry remembered Cy saying, "No one can be angry for more than a few minutes with our Juno Baba."

That innocence had afflicted many well-to-do Indians like her grandmother who had watched from afar Gandhi's revolution with retina detached from the eye. In the wake of British withdrawal from India in 1947, the task of keeping the Raj show on the road fell to the lot of Perrin and her privileged cohorts. While Juno's parents were busy with their patients, her doting grandmother took her to elaborate house parties, whist drives, and fancy-dress balls and even to the straggly race-course where once a year the Umeed gentry assembled to cheer their out-of-form colts. It was against this entrenched apathy to those less fortunate that Cy and Gisela had had to wage a constant war. But they had somehow failed to curb Juno's habit of personalizing her understanding of the good. She was a perfect fit for the 'I'm all right, Jack' England of the late Seventies.

She would inflate the talent of an artist she'd set her cap at till the sod began to lean on her for inspiration. She fixed her emerald gaze on him and listened with such soulful attention that he was convinced he was the center of her being. If a non-English painter or sculptor explaining his work to a group happened to glance in her direction she would smile and nod as though she were the only one being addressed by him; she would often complete his faltering sentence as if the two of them were kindred spirits trapped in a crowd of philistines.

For expat Indians in London trying to break into the insulated British art-world, she was like those lovely nymphs who descended from the skies in mythological times to help them cross a threshold guarded by a vicious cobra or a curmudgeonly sage; for nostalgic Englishmen grown old on modest talent she was 'pale hands' they loved beside the Shalimar.

Immigrants arrived in England in two distinct streams; those who needed work found their way up North to factory towns, and those lucky few who came to play headed for Mayfair and Carnaby Street. But the ones who fell between two stools landed in places like Wimbledon Park.

Terry was sure she would have amounted to something had she not wasted her time socializing. The work Terry had seen in Umeed hanging from the walls of Kunj, was arresting. Her *Sunset on Lake Umeed*, which adorned the wall over their fireplace in Wimbledon Park, always made visitors gasp.

Her elegant bearing, green eyes and European pallor set Juno apart from the sari-wrapped, heavily-cardiganed immigrant women toiling behind the counters of corner shops in Southall and Brick Lane. Juno's body language with a hint of temple dance held a special challenge to artists bored by the gamine incarnated by Twiggy in a baby doll dress designed by Mary Quant.

Keeping someone on a leash while throwing at them tantalizing scraps was the secret of her power. Growing up in Kunj with musical parents who read books, she could hold her own on almost any subject at a cocktail party.

In Terry's war-time childhood spent in Mam's homiletic company the consequences of not doing the right thing had not only social, but deeply personal implications.

But swinging England of the Seventies to which Terry had brought his Indian bride was a nation of ethical free agents and Juno took to it like a duck to water.

Gradually the lingering Indian consonants disappeared from her speech and her sentences acquired the huskiness of a London socialite to whom both close friends and casual acquaintances were 'darling' this or that.

The day before he was discharged from hospital in Nottingham Juno brought him a bouquet, sat down on the bed, plumped his pillows her cheeks brushing his stubble and said, "Terry darling, you must know I absolutely adore you, but really everyone knows our marriage went pear-shaped long ago. Let's throw off these burdensome shackles and stay forever united in cherished friendship."

Though seemingly improvised that last sentence had the syntactic balance generally achieved after a number of drafts chucked in the waste paper basket. It was vintage Venables doing Brutus, 'not that I loved Caesar less, but that I loved Rome more.' Next moment the wizened face of the Lodger, gobsmacked at being accosted one night on the doorstep by the wife he'd deserted long ago swam, into sight.

"Well butter my butt and call me a biscuit."

Juno's emerald eyes widened in puzzlement.

"Really now, what's all this about?"

"Nothing, I remembered someone who was given to reciting Shakespeare when he was drunk."

"Darling, this is no time to go all literary on me. It's all too complicated, besides I am a bit pressed for time and have to dash to London before the solicitors who drew up the papers close for the day. They will file the petition tomorrow."

"As you wish," Terry said. No sooner were those words out, she snapped open her leather shoulder bag and pulled out a neatly typed document. As if on cue, Nurse Appleby and the Philippine nurse Selenga trotted in and stood by as witnesses to the signing.

All of it happened so suddenly that Terry had little time to absorb the contents of the five-page document full of 'whereases and whereofs' citing incompatibility as the prime cause for separation. As usual Juno was jockeying him along but he didn't care. Now he was free to marry Jeanette and bring back Sissi to England. It was time the two most important persons in his life got to know each other.

****** ******

(ii)

Kunj has memories too. It remembers the time I arrived at its threshold for the first time. It remembers the car coming up the long driveway with me sitting upright at the back. An instant recognition had passed from the house to the newcomer. My confusion over being in a strange land disappeared as doors opened on their hinges. Now the house and I have a common past. The left side of the veranda looking through the mango orchard was my Vienna corner meant for daydreaming. The right, leading to the servant's quarters and the chowkidar's outhouse, was the Umeed section where I went over my day at the clinic. The driveway in the center was always the vista where Sissi appeared as a small dot after the school bus had dropped her off at the main gate. It had begun as a silly game under growling monsoon skies; orchard-Vienna, outhouse-clinic, driveway — loved ones returning from schools and offices.

Though I had trained them to stay within their spheres, memory pollens from the right would sometime blow to the left and vice versa in a cross-fertilizing dance. Baby Sissi would appear through the mango trees with a doll and scamper to the clinic side, touching everything in it with laughter.

Now it is getting even more difficult to keep memories confined to their respective corners. They swarm like a crowd of pilgrims storming the doors of a shrine, trampling the lame and the decrepit. Then there were also forbidden memories never allowed to escape. They were locked up in the dark room where I hid old photographs. Once in a while I would go down and hold them against the light. I kept my souvenirs in that room, a few books Papili had given me, Mutti's shawl, the embroidered peasant jacket Rudi wore when we went for a holiday in the Alps and the copy of the *Rainerbub* with which Hans the aspiring painter had settled his outstanding *Marcus Aurelius* bill, one of Papili's many impractical business practices strongly disapproved of by Mutti.

In Jehangir's Museum were Mugual and Rajput miniatures; comely maid-
ens in skimpy Indian cholis releasing pigeons from their latticed zarokhas to
fly to their far-off beloveds and bring back confirmation of their well-being.
But that copy of Schiele's *Rainerbub* was my only memento from Vienna keeping alive my hope of seeing Rudi again. It protected my past from becoming
disposable junk. Entering that little room was like being in a shunting yard,
with sudden turns, flashing signals and backtrackings. In this dark underworld
retreat I let the torch beam wander and pick at random scattered fragments
of my past.

What stopped me going out of my mind at the clinic during my early years
in Umeed was the professional pride I felt watching those thrashing frog-like
beings in swaddling clothes smacking lips with tiny red tongues long after
emptied milk-bottles were removed by nurses from their mouths. Having Sissi
to go home to heightened the joy I felt in being able to send a mother home
with a child who had a fighting chance of reaching adulthood. Not all the children born in the clinic went on to become doctors or engineers, some fell by
the wayside; some like Subhadra's Kirpal became rickshaw drivers.

There were days when despite my best efforts a new-born simply slipped
through my fingers or was stillborn. My heart would thump like a pump when
I looked up and shook my head, causing the mother's white eyes to sink even
deeper in her brown wrinkled face. The woman would nod her head mechan-
ically. In that simple gesture was foreknowledge beyond despair. That nod
made it easier to break the bad news. Later on Savita would explain the cause
of its death to the bereaved woman. The child was too far gone when they
brought it in; its vital signs had weakened to a point where even God couldn't
have revived it. The woman kept nodding her head; sometimes her lips would
quiver into a smile as if to say where she came from such explanations were
redundant. One thing less to lose.

Going home that evening through the old poor quarters of Umeed I saw
banyans droop like a herd of parched elephants by a waterhole and all around
was broken statuary from its royal past, crumbling masonry covered in monsoon moss, the short-lived gray of here-today-gone-tomorrow winter, the
rustle of old fugitive sorrow in new-grown leaves.

Under a louring sky, caught in a traffic jam, air-conditioning fogging the car, I would roll down a window just when an auto-rickshaw blaring a Bollywood item number screeched to a halt inches away. In the gloom, the interior of the rickshaw glowed with lurid colors streaming from tiny light bulbs on the dashboard, a joss-stick burned before a framed image of Sai Baba whose blessing often saved more lives than I did. Bosomy Bollywood starlets vied for space on the inner frame with cricket heroes. The rickshaw was both temple and chariot for its chattering passengers. The car inched forward only to stop again at the old city gate with its twin archways for up and down traffic.

Flush against the plinth of the nearest archway, barely missing the mud-slinging wheels of the rickshaws, scooters and lorries, sat Rahimat Khan the cobbler, father of six girls, all born in our clinic, hammering nails in the heels of a shoe on the cast-iron anvil in front of him. Rahimat's stubbly face would break into a betel-red smile of recognition and he would tap his temple with his hammer to throw a courteous salaam at the car moving forward.

The still-born baby weighing on my mind, I would draw back from the window with a tentative wave of the hand and a tiny returning smile; not to do so would have been peevish and hurt Rahimat who, despite the meager pickings of a street cobbler, dressed in his embroidered Pathan outfit delivered at Kunj two kilos of halal mutton every Eid E Milad Festival.

Witnessing the ordeals of motherhood day in and day out helped me form the habit of stowing away my own pain for longer periods, enough to get by temporarily. And waiting to see Sissi every evening gave me a goal. Every morning her laughter traveled with me to the clinic and fluttered around as I bent down over a sick child. My granddaughter's shrieks of merriment ringing in my ears, I'd feel the heartbeat get stronger in the ribcage of the child in the incubator. Then I'd look up and meet the anxious gaze of the woman in a threadbare sari and nod my head emphatically leaving little doubt that her child would live. My compulsion to work at the clinic remained strong, a new mother proudly holding her child in her arms for the first time still made my eyes glisten. In that simple look of unarticulated gratitude were powerful life-building tissues.

****** ******

When Terry sent me a copy of that old photograph of Gabby and me as children, it was hard to believe there ever was such a blessed moment in my life. What finally persuaded me to leave Vienna with Cy after he risked his life and came to fetch me, armed with my brand-new British passport was Papili saying, "Mutti and I would like to know that something of ours will continue to live in you, whatever may be in store for us."

May be it is only a dream, mere clutching at a straw or wish-fulfillment as the Viennese Freud, Papili's hero would have said, but this I know — without what I do I'd have killed myself long ago. At the very least it gave me a tentative reason for living. Now I am determined not to 'kick the bucket' as Cy would have said, before holding my Bienchen Sissi in my arms for the last time.

I entered a dream as soon as I stepped into my clinic for the first time; it didn't acquit me but merely pointed out an alternate route, the might-have-been of history. I knew as a narrative it was too fragile to last a decent amount of time, but then Juno arrived. The birth of my daughter was the splint that secured the broken bone.

Perrin misconstrued my silences as lack of maternal affection. I couldn't open my mouth for fear of crying dementedly. Silence was my heavy shield against my past but it stood like a wall between my child and myself. Having Juno kept me from giving myself a lethal injection. To hold my own flesh and blood got me out of the pit.

As Gabby says I was spared my gracious parents' ultimate passage through Hell, but I could make what they call an educated guess as to the final humiliation that shattered my parents' proud hearts. After their incarceration, their physical extinction seemed like a terminally ill patient's release from pain.

History books however thoroughly researched do not explain why my

Mutti and Papili, the kindest of people that ever lived, had to die in the way they did. I have no use for explanations. They are simply echoes repeating themselves. Pictures of baby Hitler in the crib and the Fuehrer on the podium cannot explain why I am where I am. When in my clinic, I look into the eyes of a woman with a swollen belly rising from a thin wreck of a body, I feel, how shall I put it, a gut kinship with the young Jewish nurse in Auschwitz who removed a squealing infant from her mother's arms and drowned it so that her life would be spared. No matter how many children I bring back from the brink it does not fill the void left by the one drowned in a shallow tub. There is no salve for gaping wombs. Often watching the matron wash a placenta-covered newborn, I have come close to wondering what if she held it down a moment longer till it choked. Thoughts of extinguishing tiny lives have plagued my lonely vigil.

The day after the *Anschluss* when Papili had been dragged out of his shop, forced down on his knees and made to wipe out the pro-referendum slogans painted on the street, I was monitoring the difficult delivery at Hammersmith Hospital of a cockney housewife addicted to gin, and shaking my head in sorrow for the stillborn infant. A few weeks later when I returned to Vienna there was a noticeable scar left by the ugly bruise on Papili's temple.

Unlike his cousin, Uncle Franz, and friends who had been completely crushed by the sudden collapse of their world and sat staring into the distance, Papili had shrugged off the incident as an example of passing anarchy.

During *Kristallnacht* Cy and I were being wined and dined on board the ship sailing majestically through the Suez Canal. I wasn't there to see Papili's shop being gutted, those handsome volumes bound in gold-lettered Moroccan leather gleefully tossed into the fire by savage louts.

Two days before I left Vienna for the last time the three of us had waited in the lobby at Steinhof to be ushered into the lounge. The young woman behind the reception desk had a fixed insolent smile of official courtesy on thin lips.

That day has been lodged like a piece of shrapnel below my heart all through the years. Whenever I remember Rudi's last smile as he leaned against nurse Bernard who put her hands on his shoulders protectively, I think of my clinic and a mother in an old sari, hiding a hole in the shoulder of her blouse, trusting eyes focused on my face as she tries to read danger signals, her husband hopelessly scanning the ceiling or the floor, never daring to look straight into my eyes.

Miracles are performed under such intense appeals from the hapless. It is no longer a question of science. Their faith pushes me to try the impossible against all science, to force myself into a state where magic and medicine become synonymous, fueled by a trust so pure as to make you feel like god. We are in the business of breathing the breath of life. I am convinced it is their faith in me rather than my medical knowledge that saves a life, brings a dying mother back from the brink of death. But when you have traveled so far with your patient, coming back is not easy. You cannot explain how you did it, especially in these times when no one believes in miracles, least of all you who are credited with one.

Some feel compelled to chronicle murderous history, finding new language to express the inexpressible; I save victims of another cycle of oppression, in another part of the world. Not much thinking goes into it. Writers write, Doctors save patients. It's as simple as that. I do not aspire to comprehend the historical dimension of suffering inflicted on Jews by the Holocaust. The saving game is old and beyond history. Is there a connection between the two? Probably not.

But in that state when I slip my surgical gloves on my hands and bend over the writhing woman I feel utterly free. It's that freedom when every thought disappears from my mind save the one that matters. My mind is like a motor running full speed and all the sunsets in all the skies stay frozen as if somebody had hit the pause button on a remote, and in that still sky I am only a pair of hands freeing a woman from her newborn. I don't hear anything. Even the infant's little mouth opens silently in a first cry as Savita slaps its back. I come out of that dream only after I have peeled off the gloves as though sloughing off the trance of freedom. The new child brought into this world might not be a substitute for the one lost long ago but I imagine it to be a continuation of the process we call life. It's like watering a plant in a parched soil after a drought when it brightens up and looks slightly drunk on the little puddle that gathers in the disturbed soil. You can hear its leaves opening like a baby's fingers in the incubator.

It does not work every time, some babies survive the worst of conditions, some do not despite everything being done right. There is no way to explain how the miracle works. But when it does you are not the one who made it happen. Maybe the baby had something to do with it, an extraordinary will to survive, an instinctive grasp of what the process of living requires when your back is against the slum wall. A crack opens in the universe and closes with the gash sutured.

In the death camps, cruelty masquerading as science killed babies, but each newborn infant in my clinic is like a bottle with a message of hope washing up. No matter how poor the parents, there are flickers of joy — even if it's a girl child — before reality sets in. Work-hardened nurses grin from ear to ear as they wash the infant before wrapping it in swaddling clothes. And the mother drained of physical agony sleeps, her smile gathered in the corners of her eyes. As a doctor I feel implicated and when I talk to the poor husband whose calloused fingers peel off crumpled and soiled currency notes outside the accounts office, I tell him to forget about the payment, buy oranges and milk for his wife. I feel I have earned the right to tell him not to burden her with any more pregnancies. The man grins embarrassedly, nods his head and bows low. I know that he will send his wife back swollen with a new life.

Alone at night a scream wakes me, I do not know whose scream it is, the one heard yesterday in the clinic or the one, which comes from afar, traveling through space like a meteor showering particles tipped with light.

I had inherited Papili's Nordic looks, but Mutti had passed on her silken black curls and large sparkling opal eyes to Rudi. That day at the Steinhof, when they brought him in to the sunlit visitors' lounge where I waited with Papili and Mutti, has not faded from my memory one bit. Rudi wore his lederhosen and old tweed jacket; his softly curling hair brushed back made him look grave and adult. Nothing much was said that day by any of us. When I told Rudi that I was going on a long trip, he seemed to understand.

"Schick mir eine Ansichtskarte?"

He fumbled in his pocket and pulled out the card I had sent from Rome, where I had gone to attend a conference on tropical diseases. After holding it up for everybody to see, he turned to me and said seriously, *Ich gehe nach Rom, mit Papili und Mutti, wenn ich entlassen werde."*

When I try to mark the location of that moment on the map of Vienna I feel invincible. We were a complete family huddled together over a picture postcard.

Old Nurse Bernhard, who was discharged a few weeks later by the Nazis when they found out that she was married to a Jew, had brought Rudi to the Lounge and said he had shown great signs of improvement. During the past two months he had not turned violent even when provoked by other inmates who picked on him while playing football and was taken out on a tour of the Prater along with his ward companions.

When I hugged him he said,

"Ich bin ein braver Bub gewesen."

Nurse Bernhard smiled and nodded her head,

"Ya, ya, Ja, tatsächlich. Rudolf ist ein guter Junge."

No more bed-wetting, no more fighting with others. There were tears of joy in Mutti's eyes and Papili shook the nurse's hand warmly. When Rudi refused to let go of Mutti's hand he was allowed to walk down with us halfway across the lawn outside the building. We said goodbye under the charming two-faced clock in the little garden that led to the gateway. Mutti began to cry. As Papili led her out I turned around and saw Rudi looking up with intense curiosity at the twin dials of the squat clock tower that stood like a benevolent custodian of the children's hospital. Perhaps the nurse was explaining how the four hands on the dials kept perfect time.

That image of Rudi on the road to recovery under that sentinel of time has clung to my sight. It tells me Sissi will be here soon.

I liked to think that all these long years in Umeed had given me enough expertise in absorbing pain. Now I am not so sure. As long as I could wield the scalpel to save lives I felt secure, now lying here helpless in bed I feel exposed. I fight, try to align my distress with that of my lowliest and most abused patients, to temper it by comparison; but I am too good a doctor not to know that my case is hopeless.

When I was in the midst of losing things dearer than life I had no inkling of the enormity of that loss. I never thought separation from Rudi that gray afternoon would stretch into forever. If I had serious doubts about being able to see all of them again, I would not have allowed Mutti to persuade me to leave Vienna with Cy just a month prior to their own incarceration.

While waiting for the Orient Express at Westbahnhof Papili had kept fidgeting, running up and down to get me the day's papers and chocolate while Mutti cried silently into her handkerchief. Then amidst the clanking of trains arriving at other platforms I watched Mutti's face blanche, eyes straining to smile as I boarded the Express. Cy maintained an embarrassed silence. Later he confessed he felt like a cad whisking me away from my family.

By the time he helped me board the train Papili had gained control over his voice. It didn't shake or falter when he spoke walking alongside the moving carriage. Like someone imparting news about a minor setback at work he said, "My cousin Joseph wired to say he can sponsor only two persons for an American visa. Don't worry," he shouted. "I have saved enough to go with Mutti and Rudi to Italy at the first sign of trouble." He was panting with the exertion of keeping pace with the moving train. "We'll stay in Rome with my dear friend Nello and his family till we have found a sponsor for Rudi as well."

**** ****

<h1 style="text-align: center;">(iii)</h1>

In 1989 when he was in Dubai en-route to Asmara Terry was cautioned against going there because the war for Eritrean independence had entered its bloodiest phase. He decided to head for Umeed earlier than he had planned. Terry had summoned all his courage and told Cy and Gisela that in two years' time Sissi would be eligible for an entrance test for admission to Roedean near Brighton in Kent. He believed the latter being smaller would be a better fit for his daughter. But the thought of Sissi going away plunged Cy into a profound melancholy. He sat there quietly, fingers engaged in his familiar beard-plucking routine. Gisela's eyes grew perfectly still, her blond head drooped, and food remained suspended between plate and mouth till the fork dropped down with a clatter. She kept tilting her head looking sideways at the door as if she had woken up in unfamiliar surroundings. Terry realized he had not chosen the moment wisely.

But the rest of his stay Gisela and Cy couldn't have been more gracious. If Terry refused Subhadra's caramel pudding because he had a slight indigestion Cy would subject him to a thorough examination and Gisela would allow Sissi to stay up well beyond her bed time.

The fifth anniversary of the Bhopal Gas Leak was round the corner and the Opposition was lambasting the Government for its failure to provide adequate compensation to the hapless victims. But their cries for help were being drowned in a war of words. Terry was struck by the underlying similarity between Umeed and Bhopal. Unlike the latter where change had come in one snap Umeed was being throttled slowly but just as viciously by a faceless evil. Still, it would be interesting to know how the survivors in Bhopal, that old Nawabi Capital, were rebuilding their lives. Terry's journal was quickly filling up with entries that would accrete into a script — *Umeed and Bhopal: A Tale of Two Princely Cities.*

Back in London even as freelancer he was required to wrap up a story in a hurry, to make it fit the segment contributed by him for that evening's program. He missed the thrill and excitement of his younger days in the East, interspersed though they were with lean patches between assignments.

Being camera-shy he never could picture himself as part of the production team investigating and exposing unconscionable acts of imperial fantasies like the Falklands War. From his little perch in the Television Center he watched with growing admiration his colleagues in the neighboring Broadcast Center present with absolute fairness the Government's as well as the IRA's versions of the bloody events unfolding in Belfast.

Deciphering the garbled lexicon of aftermath with innocents caught in the wrong place at the wrong time needed a period of gestation, quiet reflection, sifting the grain from the chaff. It was a luxury the Newsroom couldn't afford, next day was abuzz with a new train-wreck in another part of the world from where the silting Empire had receded. A story coming over the wire had to be filleted and microwaved, its rough edges pruned to match the BBC's standards of strict neutrality. Details that did not at once grab attention had to be squirreled away for later use. He wanted to sit with a frothing beer mug by his side, trying to roll the story back to its fetal stage when an incautious bystander in Belfast, Soweto or Yemen had walked into the path of a sniper's bullet.

Then Timothy Shaw, an old college friend who was very pleased with Terry's performance as guest speaker to his class in Media and Communication, asked him to apply for a part-time lectureship at Goldsmiths. Terry put in an application and waited. There was no word on it for nearly five months. In the meantime he had to resort to all manner of subterfuge to weed out potentially combustible material from his assistants' reports and redraft them.

To his great relief Tim rang one day in July to say his appointment had gone through. Retaining his connection with the BBC as a freelance scriptwriter for documentaries Terry began to teach three days a week at Goldsmiths helping students develop editorial skills in preparing reports that fleshed out the truth without treading on the toes of higher-ups. His long stint at the BBC came in handy when teaching young students how to achieve a rhythmic match-up with the outgoing news sequence or to invert the order of words in a sentence to blend with the segment to be aired without fudging the truth.

Finally after some dithering the BBC accepted his proposal for the script with a caveat that 'it should be vetted by Mr Craven before Terry started shooting *A Tale of Two Princely Cities*. The Government of India was quick to take offence when it was caught with its pants down by foreign media.

Time was ripe for a visit to that stricken place — Bhopal.

In Umeed Cy and his friends had been waging a last ditch struggle with the builder's lobby intent on wiping out their city's monuments. Those old-timers instinctively understood the plight of the Station Master of Bhopal Junction who on that fateful night had tried unsuccessfully to halt the mail train at the outer signal to forestall its passengers' asphyxiation.

Was there an evolutionary error running like a common thread through all the episodes of things falling apart in different parts of the world on which to build a master narrative? Were certain cultures more prone to self-destruction than others? Terry had never felt entitled to any eminence in life, but in a sudden flare-up of ambition he saw in *A Tale of Two Princely Cities* the makings of a luminous epic.

Despite his many forays into distant lands Terry had been reluctant to pronounce big judgments on momentous events. He had always been in awe of Camus for the easy grace with which he conflated the rat-infested Oran of his native Algeria with ancient plague-stricken Athens buried under stinking heaps of corpses while taking a sideswipe at Paris pullulating under Nazi collaboration. The shadow of Lucretius flitted lightly across his text to signal it was in the 'nature of things' for one dying city to resemble another in a different time and place.

He often dreamed of retiring to Manchester, buying an old cotton-baron mansion in Didsbury, Mam's Salford under an hour's bus ride away. At night commuters going home would see a glow on the dormer window of his study where, enveloped in a cloud of smoke, middle-aged Terry sat brooding at his desk. The only sound would be the clicking of his keyboard, eyes following the script emerging on his PC monitor while his imagination made daring leaps to bring all man-made disasters in the modern world under one caption.

There was enough footage in the BBC archives of the event in Bhopal but journalistic chatter in bar-rooms hinted at new evidence that pinned responsibility on the Gas Company. Terry had no definite plans but to go see for himself how a mishap of such magnitude could have occurred in a third world city under the watchful eye of a Western Industrial Unit.

Every anniversary of the gas leak revived horrific memories of that day when according to impartial observers almost 20,000 people had perished in a city very much like Umeed, a city of palaces and gardens turned a vast gas chamber. One day in late January he boarded a train to Bhopal armed only with his new portable video camera.

Bhopal had joined the club of cities that had witnessed mass extermination of its inhabitants under starry skies. Terry wanted to keep an open mind, look around and see if the event itself was not a culmination of some slowly unfolding historical process grinding toward a tragic impasse.

But every one from smooth-talking ambulance chasers to urchins sifting garbage by the railway tracks seemed well rehearsed in finger-pointing.

Cities that skip centuries possess only short-term memories. Like the old and new Umeeds there were two Bhopals: the Arabian Nights town with lakes, gardens and graceful minarets, and the new multinational hardware city under smoke-shafts. A first-time visitor was fascinated by the contrast between the timeless calm of the Upper Lake, the majesty of ruined temples and mosques frozen in moonlight suddenly looming out of the mist and the other Bhopal of streets littered with twisted corpses laid out in orderly fashion by hospital walls like some industrial waste to be carted off for recycling. Ground zero was a wasteland littered with gaping tanks entangled in the ganglia of pipes rusting in the harsh noontime light.

In history it was known to be just a notch or two below Umeed and almost certainly better run than many other native states under despots who visited their capitals only on ceremonial occasions to collect and squander their revenue on stables of race horses and fleets of cars in Bombay and Calcutta.

Like Umeed, Bhopal too had welcomed entrepreneurs bearing Ali Baba promises of instant riches falling into its lap. Was the gas leak just a one-time affair, a wrong foot put by a town eager to join the march of time?

On the day when their town was about to be enveloped by an evil cloud its citizens were said to be hosting a mass ingress of pilgrims from halfway across the world, celebrating dozens of high-profile weddings or playing card games at exclusive Raj-era clubs. While in the shanties by the railway tracks raggedy daily wage-earners curled up in their tin shacks, as a desperate station master and his panicked crew frantically waved lanterns on a lonely track to prevent a long-distance mail from pounding in at the precise moment when methyl-iso-cyanine-turned cyanide began exploding thousands of lungs.

Osman Chacha, who had contacts in Bhopal's Nawabi aristocracy, had secured Terry a spacious suite in an old haveli-cum-hotel with peeling paint. Managed by a hookah-smoking aristocrat whose immaculate courtesy to his dwindling clientele was legendary, the place itself was comfortably located in the central 'Chowk.'

Terry found that the moment he stopped and pointed his camera at a carved old wooden balcony or a comely minaret piercing the evening sky a gawking crowd of onlookers gathered around him. The sad absurdity of modern Bhopal was that many of its inhabitants found it odd that anyone should be interested in its past. They stared at Terry, their eyes filled with distrust.

According to reports, the morning of the leak had been bracingly cold. Pictures showed the corpses stiff and silent, twisted mouths framing questions. The ghost of a bygone chevalier hung over a precipice. In downtown Bhopal a lyric-besotted crowd swayed, clapped hands and threw bouquets at masters of nuanced words and subtle rhythms. A town drunk on poetry is already an archaeological site primed for tomb-raiders.

Destruction of European cities pulverized by the World Wars was horrific but Indians had glimpsed it from a safe distance in slow dissolve. Bhopal was like a giant close-up of carnage.

Terry's host Janab Valiulla drew steadily on his hookah but his breathing quickened when one evening Terry sketched the horrors of gas ovens, which had incinerated Jews. The man just couldn't get his mind around the fact that people in Europe would deliberately release gas in chambers filled with men, women and children.

Osman Chacha's nephew Parvez who lived in Bhopal and served as a local tour guide said, "Inshalla, here in Bhopal people at least had a chance to run away from the cloud closing in on them."

"A fat lot of good it did them," Nawab Valiulla retorted. But Terry thought young Parvez had a point.

Bhopal was also too stark not to be uniquely Indian, brazenly buck-passing while people living in shacks by the railway tracks, porters bandy-legged from years of carrying loads far beyond their endurance level, vendors of chai-pa-koras from refreshment stalls and weary passengers waiting for trains choked, gagged and dropped like mice felled by bubonic plague.

Those who lived through the killing moments had their lungs filled with toxic fumes, which failed to expand to regulation limit until nausea and nose-bleed set in. Bhopal like Umeed was a partially capsized ship, one side smashed, bits and pieces strewn about, the other intact rearing up, its deck festooned with buntings, its plush cabins lined with embroidered bolsters.

A whiff of ash and dust from mass cremations and burials still lingered in the air. As in Jonestown there was nothing left to shoot. Terry thought man-made disasters do reincarnate as cautionary tales, but with a fell suddenness even as the chai-wala hands out disposable clay cups to long distance passen-gers. Five years after the poisonous gas made that swift transition from leaky tanks to grungy shacks, the engines of superfast trains hooted just as impa-tiently at the outer signals of Bhopal.

It was 'a needle in the haystack', so Terry decided to explore the section of town by the lake, old palaces with rotting rafters, gilded furniture with broken finials and bolsters covered in dust.

In such a myth-sodden place one could chance upon an old inhabitant with flowing white beard and one withered finger on the pulse of the city with which to draw in sand a rough approximation to what really happened. But after three days in Bhopal, Terry was assailed by serious doubts about Mike Bartlett's method, telltale clues found in old photographs or a passer-by's casual remark taking one straight into the heart of darkness. The strategy that worked for Mike in Beirut failed to crack the syncretic codes of Bhopal. The idea of a single all-encompassing monolithic pattern underlying all man-made disasters was yet another chimera. What did Terry expect to find here years on that had not already been cataloged by scientifically trained inquirers? Despite a whole cache of photographs to fill a Bhopal memorial museum he remained clueless. What did he know about the chemical reaction that turns methyl-isocyanine stored in tanks into deadly hydrogen cyanide? What was he doing here anyway?

**** ****

Terry's last day in Bhopal found him in the old township of winding lanes where as in the historic sections of Umeed shops selling joss-sticks, rose and jasmine attars stood cheek-by-jowl with mutton shops, ribcages hanging from hooks. Often his step faltered, and eyes lingered on all those peeling mon-uments, frozen in spent grace like Jehangir's Museum. The abject hangdog look of unkempt palaces and mausoleums brought to mind empty shells of desanctified churches and abandoned warehouses marked for demolition in post-War Manchester; they had that fleeting, transitional look of buildings silhouetted at dusk in time-lapse footage, moments before fire-bombing.

Bhopal and Umeed had retained the contours of a medieval citadel ruled by a just ruler. Many disparate strands began to coalesce around that iconic image. Far from the calm waters of the ruler's twin lakes and gardens rolling down the hills, Shaukat Mahal in the center of Bhopal was like the Great Hall of Justice in the heart of Umeed, a people's palace. The annex in red brick next door where the sovereign gave audience to her subjects irrespective of rank or status indicated the hand-on-the-people's-pulse tradition exemplified by the wise Harun-al-Rashid of Baghdad. The Bhopal-Baghdad link rein-forced Gisela's Umeed-Vienna conflation.

Behind the tourist brochure blurbs extolling monuments lurked an old fashioned idea of the 'polis' ruled by 'Mai/bap' or a parent/sovereign; feudal nepotism tempered by true benevolence. Perhaps people who lived in such places were not streetwise enough for democratic self-governance.

The monarch combined the discipline of a father (Bap) with the heart of

an all-forgiving Mai or Mother. Calling such filial androgens proto-Keynes-
ians running a welfare state might lend the documentary a bit of intellectual
sophistry; nevertheless subjects reared under such dispensation tended to be a
credulous lot. It made them particularly vulnerable when they passed into the
care of elected officials intent on lining their own pockets. The many stories
circulating in the bazaar had one common thread; a Cassandra like warning
repeatedly issued by those who had caught an early whiff of the noxious gas
hissing in the belly of porous containers on the outskirts.

Terry thought of Juno as he walked under a pair of minarets mirrored in
the lake. His biggest folly had been not to have caught on to the fact that Juno
was a lakeside figure fading in and out of overlapping mists, while he remained
at heart a Lancashire lad fishing in the dank canal. The ruins of Bhopal and
Umeed bore witness to monumental mistakes made by the cities at the shank-
end of their career. Time to bring on the clowns.

Does a city so filled with dupes deserve any better?

Along this road or that they'd fled early that morning, screaming vomiting,
a mother not fully dressed holding a child just keeling over and dying. The
question was who opened the gates? Bhopal had seen many sieges, had had
its share of bloodshed, shipwrecks and yet suddenly the night of Dec. 3, 1984
had made that foreknowledge obsolete.

Back in Umeed Terry's Bhopal stories sucked out all sound from the dining
hall of Kunj. When Subhadra came in with the coffee pot Gisela addressed
her in a formal manner; the poor woman shot a bewildered look at Cy as she
passed through the door. Bhopal had the voltage to be a proxy nightmare for
those with memories of mass extermination.

Terry had only a week in Umeed before flying back to England. One day
the Sorabjis invited all their friends to have dinner with him at their club. He
found that the Umeed Club had not changed much except that Pereira the
bartender wore a sour face. Terry had reached the club much earlier than
planned; the Sorabjis and their guests were not expected for another hour.
Terry stepped into the bar for a beer. He found a dejected-looking Pereira
standing alone behind the counter polishing glasses. After settling down with
a beer Terry asked him how long he had been with the Club. That brought

a smile to the old wizened face. It turned out that for Pereira bartending at Umeednagar Club had been a family tradition, stretching back to its very inception in 1827. Pereira spoke fluently in what the British in India called 'chi chi' accent.

"We learn early, you know. To mix drinks. With mother's milk. This has been our family's post for over hundred years. Even more, who knows? Pater's great granddad first served here. Wounded in the Mutiny. Lost one eye."

He droned on squinting at the glass in hand. His grandfather had been the most illustrious of his forbears.

"My Granddad was a baccha when he started. His pater had started training him when he was thirteen or something. The padre was hopping mad. But when the old man died suddenly just a day before the Viceroy's visit and no one to serve drinks to his staff, whom did the Resident Sahib send for in juldi?" Pereira paused dramatically.

"My Granddad. Who else? Mr Perkins," says the Burra Sahib to his secretary, "this is no job for any amateur bhisti, he says. Egad Sir, the entire Viceregal party will arrive by the Mail tomorrow evening. Lord Dufferin is their Highnesses' Guest at the Palace, but the rest of the staff will stay at the Club. They will start bleating for chotta pegs before dinner. Fetch Master Joseph at once, chop chop. You know how old my Granddad was? Just fifteen. You were a man at fifteen those days. No one could shake a gimlet like him. He was a legend all the way from Mhow to Poona. Ah, those were the days. No Indian except the Maharaja Sahib was allowed in here. And he came here only once a year. On Empire Day. To drink to the health of their Majesties. But look at them now. All they guzzle is whiskey. Drink like a fish. And now they have let in fellows who play rummy and nothing else. They play for cash, huge amounts, I tell you; these shethjis have turned the Club into a satta-bazzar. I can hear my granddad turning in his grave."

Cy told Terry that even Osman Chacha had sold his estate, retaining only his bungalow surrounded on all sides by apartment houses under construction. There was no space even for wild flowers to grow during the monsoon.

Cy and Gisela had already refashioned their lives and because of their daily contact with the underprivileged they had a healthier perception of the changes taking place beyond their flowerbeds. But they too were becoming irrelevant in other more dangerous ways.

With Jehangir's widow moving to a Parsi retirement home in Bombay and Col and Mrs Mehra spending three months of summer with their daughter in the US there was practically no one with whom Cy could spend time talking about music and books. Others had moved to the new gated society in the only quiet section of Umeed and Cy and Gisela now saw them only once in two months.

Juno breezed in every two to three years from an unexpected corner of the world in the company of some unkempt penniless man whose ego needed a booster shot with free meals and lodging. During her last visit she had withdrawn all her jewelery inherited from Perrin from her bank vault.

Cy yearned for company after he returned from the clinic but Terry could not delay his departure for London and told the Sorabjis that he'd finally decided to take Sissi to England the following Summer when she'd be ready to enter Ashenden. He was also beginning to miss Jeanette with her gentle brown gaze and shy blushing smile. She was back in London after her month long Christmas break in Hamden, Connecticut.

✸✸✸✸ ✸✸✸✸

'All is fair in love and war' may sound like a battered cliché but it wins modern day elections as Cy and his confederates learned the hard way.

The following August as he prepared to fly back to London with his daughter, Terry thought the air inside Kunj behind its Doric façade was heavy, and a vague foreboding generally felt around a body lying in state clung to the Sorabji residence. Cy seemed distracted and once Terry walked into the big hall to find the old man engaged in an imaginary conversation with someone visible only to himself.

"A few years back," Cy was saying, "I would have gladly referred a patient whose appendix was in danger of being ruptured for surgery at the government-run hospital. Now I hesitate because it is like passing a death sentence on the poor patient. Overcrowded and filthy, the place is a charnel house."

The reputation for honesty and integrity enjoyed by Cy's friend Dr Upadhaya should have ensured his victory at the election for Mayor but Pavanlal's money flowed like water in the bustees and on election night his son donned the mantle of Mayor.

On the stumps Dr Upadhaya valiantly vowed to re-investigate an old complaint lodged by parents of two children who were buried when a single wall which was made to support two high-rise buildings hastily put up by Pavanlal's company had collapsed during a monsoon squall.

In a rare display of heroism an independent corporator had demanded a thorough investigation into how and why Pavanlal had been granted permission to construct two tall buildings with one common wall. A local Hindi paper in a sudden fit of righteous indignation editorially censured the speed with which approval was granted to erect such a flawed structure. When the opposition insisted on a meaningful inquiry the incumbent mayor-turned-oracle delivered a curse on them for violating his sacred ground.

Finally the investigating committee appointed by the mayor came to the conclusion that the corporation on the basis of the civil engineer's recommendation had approved Pavanlal's application. There ensued a Kafkaesque sequence of finger-pointing from the civil engineer down to the surveyor and on to a never-ending train of junior clerks lurking behind dusty files in the bowels of the records office.

The surveyor and the civil engineer were let go with a rap on the knuckles instead of being charged with involuntary manslaughter as demanded by the opposition.

But Cy and his friends were completely out of their depth in dealing with Pavanlal whose reach extended all the way to the Chief Minister of Devasthan. The builder could not be touched as long as he kept cash flowing into the CM's reservoir for securing dissident politicians' votes in favor of the ruling coalition.

Cy and his vanquished knights sat in their corner of the Club staring into empty glasses; they were no different from the colorful exotic birds embalmed in the taxidermy section of Jehangir's museum.

Very few people in the audience could understand what Cy said on campaign stops. Some of Upadhaya's younger party workers even tittered, to their ears his public school accent sounded strange. Some imitated his deep baritone after the rally while he was descending from the podium.

The week before election Cy hosted a big dinner at the club for prominent members of Umeed society, which included writers, artists and well-known cricketers. Echoing the words of Nehru uttered on the eve of India's Independence from the Red Fort in Delhi, he reminded them once again of their 'tryst with destiny.' He repeated Edmund Burke's warning to those who remain indifferent to cads and bounders getting the upper hand in administration, "The only thing necessary for the triumph of evil is for good men to do nothing."

Then he'd proceeded to remind them of their responsibility as citizens of a free country with words from Pericles' Funeral Oration as recorded by Thucydides, "Democracy allows men to advance because of merit instead of advancing because of wealth or inherited class."

He warned his listeners of the dangers their children might face if they didn't make the right choice at the election and he concluded with a metaphor from Demosthenes which was spot on for Athens, a city on the Aegean, but hardly relevant for land-locked Umeed. Nevertheless people were entranced by the sound of his fruity voice blending with that of the fabled Athenian orator.

"While the vessel is safe, whether it be a large or a small one, then is the time for sailor and helmsman and everyone in his turn to show his zeal and to take care that it is not capsized by anyone's malice or inadvertence; but when the sea has overwhelmed it, zeal is useless."

There were very few in the audience who had heard of Demosthenes or Pericles for that matter but the words chosen by Cy struck a chord and he received a standing ovation from Col Mehra and his friends. Without mentioning any names Cy was able to imply that Umeed was under siege from within. What he did was quite simple. He tried to induce in the listeners a sense of their proud past and judging by the thunderous applause at the end many, including Col Mehta, concluded that Cy had carried the day.

But Pavanlal's men ferried busloads of voters to the polling booths. In the end the words from ancient Athens proved to be the last hurrah for Cy's generation.

Despite the threat of eviction hanging over their heads, the majority of poor bustee-dwellers voted for Pavanlal's son and put him on the Mayoral throne.

Within five years the entire area from which they were evicted was dense with towering apartment buildings.

Dr Upadhaya's defeat was the final nail in the coffin of old Umeed as far as Cy was concerned. Gisela tried her best to ease his pain playing Schumann's *Träumerei* but it brought only a forced smile to his face. It hit him all of a sudden that his much-loved town known for its unique blend of elegance and simplicity had turned into a satellite of the State Capital Surajnagar where the stink of corruption had been building up since 1970. Surajnagar had always been a manufacturing town where Indian merchants had set up huge business enterprises by greasing British palms.

Cy had fancied Umeed to be different. For centuries it had been immaculately administered by art-loving Mughal rulers followed by Rajput princes; the latter mentored by puritanically strict but intellectually enlightened British tutors or their Indian counterparts like Sir Jamshet Sorabji.

The old world had been plodding along without stumbling thanks to Dr Upadhaya, Col Mehra and a distinguished array of individual administrators who steered its course for almost two decades after Umeednagar merged in the Indian Union and became part of Devasthan.

The rot had set in deeper than Cy had thought possible for a town where symbols of its great tradition were still to be found in the graceful Palladian architecture. Some of these domed structures gawked at from street level by the common man in centuries past now looked like oversized inverted begging bowls to intercity bus passengers crossing the massive flyovers soaring above them.

It was painful for Gisela to watch from the comforts of an air-conditioned car, the long slow moving line of squatters, their grimy bundles and chicken coops secured by ropes to carts and cycle rickshaws, making its way to a scrubland for resettlement. They were being shunted off to a place too far for a commute on foot to earn their daily wages. They walked silently without looking up, like evacuees in wartime Europe being led to the ghettos.

The Sorabjis stayed at home the day Sissi left for England with her father. The sight of a train carrying one's young one away is disquieting like something vital passing into nothingness, a childhood ending. Eyes staring from creased old faces they stood on the veranda, the little Gurkha woman crouching by their side keening in the fold of her sari as Sissi climbed down the steps to the waiting car. It was like watching a farewell scene unfolding in a jungle, a pack breaking up, wet snout and shriveled pelt slinking back into the lair.

Terry thought of all those thousands of British children sent to England for schooling. Spoiled and cosseted by Indian servants, particularly by their ayahs, many of them carried the scars of that separation all through their lives.

English and Maths were Sissi's strong subjects and she had a good chance of securing admission to Ashenden where Jeanette's friend was Head Mistress. She had received a sound schooling by just being in the company of her grandparents but she needed to get used to a system that allowed students to develop their own capacity to think. Learning by rote still prevailed even in the best of schools in India. Terry had assured Gisela Sissi would return to Umeed during her summer vacations.

Gisela maintained a brave smile till the end but one simply had to look at her eyes to know that her heart was in her clenched mouth. Only that Gurkha lad Kirpal perched on a branch of a banyan tree watched them leave without being seen. Sissi had paused and looked all around for him that morning before getting into the car.

As Mahmud pulled out of the porch and started down the driveway there was a sharp report of a stone hitting the boot, causing Mahmud to turn back and look over his shoulder. Terry caught the name 'Kirpal' as the driver cursed loudly in Urdu. Sissi got up, leaned forward and whispered something in Mahmud's ears. On their way to the station, the driver steered the car with one hand and kept gesticulating and shouting at men driving two-wheelers who seemed determined to throw themselves under his front wheels.

Sissi's eyes welled up as the train picked up speed and Umeednagar became a dot on the horizon disappearing behind fields of gazing grain. As the air-conditioned carriage began to rock gently her eyes red with that morning's crying closed gradually. Terry let her sleep till teatime when she nibbled at a biscuit without looking up and slumped back in her corner.

✶✶✶✶ ✶✶✶✶

For the first time in his life Cy felt the world he had known slip away from his grasp. Juno and Pessy belonged to a generation with an etiolated sense of the past. For them what mattered was the future and to secure their position in it they could without any qualms sign a deal in blood. Even the young His Highness seemed to be cut from the same cloth. He never returned from his comfortable retreat in Ireland to attend the last rites of his mother, and Gisela's friend, when she passed away after the Emergency. His fears of being arrested by income tax sleuths unleashed by Mrs Gandhi on the rich and famous were not unfounded. The Royal house of Jaipore had felt her wrath for supporting the opposition People's Party. Besides the Young Highness's French girlfriend had spirited away some of the most precious jewelry that rightfully belonged to the Umeednagar State Treasury.

All three were scions of illustrious families, had grown up in homes which were not just settings for noblesse oblige but its embodiments. Even their old retainers were groomed to blend seamlessly with household goods. The alacrity with which the young succumbed to the notion that heirlooms like Jehangir's china wore price tags was a real eye-opener.

In an ultimate act of renouncing his Parsi ethics Pessy courted the leuko-derma-afflicted daughter of Manishankar. Laxmi was named after the goddess of wealth. Her father held an absolute monopoly in the trucking business. Laxmi, who had large brown eyes and pleasant features, had a secret. A couple of years before she enrolled in the Women's College a white freckle had appeared on her brown neck.

Under smart make-up it remained undetected for sometime, but as soon as green-card holders from America lured by Manishanker's wealth began to make a bee-line for Umeed to interview his daughter, tongues of nubile but financially insecure cousins driven by jealousy began to wag as to why even at the height of summer their Laxmididi wore long-sleeved blouses buttoned up to the neck. From then on it was a matter of time before the cat was out of the bag turning, the once sought after Laxmi into a recluse.

By the time Pessy appeared on the scene Laxmi's parents had reached the end of their tether and were on the verge of giving their daughter permission to join the Sadhvi order of Jain nuns. Despite offers of gold ornaments weighing two kilos by way of dowry, her father had been unable to persuade any young man from the Jain community to marry his daughter.

Armed with her parents' blessings Pessy eloped one night with Laxmi and returned to Umeed a week later waving a civil marriage certificate from Kandivali near Bombay.

Laxmi's mother pounded her chest and tore at her graying hair, Manishanker threatened Pessy with a lawsuit but no one was fooled by the charade. The Manishankers gave new meaning to eating the cake and having it too by palming off an unmarriageable daughter while making a racket over her elopement with a goat-eating Parsi.

It is fair to say that there was outrage in both communities, Baniya and Parsi. The Baniya women mourned Laxmi's death as a Jain and wailed "Hai, hai, the wretched girl has brought shame upon us all by marrying a meat-eating non-Jain mlech."

Not to be outdone the Parsis who frowned upon miscegenation, which led to a further dip in their shrinking gene pool, hastily called a meeting of their Panchayat and passed the following motion, "Mr Pestan Sanjanwala is hereby informed that his wife shall not be allowed to enter the Parsi Agiyari. He himself shall be free to enter, if he chooses to come alone. This ban shall remain in force in future and will apply to the offspring of this unholy alliance."

Pessy tore off the copy of the resolution and threw the pieces in the frightened face of the poor courier who'd been ordered to deliver it.

"Don't you dare set foot in my house again," Pessy shouted at the scuttling courier, "and tell the worthies of the Panchayat not to send you again with requests for donations."

Pessy was under no obligation to contribute to the Panchayat which ran several charitable activities to help poor Parsis with their hospital expenses.

Since neither Cy nor Gisela practiced any faith they had never faced the ban, but Pessy made it clear that he could hardly be expected to part with large sums of money to shore up the dwindling coffers of the Fire Temple that stood in dire need of repairs. On his mother's plea he sent a team to mend the leaky roof but that was that.

Laxmi soon realized that the love-smitten Pessy of their courtship period was a heartless joke perpetrated by two ruthless men, her husband and her father. She had been a brilliant student and continued her studies acquiring a Master's in English. After teaching at the Convent for a number of years she turned spectrally white, prompting Pessy's drunken comment that his wife was fairer than any true-blue Parsi woman in Umeednagar.

In the Nineties when Juno sold the parkland to him leaving a narrow wedge for the entrance to Kunj, Pessy engaged a young architect called Majeethia to draw out a plan for housing aging parents of US-based professional men and women who had started looking for a way of providing comfortable living space for them in India. He named the new housing complex New Jersey Society.

By the time of Cy's exit from this world in 1998, the majestic façade of Kunj was eclipsed by parallel rows of box-like apartment buildings on stilts. Gisela's only consolation was that Cy was not there to see the devastation of their garden and the eclipse of the fan-shaped veranda by backs of apartment buildings with jutting balconies, wind lashing the clothes hung up to dry. Generations of pigeons who'd nested in the vanished mango orchard and banyans now flew in and out of those balconies looking for a niche.

Some of them managed to sneak into the bedrooms of Kunj. Subhadra kept the windows shuttered down since with Sissi gone to England her mistress was the only one who still slept upstairs. Gisela felt sorry for the homeless pigeons but Subhadra was tired of scrubbing off their droppings and would not open a single window. Finally Gisela's bedroom windows were screened and flocks of angrily guttering pigeons having grown tired of battering their heads against them turned around and began to mount periodic aerial attacks on the New Jersey Society in retaliation for their demolished homes.

****

(v)

Spending inordinate amounts of time with one's ex-in-laws doesn't sit well even with the most considerate of current spouses. After Sissi came to live in England Terry made only one trip to Umeed; it was a quick dash to see the Sorabjis while returning from Hong Kong in 1997 when that last imperial post east of Suez was ceremoniously ceded to China by Prince Charles. At the Club, old colonials like Pereira who had not forgiven the Labor Government of Prime Minister Atlee for abandoning his kind in 1947, directed their ire at Margaret Thatcher for betraying the people of Hong Kong.

However unctuously Pereira's tail wagged for the Empire, he served contraband whiskey to the new masters of the club with a lot of bowing and scraping. He may well sneer at their 'junglee' behavior when he was alone but he knew that one gesture of reproof for the way they spilled their drink all along the counter would get him the boot. Unlike the superannuated upper crust of Umeed, Pereira belonged to that band of unflappable underlings who in ancient Rome knew instinctively how to adapt to their new masters when the old ones died.

The mendicants of yesterday who appeared at the door clanking long metal forks were replaced by moving columns of beggars. Stepping down from a cafeteria you ran smack into a family of alms-seekers, a mother in rags pulled her legless husband perched atop a skateboard, a child clinging to her side. They thronged entrances to the new eateries with fancy names like Taj Palace during lunch hour only to recongregate in the evening outside temples and mosques.

Terry remembered the mild early morning sounds of old Umeed, the muffled whistle of a passenger train about to pull out of the station, the clip-clop of tongas on the road, the ululations of vendors in the sunlit forenoon, the occasional rat-tat of a scooter mingling with the roar of a three wheeler called 'tempo' ferrying villagers into town to sell watermelons, and the patter of rain in July with vapors rising from the paved roads.

Maps of destruction do not always tally; scales are different, mountains not as tall, valleys rarely as deep. Two recent events in Umeed seemed ominous; a baby sleeping in a construction worker's tent was dismembered by stray dogs crazed by hunger, followed by the goring to death of a senior citizen by a mad cow just outside the Station.

The wooden horse was galloping towards Umeed.

There was one final flare-up of hope before the flame went out. In his retirement Col Mehra dusted off an old ordinance from army archives that outlawed high-rise constructions in the vicinity of regimental firing ranges. That evening there was much rejoicing in the Umeed Heritage Society corner at the club and hand-wringing and muttered obscenities in what Pereira called 'the beer and pakora' section where members of the building mafia supped.

Cy's life-long exile from the language of the masses had made him socially deaf. Codes of conduct had changed; playing with a straight bat was out-moded. His white flannel trousers and bosky shirts were like period costumes to the ready-made generation. His repartee remained a private joke and those who laughed did so for old time's sake. Cy himself was like an old palatine villa, white marble surrounded by garbage dumps. His world had ended before he could make an exit.

Elsewhere in Umeed were half-demolished bungalows through which the wind blew whistling like a daily wage-earner at toil. Since cheap labor made it unnecessary to buy heavy wrecking equipment, an old building was clawed down gradually over several days with pickaxes and chisels. Behind the hacked-off sections the rest of the interior seemed eerily tranquil under high gilded ceilings; a framed photograph or two still hanging untilted on both sides of a casement, moats whirling in shafts of light. Underneath the gabled roof of a portico sparrows chirped at nest-building unawares that the very next day their hatchlings would come crashing down with the rafters.

At night the phantom bungalow awash in moonlight seemed like a secure place for a family till you turned the corner and the rest of its half-eaten rump came into sight. House lizards darting from the intact to the hollowed-out part hit the floor and lay stunned, their tails still twitching. Terry remembered the bungalow from earlier visits and the garden where the rose-mad Osman Chacha could be seen stirring the soil on creaking knees.

The Georgian revival villas with stucco moldings and cornices which had once housed Parsi merchants and compact white-washed bungalows of Goan Catholic bakers and tailors had all like chimney sweepers gone to dust. Against Cy's urgent pleas most of his friends accepted the builders' offers of free flats plus large packets of cash to augment their bank balances.

The local rags controlled by builders said preserving reminders of the shameful colonial era would deprive the swelling ranks of middle class and lower middle class families of decent housing.

To ease traffic congestion the entire banyan population with its hoary past visible in every twisted root and copious umbra was decimated. The bust of Dadabhai Naoroji, which greeted passengers crossing the bridge into town, was carted off to the Museum. The corporator responsible for the ward to which the bust belonged was reported asking 'who the heck is this bawaji Naoroji?' Cy simply tapped his forehead with his pipe.

Removing statues of Queen Victoria and the Viceroys during post Independence euphoria was one thing but bundling off the bust of one of the founders of the Indian National Congress to the knackers yard was too much for him. He would close his eyes as soon as he got into the car and not open them till Mahmud held open the door for him at the club. There were whispers emanating from the mafia dens about Cy being a spy implanted by the British for paving their way to recolonize India. The conspiracy had the supposed backing of some ex-Royals whose annual purses running into millions of rupees had been drastically slashed by Indira Gandhi. But what really broke the camel's back, so to speak, was Mr Kazmi's revelation that even those patients whose fees had been written off by Gisela and Cy had accepted cash and voted for Pavanlal's son.

A kind of gloom overtook Cy and nothing Gisela or Subhadra could do helped dispel it, his bruised spirit never regained its jauntiness. In the morning dried saliva gathered at the corner of his mouth.

At breakfast Cy's hand trembled, the saucer filled with spilt tea. One could sense that something vital had cut loose within him when he resorted to crude plebeian humor to cheer Gisela up. In a brassy Sam Wellerish vein he would declare, "Don't you worry, ducks, everything'll come out alright at the end, as the man said whose son had swallowed the button."

For centuries the bazaar had gossiped at sweet shops about Umeed's 'burra log'. Men about town lingered at groceries long after their bags had been filled and the afternoon sun elongated their shadows. It was now Doctorsahib's turn to be the butt of their scatological jokes.

"What possessed him to venture into politics only to get castrated? Why didn't Madam stop him from exposing his fat Parsi bottom in the bazaar like a rampant bull?"

Old Umeed used to welcome Kerala Brahmins and Bengali professors to teach at local colleges. The new university now had only regionally-bred faculty who could be bought and sold like rotten onions at knock-off prices in the open market. One by one the city was emptying of its cosmopolitan class.'Jacobs,' the delicatessen owned by an old Jewish family from Bombay which provided snacks like Sacher Torte cakes and plaited cheese, Goan Catholic bakeries selling Portuguese bread and buns under a garish print of the Sacred Heart, Hong Kong tailors who could fashion skirts and blouses from pictures in glossy catalogs, and Chaglas', the family-owned Khoja sports shop, were all made obsolete by cavernous malls. Chimney-shafts of factories along the highways spread a thick sooty cloud over Umeed.

****

(iv)

Shipwrecks don't occur within a blink of an eye. You sail towards them in the dark mile by nautical mile. I should have pulled Cy off to safety, but his faith in the sturdy construction of old Umeed had put me off guard, till it was too late to avoid a head-on collision with the iceberg looming suddenly out of the mist. This Indian town where no invading armies had battered down its fortress of solid black stone for over three centuries had induced in me a false sense of security, reinforced from time to time by generous patronage from the Royal House of Umeednagar. Living within the protective walls of Kunj with household staff bowing and scraping in every corner, life had seemed impregnable.

I had lost the sixth sense that used to make my ears burn when danger went into a feline crouch on the window-sills of Vienna. From snatches of conversation between my friend Sophie's parents about my unusually blonde hair and blue eyes, I'd been able to surmise what today is called racial profiling that echoed through the most elegant coffee houses of Vienna in 1933 when Hitler took power in Berlin. The kid-glove treatment of Nazi bullies by the Medical Faculty in Vienna was enough to send me packing into exile in London well before the Anschluss.

But I was totally unprepared for what happened in Umeed. I was not attentive to the pressure building up within Cy who had been fighting a lonely battle to save his father's town from being destroyed. Then the inevitable happened, he suddenly went to pieces.

One day a couple with eyes like fading embers came into the clinic. The man holding a dead boy placed the limp body in Cy's arms fell at his feet and said 'save him.'

This wasn't the first time Cy had come across patients expecting a miracle, but the child had been dead at least for an hour. He had no remedy for parents refusing to mourn. When told it was impossible to revive his dead son the man just as suddenly got up and walked away leading his stricken wife by hand. Cy was frozen to the ground with the dead stiff body in his arms.

Timely intervention might have contained the typhoid that had raged in that little body already emaciated by grinding labor at a brick-kiln.

Cy kept shaking his head and mumbling to himself incoherently as Kazmi slowly took the body from him and laid it down on a gurney. He looked all around for the parents but they had simply disappeared.

I found Cy slumped in his chair pale as his bosky shirt, staring glassy-eyed at the ceiling, lips trembling. I had never seen him so desolated. Then he started banging the desk, sending case papers flying. The dagger of that father's bereavement had penetrated deep into his heart; he was having a nervous breakdown.

He'd been my life-support pulling me back from the abyss. Imperturbable in crisis, he had been reduced to a shaking muttering old man. I was taken aback by the sudden collapse of his monumental confidence, and stood there patting his back, unable to get out any words.

Kazmi was the first to recover and brought in a steaming cup of tea from the kitchen with a biscuit. Holding the cup with trembling hands Cy gulped down the tea. Slowly color returned to his cheeks.

What had so shaken him was the fact that the father after being told that the boy was gone had merely stared at him blindly and walked away like an onlooker in no way connected to the dead body.

That night Cy slept fitfully, suddenly sprang from bed and sat up, his face wore that haunted look I had first seen on entering his office that afternoon. What had so unmanned my valiant husband was slowly dawning on me as the night wore on. Every time he woke up, the ravaged face of the dead boy's father appeared before him and became a mask of his own shame. The man had stumbled into the clinic and thrust his son's body into Cy's arms like an offering to a god. In popular imagination Cy's English upbringing and training had made him infallible, his past successes as doctor had metamorphosed into a miracle cure.

Neither Cy nor I had taken our beatification in popular imagination seriously; we had treated it as a robust expression of faith in our diagnostic acumen. Perhaps we had been remiss in not discouraging unrealistic expectations from building up within the poor, illiterate community.

I could see that Cy was haunted by the image of the man desperately trying to thwart fate from snatching his son from his arms. The sudden extinction of hope in the father's eyes followed by the icy stare of faith betrayed got hold of Cy's heart, and kept gnawing at it. The man had simply walked away, leaving behind his raw pain distilled into silence beyond words.

Into such a stark, gutted place I'd stumbled accidentally when I was fourteen. It was late evening; walking past a half-open door of the music room I heard someone crying to repeated pounding of the octave at the outer limit of desolation.

'*Mein Vater, mein Vater, und siehst du nicht dort…*'

The tenor's voice spread an appalling gloom through the dim-lit corridor. Leaning against the wall I somehow managed to reach the lone bench at the far end and slumped down.

Dire forebodings rocked my frame, I had come face to face with *Der Erlkönig* through a routine practice session at the conservatory. As Papili explained later, after sketching briefly that strange Goethe poem, even Beethoven had abandoned the effort, leaving it to his acolyte Schubert to capture a father's grief on his son being cruelly wrested from his arms by an evil spirit lodged in '*Es scheinen die alten Weiden so grau*'.

That evening Cy couldn't eat anything, got drunk but those two pairs of besotted eyes kept drilling into him. 'One has to be an *aulia* or a healing prophet,' he said 'not to be scared when mistaken for God's omnipotent emissary on earth.'

Next day the nursing staff and ward boys missed that smile breaking through Cy's gray-peppered beard. The usual buzz and murmur of patients in the waiting room, the rustle of crisp uniforms through corridors, even the cries of the newborn got muted. Driving home that evening was like following a funeral cortège. I leaned over and squeezed Cy's hand but couldn't bear to look at his face. Till then I had drawn strength from Cy, now the roles were reversed. I would be on my own for the rest of my days on earth.

As the traffic moved inch by inch amidst honking of horns, I would catch a look of intense loathing on Cy's face. The city clanked incessantly like a machine no one knew how to switch off.

I looked back longingly at my early days in the newly independent Umeed after the British had packed up and left, the slogans had died down, the freedom fighters pensioned off and people were busy picking up the pieces of a fractured nation. I remember strolling down to the Park on warm summer evenings, the smell of freshly mowed lawn rising from the ground, Cy flanked by Perrin and me, exchanging greetings with couples in their Sunday best, smartly turned-out men in tropical suits and wives in Georgette saris with shyly smiling faces saluting the three of us. The bandstand was the place to be to feel the thrill of a new nation in the making.

There was a decade when Cy and his friends swayed between nostalgia for the knightly world, which had tumbled into the grave, and euphoria of being part of a wider, all-encompassing nation. There was no going back, the future was limitless and as long as yesterday's freedom fighters grown old behind British prison walls stayed at the helm of government the atmosphere remained charged with hope.

I had learned from Cy how to restore a woman's confidence in her own self. I would watch Cy's gloved hands as they moved swiftly cleaning a wound with long slender fingers; when finished, he'd look at the patient with his hazel eyes and give her a sudden reassuring smile.

In the old days we only had to step into a shop for the owners and their staff to come forward to attend to our needs with broad smiles. Now when occasionally Cy did open the heavy glass door of a brand-new shop selling electronic goods no one even looked up.

Cy lost interest in bridge and his arthritis prevented him playing a game of tennis. He gained weight and spent his evenings reading old copies of *Punch* and *The Saturday Evening Post* borrowed from the Club library.

**** ****

It is now open war between the Umeed Heritage Society and me as I said to my friend Pessy, I won't rest till I bring them to their knees. Let them try and stop me; I will pickle their balls, as we say in our village.

Pessy tried to calm me down, offered to intervene but I said 'No, it's too late now.' They tried to have my Munna arrested for the collapse of that building even after I pleaded that he was misled by that no-good Sandeep Pakwasa his friend from college who had worked as contractor under a builder known for shoddy constructions in the past. Sandeep was Munna's boon companion but that was no reason to take him on the team.

Sandeep had contacts in Bombay and had helped Munna organize that extravaganza with his favorite actor Parvez Khan dancing and shrieking on the stage with his girl friend Bulbul like demented cats. Though why a Hindu girl from a good family – her father was a General in the Indian army – should swing her ass for that 'katta' Parvez is beyond me.

The concert wasn't anything to crow about. Too many blinding lights criss-crossing on stage with Parvez and Bulbul caterwauling like mad. Wife Sundari and I went because we cannot say no to Munna. After all he is our only child, a gift from Balaji himself.

Bulbul was so heavily made up that she looked like a Bhootani sprung from the burning ghats.

When the waiters handpicked by me at the club relate to me how the Umeed Heritage Society geriatrics mock me for not speaking English/Winglish and say I have no ear for music it really hurts like somebody had landed a kick in my crotch. They forget that I have stacks of records of Mukesh and Lata Mangeshkar. That's real music, celestial and beautiful to the ear even till today. And I rated Dilipkumar much higher than Dev Anand even though Dilip was a Muslim, a Pathan. His acting in *Devdas*, his sad smile in *Andaaz* when Nargis ditches him for Raj Kapur ah ha ha, I still get a lump in my throat. But that's neither here nor there. And what about Madhubala eh, I saw every picture she was in. Now that was a true beauty, god-given or in her case, Allah given, for she too was a Pathan like Dilip Kumar. What of it, where genuine beauty is concerned there is neither Hindu nor Muslim. This Bulbul that Munna swoons over would look like a nokrani by Madhubala's side. So to say that I am a Hindu fanatic is wide of the mark.

It is positively insulting to equate me with those saffron brigade fanatics. Why you remember two years ago when a Hindu mob dragged Mahmud the Sorabjis' driver out of his car and were about to set him on fire after dousing him with petrol? When word reached me, I jumped on my old scooter without waiting for my driver Mansingh to take my car out of the garage, rushed to the spot and stopped the mob before it could make holi of Mahmudmian. The man was so overcome with gratitude that he touched my feet afterwards when I carried him on the pillion all the way to his house in the Mughal Wada. How many people would have the courage to go into that Muslim mohalla on scooter in the dead of night? I knew I would be safe because all the dadas and gangleaders in the Muslim community respect me. Everyone knew that the riots were the handiwork of Pessy's father-in-law whose truck business had suffered for lack of patronage under the new Chief Minister.

I am nobody's fool and draw a line at sacrificing innocent lives. As a Hindu I consider it a grave sin. Do I see a smile on your face? I'd wipe it off if I were you, because I am dead serious. I hold all life sacred including that of Muslims and Dalits.

Look, I can say boldly that I have never done anything to hurt people deliberately. It's not in my blood. We Baniyas have made a lot of money, we have a special gift for it but we always play by the rules of trade and commerce. We make compromises only when they are in keeping with our family tradition. How do you suppose we prospered even under Mughal rulers in the past even though some of them were quite wicked like that Aurangzeb who levied unfairly large taxes on us for not converting to Islam? Compromise is our family motto.

We all respected the Old Highness who modernized Umeed but the rest of the Maharajas were sex maniacs, drunkards and gamblers. So don't tell me how good it all was. How did all those thakurs who had to finally sell their farms to Pessy get hold of them in the first place? Wasn't that a form of land-grab? Their great-great-great grandfathers just took over the farms from the sultan after they defeated him at the Battle of Umeednagar.

The Umeed Heritage Society dolts not only turned up their noses, they had this utterly foolhardy notion that they could defeat my Munna at the election for mayor. In the process they hauled poor Dr Upadhaya over coals and made him a laughing stock in his old age. I sent message after message to the good doctor not to rush in where better men than he had their noses bloodied but that old bawaji Sorabji lost his marbles and kept him in the race. They were just a bunch of oldies fielding against a much better team and dropped catches till they were defeated by an innings.

And the fuss they made when some of us who still believe in our own Dharma erected that statue of Swami Bholeram at the club entrance you'd think we had committed some sort of heinous crime. Aré baba, this is our country and our religion and from now on we will build our own statues instead of importing them from Europe like that 'Nanga' David installed in the Museum right in the path of women and children. Don't talk to me about Khajuraho, it was part of Suraj worship in ancient times and anyway it is safely tucked away in the forest. This David-Shavid in the Museum was right there in your face flaunting his handle saying here I am, lead me to a woman and I'll show you how to make babies.

This is slavery sir, sheer slavery to the British who brought their shameless art with them when they were here. Now you tell me what makes Davidsahib in any way better than our Swamiji, fully clothed and all, giving blessings to everyone passing under his eye, be it Hindu, Muslim or Christian?

Listen, our gods when they are standing right next to their goddesses don't even look at them and are always fully clothed. Have you ever seen our Ganesha and Hanumanji whom you insultingly call our elephant and monkey gods going about their business in the altogether? If you want naked statues you go back to England, here there is a dress code even for gods. And don't throw the Lingam in my face. There is a difference as Swamiji explained to us; Mr David's is like a cricket bat attached to a human form. And that is not right.

**** ****

The new Umeed was a town drained of all color, gun-metal gray and hard as steel.

In England whenever Cy discussed his plans to return to India, his colleagues at Hammersmith Hospital would all say in a single voice 'Don't go old chap. You are one of us.' But with the threat of war looming on the horizon he had no choice but to return to fulfill his Dad's last wish.

The people of his father's generation had created little surrogates of London and Paris in their cities. Now the model was conurbation, a series of townships strung together, a chain of glass-fronted shops along its flanks.

The new Umeed of skyscrapers and flyovers was only nominally linked to the walled city, with its cobbled streets and twisting gullies.

I had known all along that one day my Sissi would go to England to live with her father. But I had not imagined fate would bring me so far in time and space just to witness yet another man in my life destroyed by his city. One by one our friends sold their large houses with gardens to estate agents and moved with their black money to suburban housing colonies or migrated to distant lands to be with their offspring. Cyrus, with untrimmed beard, sat staring at the remaining trees in our garden while his old friends began to abandon their homes. They said they were tired of being made to run from 'pillar to post like a peon' for their pittance of a pension by corrupt officials.. Even Collector Chaudhary secured his pot of gold and went to live with his widowed sister in Calcutta. Col Mehra's decision to sell his bungalow and leave for California was the final blow to Cy's hopes of spending the evening of his life in the company of like-minded friends.

He was utterly bewildered that the old world had vanished so suddenly. He had been too busy to notice the slow fading of civic pride, a little act of chicanery here, a small let-down there, the infinitesimally gradual but inexorable rotting and erosion of institutions from within, the fudging of facts in a Government inquiry when innocent lives were lost at the site of an ill-constructed building. All through this he had kept his head, maintained his poise, stayed calm like a soldier in a combat zone, but now as he put it 'the Gatling's jammed and the Colonel's dead.'

I would catch him muttering 'idiot' under his breath when a cyclist or a man driving a scooter cut Mahmud off from the front or a truck came charging at our car from the wrong side of the road.

In the end he stopped going out all together. Until a few years ago he would head for the Club in the evening to play bridge with Col Mehra who would drive down along with Dr Upadhaya and Osman Chacha all the way from their so-called luxury flats on the outskirts of Umeed. They knew how their moving out of town had hurt Cy although he was careful never to remind them of what was a betrayal of their heritage.

The Club was the only spot where the old Umeed had not yet been wrestled to the ground. Sometime an old half-forgotten acquaintance dropped in unexpectedly. He was no longer a member but had no memory of having been expelled for non-payment of dues. He would sit at his usual table, study the menu and say, "Hum kutch meetha lénge."

The waiters would look at each other in silence, and then the Head Bearer would quietly slip into the kitchen and come out with a plate of 'khuba-ni-ka-meetha,' the gentleman's favorite apricot and cream pudding.

Cy watched the scene as if in a dream, knowing full well that the retirement of the Head Bearer would mark the last gasp of a civilization.

Meanwhile the new members of the Club tolerated the old fogies acting out the final scene of their tragi-comedy with the waiters. The future belonged to them; they were in no hurry to get rid of the old codgers as long as they paid their dues. I suspect they were secretly proud of them in their own way; their eccentricities, quaint broad-bottomed trousers, bosky shirts and ties lent the Club a touch of class.

In their last years the Club was the only escape for Cy's circle into their past; there for couple of hours they could inhabit their old stylish world until I picked up Cy on my way home. I had this odd feeling of once again witnessing a primal scene of defeat where four old friends huddled together silently play-ing cards. There was now so much shouting and hilarity around, the card-play-ers communicated with each other in something like sign language, gesturing with raised fingers or mouthing words. Four deaf-mutes in white shirts and institutional ties enclosed in their own world, oblivious of the sound of debris crashing around them.

Once when I walked into the lounge to take Cy home, I heard him say to his friends like a war weary veteran, 'I am defunct, and am simply bobbing along in the wake of my wife.'

At night by the window his old Umeed appeared like a skulking ghost, a shadow returning to its own earthly habitat begging to be let in.

Kunj was now the only refuge left, the club had long since turned into a bordello.

If you are a stranger in a new town or country you are perhaps less bewil-dered; you may have to learn a new language, master alien social codes but gradually you learn to negotiate your passage, avoiding dangerous neighborhoods, staying within well-policed zones. Becoming a refugee in your own town is like waking up every morning to find yourself in the dock for an unspecified crime. The self is perplexed, the house is the same but the scene outside is different. The familiar world has contracted to your living room and outside rages a new planet.

Cy recalled a very special night when he was a boy. One of his Dad's guests had to catch a mail train in a hurry. Sir Jamshet simply picked up the telephone and requested the stationmaster to delay its departure by ten minutes. That night the Bombay Mail did not steam out of Umeednagar Station without Sir Jamshet's guest.

The pain in Cy's knee grew steadily worse, but what plunged him in utter despair was the loss of hearing, first in one ear and then the other. At first he considered it a blessing in disguise because the incessant honking of horns of auto-rickshaws and cars did not hit his tympanum with the same force, but he was now unable to listen to music, especially when I sang his favorite Schubert *Lied, 'Auf dem Strom.'*

Every evening I returned to find him sitting alone in his old wicker chair in the small patch of garden at the back of Kunj. Only one gnarled old banyan stood there surrounded by weeds. It predated Kunj itself by a couple of centuries and had a vast network of roots, contorted trunk and giant limbs entangled at the top to form a leafy dome.

Cy sat under its yellow leaves gleaming in the dim light of the lamp, fanning himself listening to the hoots and whistles of express trains in the distance. The fallow land at the back of the house would soon fall into the grasping hands of Pessy and be converted into a massive housing colony with squat houses that looked like a rows of identical tombs. Cy sat still under that tree like a mendicant who had given away everything.

In the quiet of the night the Indian monsoon drummed the windowpane like a tabla accompanying a nimble-footed dancer. I did not understand Indian music but I was captivated by the sensuous rhythm of Bharatnatyam. Even in the early days in Umeed, when I was invited to a concert at the Palace I was mesmerized by the simultaneous dance of eyes and hands accompanying the percussive footwork followed by moments of enchanting stillness. There was a sense of communing with elements larger than the dancer's lissome body. The classical Indian dance was so touched with an elemental beauty that it was a perpetual source of bewilderment to me why so many Indian film directors were obsessed with the crude hip-swinging and arm-flinging that passed for Western dance.

When the Convent of Jesus and Mary in an effort to acquire a more Indian identity engaged a retired dancer to teach a class in Bharatnatyam both Cy and I encouraged Sissi to enroll in it. By the time she left for England she had assimilated enough of its grace of movement to set her apart from other girls who celebrated their birthdays swaying to the loud screeching of rock bands.

Even with Cy gone and Sissi in England I occasionally found joy in watching a woman's face suddenly wreathed in a happy smile when she brought her child born prematurely the year before, for a routine check-up. The mother's pride in her child growing up healthy was all too real.

Going back to Kunj and not hearing Cy's voice filled me with dread. Even more terrifying was the memory of his sad final years. Papili and Cy deserved a better end; their departing from this world should have been more meaningful to them. Absolute *Yekkes* had survived the War but Papili with all his erudition had not. During the last two years of his life Cy was rarely sober. Drunken stupor was his only refuge despite the steep rise in his diabetic count. Finally he literally rolled over and died leaving me alone to face the new snarling Umeed.

Once I had woken up to see Cy crouching in bed staring out of the window like a frightened child. A bird was hooting in the dark.

The likes of Pavanlal had vanquished a prince among men. What does that tell us about human intelligence?

They say beautiful lives, like great cities, achieve perfection in their ruin but that is really beside the point.

**** ****

BOOK IV

(i)

Before his daughter's arrival in England Terry had been unsure how Sissi would react to sharing her father with a stranger. But it was Jeanette who managed to lift the lingering cloud of misery that had trailed Sissi all the way to England after leaving her childhood home in Umeed. She invited Sissi to join her group to see a matinée of *Under Milkwood* at the National in which the adult world dreams into being its own lost childhood in a little Welsh village. The lilting voices on stage and the miniaturized fishing village of Llareggub tidied up Sissi's longing for Kunj Bungalow and its lush surroundings and reassured her that no matter how far she went away her Oma will always be with her.

Sissi relaxed over dinner at a popular ethnic restaurant bankside in the jocund company of American students. By the time Jeanette drove her to Kent to take her entrance examination at Ashenden Sissi was calling her Mum. Juno had always insisted that her daughter should call her by name.

Jeanette taught courses on modern British Literature to American students from Greenlaurel University who spent a semester in London, attending seminars with weekend trips to Stratford and visits to various literary sites in London. After graduating Phi Beta Kappa from Princeton she had spent five years exploring the Treatment of Children in Dickens and Mark Twain for her doctoral Thesis. She was struck by the arc of destiny that landed Oliver Twist, Pip and David Copperfield under warm counterpanes in snug middle-class homes after years of scrounging and roughing it up on the streets. In contrast was the Huck Finn tribe's rugged individualism that made them 'light out for the Territory ahead of the rest.'

All her spare time was spent in the stacks of the British Library, which was then part of the British Museum. On a crowded day, Terry had shared a table with her at the Canteen in the basement of the Museum. A few days later coming out of the Underground in South Kensington he'd run into her again and discovered that her place of work was only a stone's throw away from the flat he had moved into after Juno shifted to Maida Vale.

On off days he accompanied Jeanette and her excited crowd of students on trips to Stonehenge, Chatsworth in Derbyshire (a possible model for Pemberley in *Pride And Prejudice),* Bateman's — the Kipling house nestling in the Downs of East Sussex, and 'the Crescent' in the city of Bath.

At first he was wary of joining the expeditions in case her prankish wards took him for Jeanette's bodyguard. But she could rein them in with subtle warnings against letting their country's image tarnish in the land of their former colonial masters.

Terry realized that while roaming the globe he had seen very little of England, having deferred his visits to historic cites to some vague future. He had to miss an MGS tour of Stonehenge because it had coincided with Mam's phlebitis taking a virulent turn.

It was also sobering to realize how very little American kids knew or cared about Britain's imperial past.

Only concern for her mother held Jeanette back from making any kind of commitment to England. At the back of her mind was a picture of a toiling woman who after losing her husband to the Korean War wore thrift shop hand-me-downs so she could buy her daughter a present on her birthday and a new dress for Christmas.

Terry could picture Jeanette settling down to a hard life of a pioneer teaching in a one-room schoolhouse in 18th century Connecticut or returning flushed after a hard ride on her ranch horse across the prairie. She came at you in bits and pieces, but each segment arrived in sequence adding up to a credible totality. Large black slightly protruding eyes, face framed by unruly reddish brown hair, full mouth set between slightly puffed cheeks, and a steady lingering gaze Jeanette was surprisingly trim when she stepped out of her winter coat. She made it plain that she would marry him only if her mother gave the green signal.

"Even a middle aged college professor needs confirmation of her choice of husband from a practical mother before tying the knot, just to eliminate any possible hurdles."

After her father's death her mother had lived all alone in a white clapboard house with green windows in Hamden, Connecticut, raking fall leaves at eighty from her yard in late October. She had worked as a post-mistress before retirement and had successfully steered her daughter away from two hit-and-run gentleman callers in the past.

"Mother believes that being in love is only part of the equation for a lasting relationship if you don't want to be returned all smudged and squashed up like undeliverable mail with an incomplete address."

Jeanette's mother grew forsythia and tulips in the spring along the gravel path that divided her front yard, the other side of which was filled with rows of dahlias and morning glory. But recently she had been hospitalized for fracturing her fibula while taking a shower. When Jeanette returned to London after spending a month nursing her mother she and Terry got married in a simple ceremony at the Registry. The bride's party comprised her American colleagues and a loud bunch of cheering students but his quietly smiling ten-year-old daughter represented the bridegroom.

**** ****

Any misgivings Terry might have had about Sissi and Mam getting along had vanished the moment the two of them met. The young girl simply ran into her grandmother's arms.

"Eh lass, the Lord's me witness but for years and years I was expecting y't come." Then touching Sissi's cheek she said to Terry, "Strike me pink, but she looks exactly like Princess Margaret when she was a little girl."

Her Oma had told Sissi before she left Umeed that she must never let her English granny feel less special. Even as a toddler she had been told that Daddy's Mummy loved her very much although she lived far away.

Sissi and Terry made it a point to spend her first Christmas in England in his childhood home in Salford. Mam read a cookbook and watched TV shows to master the art of making butter chicken and biryani and served it to her granddaughter along with roast goose and Yorkshire pudding.

"It'd be a sad day for all of us if my gran'chile had to go hungry on Christmas day, cause she's not used to eating our food."

Since her phlebitis made it difficult to stand for long hours in the kitchen she went shopping for Indian sweets in Rusholme and served Sissi Gulabjamun along with Yorkshire pudding.

The following year Jeanette and Terry decided to give Mam the best Christmas present of her life and bring her to London. Juno had promised to drop Sissi off at Terry's flat in Kensington on Christmas Eve. After coming down for her break Sissi had spent two hectic weeks with her mother in London during which Juno gave her a crash course in visual arts. For three days she marched Sissi through the British Museum, the V&A, the Tate, and the National Gallery. The little girl was exhausted with information overload and her calves ached owing to hours walking acres of hard museum floors.

London would often figure in the back jigger gossip of Mam's tight circle of friends in Salford but mostly rather unflatteringly when its swinging toffs were involved in some more lurid rumpy-pumpy and got nicked bed-hopping as during the Profumo Affair. When outraged, Mam's voice could easily slip into an acerbic Eena Sharples register ticking someone off for an indiscretion at 'The Rover's Return.'

Mam and her friends were all loyalists and stood up respectfully while 'God Save the Queen' played scratchily at the Gaumont. When one of them visited London, which was rare indeed, he or she became an instant celebrity and was eagerly interrogated on whether or not they had seen Her Majesty ride out of Buckingham Palace to open Parliament. Londoners had no idea how glamorous and unpredictable their city appeared to working families cooped up in terraces up North.

The three of them cosseted Mam, never allowed her to get up to retrieve her glasses and often while Terry and Sissi watched a Christmas special on the telly, Jeanette and Mam engaged in woman-to-woman chats, heads leaning against each other. On Christmas Eve the foursome packed into Jeanette's Honda Civic and headed to Regent Street. But Mam asked to be taken to Pimlico where her long dead uncle Roger had lived in a lodging house while working as an Engine Driver during the War.

The car slowly passed through brightly lit thoroughfares and little side streets till the heads of its youngest and oldest passenger began to droop with sleep.

Next day at Euston, before Terry helped her into the train that would take them to Manchester, Mam kissed Sissi on the forehead; eyes welling up with tears she could only manage to say 'Bless thee lass, bless thee.' Her voice faltered as she turned to Jeanette, "Ah'm not long fer this world, that there's a very obligin' child. Allus tek good care of her."

**** ****

To her credit Juno did not resent Sissi's partiality to Jeanette. She tried hard to make up for abandoning her daughter in Umeed by chaperoning her around London during school holidays.

There was a time when Juno acted as though she was jealous of Jeanette. The latter's preoccupied look led people into thinking she was a dull bookworm. Jeanette wore simple professional suits when teaching but going out with Terry she was an arresting figure in evening gowns of simple but elegant cut. She spoke in a calm unhurried New England voice.

Sissi's small form and adult manner contrasted with Juno's effervescence. If Sissi lingered before a painting not favored by her Mum's current arty circle she was subjected to a barrage of commentary. The little girl listened with a grave expression on her face.

Despite depleting resources Juno took Sissi to Paris and Florence with side trips to Versailles and Sienna. With her now considerable knowledge of art she gave mini lectures on works, which in her opinion revealed their genius only to those with a special eye for beauty. Later Sissi said she felt like asking Juno why if she had such exquisite taste in art did she make such bad choices in men?

Instead Sissi just nodded her head dutifully and took notes before Juno bustled her away from paintings that in her opinion were overrated.

"Really, I don't understand all this fuss over the *Mona Lisa*. Now consider this," she would say taking Sissi by the hand and leading her to *The Virgin of The Rocks*. "See — see how Leonardo sets us viewers apart from the figures surrounding them with these rocks of geological precision against the blue far- off mountains? Brilliant — at once strange and familiar. Darling you should know if there's one thing your mother knows how to do well it's that sort of sfumato work."

Fortunately for all of them Juno didn't have enough money and had to call off their trips to the Hermitage and the Prado. After playing the thinking man's crumpet for years Juno finally settled down with butter chicken, so to speak. When Prem Katyal a restaurateur whose expanding business took him frequently to the United States, proposed marriage she accepted him although he did not have one artistic bone in his pampered swarthy body. By then she had secretly been on the dole for a few months.

She had tried to woo Sissi with grand displays of maternal love when a simple hug and kiss would have sufficed. Once again when faced with a difficult choice, the chance of seeing Sissi on weekends, or following the man with a fat wallet, she chose the latter.

"I know I need a face-lift, this may be my last chance to shore up my finances. If I let Prem slip through my fingers I may be forever condemned to stay on the dole. I hope you understand. It breaks my heart but I have to do it."

Sissi who'd had long practice in nodding her head obediently when Juno was in the Mea Culpa mood gave her a hug and wished her good luck.

After a tearful farewell on the front steps of Ashenden Juno flew to the United States. She did ring from Austin Texas from time to time and sent Sissi big mail order packages of dresses insisting that she should join her in the States but Sissi spent all her summers with her Oma in Umeed.

At the restaurant Juno wore her exotic saris and played the gracious hostess. More than the food itself, what brought oil rich Texans flocking to the Restaurant was Juno dressed as an Indian princess in genuine pearl necklaces with manners to match. Soon Katyal realized that his wife was his real asset. Resplendent in clothes specially tailored in New Delhi, head wrapped in crisp blue turban, he stood by her side greeting the incoming clients and escorted them personally to their reserved tables. He would hand over the wine list and she the menu for the evening. They had carved tables and chairs upholstered with brocaded fabric to reflect their courtly-oriental background.

Having grown up in Umeed Juno brought into play all her former selves and soon the Rajmahal Restaurant in Austin Texas became the talk of the town. Mr and Mrs Katyal hosted special fundraising dinners at their restaurant and appeared in national papers standing alongside future governors and presidents.

Looking at their pictures in the clips sent to Umeed Gisela couldn't help smiling. 'At last,' she thought, 'at last Maharani Juniper has gone to live in her own palace.'

But then something happened that threatened her daughter's secure fortress. The internal revenue people slapped her husband with a penalty worth three million dollars for some lapse in filing their tax returns. Katyal tried to pass the blame to his accountant who had fled the country. The last Terry heard Katayal's application for bankruptcy had stalled pending official investigation.

**** ****

<h1 style="text-align:center">(ii)</h1>

One day an official looking envelope addressed to Cy was delivered at Kunj. It bore the printed address of the Umeed Corporation in Hindi. I took it to the Clinic where the matron read and translated it for me. At first I could not grasp its full significance. In Savita's translation the language of bureaucracy must have lost some of its bluntness and it was only when she spelled out its dire implications that my legs began to buckle under me.

"You are hereby informed," the Matron, read, "that you are in illegal occupancy of the premises which rightfully belong to the Umeednagar Corporation. All land belonging to the erstwhile Princely kingdom of Umeednagar officially came under the jurisdiction of the Corporation in 1947. The bungalow Chameli Baugh and the surrounding land are urgently required for the construction of the new State Transport Bus Depot. In view of the good work done by you and your wife the Corporation is providing an alternate accommodation. You are therefore instructed to vacate the current premises by the end of the month. Failure to do so would constitute trespassing and legal proceedings will be started against you."

I stayed slumped in the chair, stupefied, confused.

The emptiness stretching beyond the cliff-end of despair must finally wrench open the mind's eye, how else explain the clarity with which one picks up ordinary details missed during a busy day. I noticed that the house lizard evicted last week by Mr Kazmi had returned to its perch behind the full-length photograph of Her Royal Highness, the patroness of the clinic.

I remembered the colors of the buntings on the day the clinic was inaugurated in the year 1940, the smell of marigold bouquets, the fudge like Burfi, an Umeed speciality too sweet for my then unIndian taste.

The redbrick bungalow with its lawns and bougainvillea-smothered wicket gate was a gift to Cy from the Royal House of Umeed. He had been presented the title deed on that day and a copy had been kept in his desk drawer in the bedroom upstairs. Only once or twice had there been an occasion for me to see the document while helping Subhadra clean the furniture.

The corporation needed that piece of land to build a new city bus station for daily commuters to the rail station and other shopping centers, which had come up beyond the railway tracks. Shifting the clinic from Chameli Baugh to a smaller building was perceived as the only logical solution. I was allotted one whole ward with ten beds for my patients in the government-run hospital where they would be under the care of resident doctors at night. I was free to visit them at any time I wished.

As the Commissioner at the Corporation explained politely but firmly he was under no obligation to provide an alternate space to me but considering my long service to health care in Umeed, a provision had been made under a special dispensation to find a new place for the clinic.

The Secretary to the current Her Highness led me to the large chandeliered sitting room at the Palace where she waited to see me. She was in a simple white cotton sari and her widowed forehead looked bare without the small red bindi mark. Her husband never returned to Umeed from his exile and had passed away recently unsung and unmourned in a foreign land. The Palace had continued to support the clinic from its dwindling income but it could do nothing to stop the corporation from commandeering the building and the land around it.

"All official property in the city belonging to the old princely kingdom of Umeednagar had passed under the jurisdiction of the Corporation, at the time of the princely kingdom's accession to the Indian Union," said Mr Zutsi the old secretary who looked after the Palace administration bent with age and hard of hearing.

Luckily Cy was not there to see how cramped the new premises were on the second floor of a congested office block owned by the Corporation. There was a lift but it never worked and getting up to the clinic itself would have been impossible for him.

Dr Gopal Trivedi who always dressed neatly in a white khaddar bush-shirt and brown trousers, wore no caste mark, spoke the same fussy, heavily-accented idiomatic English as before rose to the occasion and assumed full responsibility for the running of the new clinic. For him bed-wetting was still 'making water in sleep' and a self-regarding boastful patient 'one who blows his own conch.' He would explain to me that there was only so much one could do about a patient who disregarded his warning against consuming hooch, "You can lead a horse to water, but he will drink toddy only."

Toddy was a heavily fermented palm wine favored by rickshaw- drivers and other daily wage earners who consumed it in vast quantities often with fatal results. Cy and I used to let Mr Kazmi decide whom to exempt from paying the fees, which over the years had steadily increased from rupees 10 to 25. Gopal soon came to be known as Dr Pachees Rupia, a title he was secretly proud of.

The new premises had only two rooms. I used the bigger of the two at the back reached by a narrow passageway as office-cum-delivery room. Kazmi doled out compounds from the cubicle facing Gopal's office. In the front was the hall where patients sat on wooden benches like pupils at school until a name was called out by Kazmi who doubled as receptionist behind his window guarding the entrance to my office inside.

Gopal's office was too narrow for a proper table for a patient to lie down for a routine medical examination. That did not faze him. He stacked all his papers on a revolving stand and had his patients stretch out on his writing desk which was long enough for children but not for men of average height

Chameli Baugh was razed to the ground but the plans for the bus station were mysteriously shelved. Paid volunteers engaged .by Pavanlal paraded through the thoroughfares of Umeed chanting death to the new bus station. The old one facing the railway station was suddenly deemed to be more convenient to train commuters who worked in neighboring towns. All this seemed to be pre-planned and once the clinic had been bundled off the old building was demolished and Pavnalal was given a 90-year lease to the property to do as he pleased. He quickly set about building a housing complex for the new professionals who had started pouring into southern Umeed from all over the country to work for various multinational corporations.

In my loneliness even the excessive civility of Gopal Trivedi seemed grotesque. Every evening I found myself going straight to the drinks cabinet and pouring myself a stiff whisky, the desi type much derided by Cy. Then one day a doctor at a posh clinic outside the old city walls turned down a poor man's request to help his daughter. Tears streaming down his cheeks he came to me and begged me to save her.

Mahamud driving the car, we sped weaving through black on white after-noon shadows thrown across by one storied identical homes stalled like a freight train on a muddy unpaved street at the end of which were a group of women all talking at once. Each one vied with the other in shouting unsolic-ited advice to the old man's daughter. One baby was born but the other had got stuck in the birth canal. Slowly with Mahmud's help Savita carried the young mother into the car.

The upholstery at the back was soon covered with blood from the pla-centa. Driving through the one lane road behind a slow-moving lorry loaded with timber valuable time was lost.

The rest was like a dream. The woman was placed on a waiting gurney and rushed to the delivery room. Savita and another young nurse held her legs, the woman was not having contractions. I injected a dose of pitocin but the fetal heart monitor whooshing over the belly registered nothing. Savita held up the child but it did not cry.

Miracles like credit cards came with an expiry date.

Mr Kazmi was taken ill but attended the clinic till he was too weak to walk. Finally he succumbed to cirrhosis of the liver. I continued to pay his full salary to his widow and a few years later Gopal helped her find husbands for their three daughters.

Between the two of them Gopal and Savita kept the clinic functioning in the way Cy would have wanted. Gopal with his quaint ways and hearty roll-ing laughter worked long hours while drink in hand I sat at the table without touching the food till Subhadra began to scold me in Nepalese. I did not understand the language but the meaning was unmistakable. She was urging me to eat the schnitzel strudel I had taught her to make. I began to nibble at it because she vowed to go to bed without eating that night. Next morning in Gabby's New York a pair of planes slammed into towers again and again.

That evening I couldn't push what was served down my throat despite the two of them egging me on. Gopal Trivedi made me swallow barium and found what he called a slight obstruction in my esophagus.

****

(iii)

The Umeed Heritage Society dead weights crossed the Lakshman Rekha when they locked horns with old Pavanlal. I was mad for days afterwards. If they had not thrown the first stone at me I would not have retaliated the way I did. The old buggers just never gave up. Sorabji and his friend Col Mehra had to dig up some old regulation and stop me from building a skyscraper. It was not going to be anything like the Empire State but certainly taller than any building in Bombay. Wouldn't that have put Umeednagar on the map of the world? The whole project was very dear to my heart. You might say it was the culmination of my lifelong effort to raise the profile of my hometown. But no, they had to get a court order and bring a stay on my project. I became a joker in the eyes of other builders. They laughed and jeered at me at the club.

I had to wait for a suitable opportunity to take my revenge. I wish I could have retaliated while Bawa Sorabji was still alive. The old sister-defilers of Umeed Heritage Society did not know that more than half of Umeed corporators owed their seats to me. As soon as Munna settled down in his job and won over all the coporators to his side we got the Sorabji Madam kicked out of Chameli Baugh bungalow in the old town. She was given only one month to pack up her clinic and move to that grungy apartment building with smelly urinals. I was sorry that poor foreign woman had to bear the brunt of my wrath for no fault of hers and that too after her husband had left this world.

My new enemies now live in Surajnagar and work in the State cabinet. I've no opponents left in Umeed, got rid of them one by one. You might smile but really I am the new Raja of the town. Why, every time the old women in the Palace squabble over their property I am called to mediate. I do that even when there are riots between Hindus and Muslims mostly staged by the

Home Minister so that people will not agitate over inflation resulting from his shortsighted policies. It's typical. Somebody throws a homemade bomb at a Tazia or a Ganesh procession and a new battle of Kurukshetra commences. An innocent laborer sleeping by the roadside or a factory worker going to his night shift is killed and 'Baas,' real Dhammal begins and not just with knives as in the old days. Now there are home-made pistols and Molotov cocktails.

Then the elders of Hindu and Muslim localities come to me and say, Pavanji Maharaj the police are not able to quell the riot, please come and make samjhota, get the two sides talking and stop butchering one another. Then I go to the Muslim Mohalla; how many cabinet minsters would dare do that? As body guard I've only our Himmatlal with me. He would lay down his life for me. I had saved his several years ago when in a fit of rage he'd cut his wife's throat. She was having bad relations with their neighbor. Himmat killed them both and came to me with the axe still dripping blood. I made him sit down, dispatched my men to clean up the mess. I sent word to the sub-inspector in the police station in his locality not to come and investigate before all the evidence was washed away. Of course no witnesses dared come forward because they knew my man was involved in the crime. I got the daughter of the murdered man a teaching job in one of the schools; her mother didn't even file a police complaint because when he was alive her husband used to mock her for being fat and ugly.

Anyway, what I do to stop them from rioting is simple. Build trust between the two sides. I invite both Hindu and Muslim leaders to my farmhouse, feed them chicken biryani, serve them real whisky and by the time they go home they are hugging and clutching each other like long-lost brothers.

That Home Minister is really getting too big for his shoes. I know he is building up a huge fortune, estimated to be 800 crore. It is all safely tucked away in Swiss Banks. Every one knows that. Such men have no faith in religion and only pretend to love our Bharat Mata. At election time they have the audacity to describe themselves as the only salvation for the country.

No one can accuse me of having a Swiss bank account. I don't believe in hoarding money. That is greed. I let it flow here in Umeed. I have established scholarship funds for bright children, run a free ambulance service for the aam admi and every Saturday, which as you know is Balaji's day, one hundred beggars are fed simple but wholesome meal with one sweet. Whatever mistakes I might have made will be forgiven because I have received so many blessings from the poor people. I am told that some poor Muslims also come and eat but I have told my men, hey as long as they do not make mischief give them food.

Every summer I organize a katha by Swami Girijashankar. Do you know how much Swamiji charges for every katha lasting ten days? Ten lakh rupees plus food and free lodging in one of my luxury apartments. I can tell you, they don't come cheap these Swamijis. He talks constantly for ten days about the Mahabharata but I go only on the day he discusses the essence of Krishna's advice to Arjuna. I like what Krishna says, that you have to tell a lie occasionally in order to rid the society of evil. If I act in a way that brings happiness to the whole community who is Dr Sorabji to lose his cool and cry 'corruption.' If my action helps people to make money and get out of poverty isn't that an act of kindness?

They say that Swami Girijashankar used to own a pan and beedi shop in a village but one day Nathji came into his dream and said Beta, 'chodo ye sab kutch,' I am pleased with you. Go to Haridwar and take a dip at the Sangam. You will get all the knowledge you will require to spread my message of hope among our people.

I am told there is a cloud hanging over his activities lately. But people are jealous and spread lies. They did the same with Bholeram but no evidence was found against him and the police were left looking like idiots. I have cautioned Girijashankar gently about the rumors floating around. They say he's got a widow pregnant. When anything like that happens, one must act promptly. Deny the charges, even if the stupid television channels do not leave you in peace. Pay money and move the woman and her family to Dibrughad in Assam or to some remote backwater of Kerala so that no one would know where they went. The rumor will die down by itself.

That Kangal Swami in South India knows a trick or two. His hungry eyes can spot a married woman nearing middle age whose husband is impotent. He knows she yearns for a child by the way her eyes are riveted to the picture of

Baby Krishna on the wall behind. It shows the holy infant floating in the river on a big banyan leaf, sucking his big toe. She looks at her husband standing next to her with deep contempt and all the time Kangal is watching and salivating. Generally idiots like the woman's husband have already tried all kinds of medicines to improve their bed-room performance, European, American, Yunani, Indian, consumed all sorts of bhasmas including one made of a tiger's paws but in the bed he sweats and grunts with no results. Then Kangal Swami visits his house, sometimes with the husband's knowledge or when he is away on business and blesses his wife and nine months later a bouncing baby boy is born. A swami has many opportunities to plant his seed, only he has to be careful not to get caught, that's all. People will forgive lechery in maharajas and film stars and even high-court judges but let a swami get caught without his dhoti in the doorway of a stranger's bedroom and the sky comes crashing down on him.

I do believe that we are all human and liable to make mistakes. Admit them and reform, as Gandhiji himself used to say. Read his autobiography if you don't believe me. If you admit mistakes and repent Nathji will forgive you. Valmiki who wrote the Ramayana was what you would call a dacoit, but Rama appeared before him one day and he was a changed man. Hey, even Dharamraj had to lie, no, when he told Bhishma that Aswathama had been killed in the War?

Our gods are merciful. They have to be otherwise most of our ministers and political leaders would have no option but shave their tops and head for the Himalayas.

Lately the newspapers have been full of reports of scions of good families raping Dalit women. It is as if the whole male population of India has turned into a giant street-dog in heat. There is only one solution. Get your boys married as soon as they finish college. I got my Munna engaged when he was still in High School to our neighbor's daughter Roopmati. As a father-in-law it wouldn't be proper for me to dwell at length on her physical assets but may I say that if you saw her on the road you wouldn't be able to walk straight without bumping into passers-by. Even at sixteen she was fully developed with ivory skin and full red mouth and breasts like…Baas, I cannot proceed further without disgracing myself. As soon as Munna passed his B. Comm. and she her First Year of College I got them married. The entire Devasthan cabinet came down from Surajnagar led by the CM to bless the married couple. Munna tried to get Parvez Khan to attend but he sent his good wishes from Tokyo where he was location shooting.

Anyway having Roopmati for a wife immunized him and ensured that he simply won't look at another woman, at least for the next ten years. Enough time to advance his career in politics. Being Mayor is just the beginning, I want him to be the CM of Devasthan and after that who knows even the first Indian PM from Umeednagar. So far only UP has produced our PMs; Mr Rao I believe was the only exception.

That marriage of Munna to a girl from a lower caste was a bit of a comedown for me but it solidified my political base even among the farmers. For centuries the Brahmins and the Kshatriyas lorded over us. Now let the Baniyas take over the reins of power. Our central creed is compromise and what is democracy without a little give-and-take. We are not hung up on outmoded codes of honor like the Kshatriyas. Our Gandhiji was a baniya but he was not pukka like me. He declined political office and I say thank God for that. He turned into a saint, and that's no good in politics. His idea of compromise at any cost was totally at odds with ours. He would have simply handed over Kashmir to Jinnah. He would have thrown his arm around old Mohamed Aali and said, *Aré Miyan kiswasté hairan ho rahe ho,* why if you desire it so very much take Srinagar and live happily in a shikara on Dal Lake. Thank God Sardar Patel was in charge and saved us not only Kashmir but Hyderabad in Andhra and Junaghad in Gujarat.

I am too old to aspire to be the PM of India but I have done enough for our Umeed and I am sure Balaji will reward me for that in the other world. I have groomed Munna properly in business practices as well as in family tradition. And come next election I want him to stand for Member of Parliament from Devasthan and go to Delhi, learn all the tricks from senior leaders, so that when the time comes he would be as formidable and shrewd as Chanakya himself. He knows how to govern a city like Umeednagar, but managing the whole country is another matter. It is like Arjuna's son going into battle against the Kaurava army. You need to combine in you the valor of Arjuna as well as Krishna's skill in manipulating the chariot of power to get you out of the traps set by your enemies.

My Bapuji used to say, what's the good of sticking a knife in a dead body? And he was right. It was I, your humble servant Pavanlal, who said to the corporators 'let us provide a decent place for Madam Sorabji's clinic', at a nominal rent. Many of my construction workers think she is a kind woman. Though come here from foreign she worked all her life to help poor people. I have respect for her. And I also remember how good she was to my wife when she was upset over the death of our daughter long ago. My Sundari did not want to see any other doctor except Madam Sorabji when she was pregnant with Munna and it was she who brought him into this world. How can I forget that? If only her husband had not treated me as though I were a Banjara.

When Munna came to me after becoming Mayor and told me that a large contingent of officials will be coming to Umeed to work in the IT Park by the Delhi Gate and there was a chance for us to recover all our money spent on winning the election by building a luxury apartment complex for all the smart techies being posted in Umeednagar, the only place nearby with some land attached to it was Chameli Baugh. As you can see I was in a quandary. On one side there was this good woman who struggled on to keep her clinic functioning even without her husband and on the other a very good chance of recovering all the money lost during the campaign. We could have won the election on a quarter of the amount we had to spend if Dr Sorabji had not kept supporting Dr Upadhaya till the end.

So once again it is logic, no? You cost me unnecessary expense so you pay for it. I am sorry that I had to get it back by kicking your wife out, but after all business is business.

You see that old bawaji and his chamchas still lived mentally in the Umeednagar of old times when the Maharaja ruled it and built new buildings for the people. All a Maharaja had to do was to take money out of his state treasury to build a college or a hospital. Then the population of Umeednagar was barely two lakh. Now it is fifty lakh.

Why um? Because all the people from nearby villages and from as far away as Bihar in the north and Kerala in the south have come here to work in the industries. They all need accommodation.

Besides there are now so many clinics. Some of them so good that Arab Sheikhs come here to have surgery whether for hernia or by-pass. There is really no need for the Sorabji clinic even for the poor. The old Umeed Heritage Society fools were completely ignorant of the new economic reality. Only if we provide the infrastructure will people invest money in Umeednagar. It's as simple as that.

The CM's demands for donation are becoming outrageous; sometimes he himself telephones at night instead of asking his secretary to do his dirty work.

"Aré Pavanbhaiyya," he says "tell your son the Mayor that if he wants water from the new reservoir for all the new housing colonies that have come up on the southern side of Umeednagar he will have to increase his monthly donation to five crore. Otherwise the height of the reservoir dam won't increase and there would not be enough water to spare for Umeednagar and its outskirts."

Now you tell me how Dr Upadhaya would have handled that piece of shit? He would have written angry letters to the *Times of India*. Do you think that would scare the CM into releasing the water necessary for the new Umeednagar? And who gets the blame when the citizens have no water in the month of May? Who but the poor Mayor himself.

I tell you Baba we live in Kaliyuga that means the epoch of Kali the goddess who sucks human blood. It is such a cruel, cruel world we live in. Now how to explain this to the simple-minded old sahibs who live in their fool's paradise?

So we have to fight on two fronts at the same time, bring in more money into Umeed so that we can spend some of it on keeping the government machinery well oiled. That is our democracy not the sort they have in England. My cousin Sampat who went to the US and made a fair amount of money running motels in Texas says that is how Amrika was built. He says most of the modern philanthropists who build hospitals and donate money to charities in Amrika made their fortune from oil they found in lands they had grabbed from poor farmers. Yesterday's 'chors' become today's philanthropists. Same as here.

Madam Sorabji still has a clinic although in a different part and smaller in size and my Munna has the money to keep the CM happy. Everybody has to make adjustments otherwise they will be simply weeded out like dhatura plants in a wheat-field.

I am not a vengeful man. In fact when Dr Sorabji died I walked with all the leading citizens of Umeednagar to the crematorium after putting a big garland of roses on his palanquin. Madam Sorabji said her husband did not want his dead body to be sent in an air-conditioned container to Bombay only to be eaten by vultures in the Parsi Towers of Silence. That was a very practical move on Madam Sorabji's part, which I applauded when the Corporation passed a resolution condoling his death. Not only that, I sent her a message through Pessy that I would be happy to arrange for a fleet of cars to travel to Omkareshwar in MP to scatter his ashes in the holy Narmada but unfortunately she refused. I heard that she buried the urn with his ashes under a banyan tree in her back yard.

But that's what I call moving with the times. If only her husband had shown some respect for me and not treated me as though I was a nobody come from nowhere. I have a new high school coming up in my latest housing complex and would have gladly named it Dr Cyrus Sorabji Academy. But he was too unbending and acted as if he was born in England and we were all country buggers not knowing anything about culture.

Now that I am also getting old and cannot move about easily after my knee operation last year, I am finished with rebuilding Umeed. It is up to Munna to take it further into the next century.

Accompanied by my dear wife I made what would perhaps be my last pilgrimage to Balaji's temple in Mehdipur and offered as a token of my gratitude a whole coconut plated with gold plus money to feed one thousand beggars every full moon day throughout the year. What more can a man do? I only hope that with Balaji's blessings along with those of one thousand hungry stomachs, whatever sins I might have committed inadvertently will be washed out.

For one thing at least I am grateful to the Sorabjis and that is to avoid drinking contaminated water no matter how holy may be the river it came from. Despite my wife's constant badgering to go to Kashi I never once entertained the thought of taking her to that holiest of our holies. Drinking from the Ganga is simply not on the cards. I know the divine Ganga is not what it used to be, neither is the river of time as our ancient Rishis used to say.

One must always remember that rule. What was good for one generation is never the same for the next.

My wife was disappointed but then I had a brilliant idea. I flew with her all the way from Umeed to Tirupati in the South where you have to wait for up to two days to catch a glimpse of the god. But what's money for? A donation of ten thousand rupees put my wife and me right at the top of a three-mile-long queue and we were escorted straight into the sanctum sanctorum awash in the gentle light of a beautiful five foot high brass oil lamp. I said to myself "It's a lot cheaper getting an audience with the Lord of the Universe than with the Chief Minister of Devasthan."

**** ****

Cy passed away in sleep one day in 1998 when Terry was in Manchester taking care of Mam whose phlebitis restricted her movement. Except for that one Christmas in London Mam never got to spend much time with Jeanette and Sissi, having succumbed suddenly but peacefully to a massive heart attack brought on by acute diabetes. Mam liked her cuppa with lots of sugar and milk, a habit she had developed very early like all working class women who had their kettle perpetually on the hob in order to fight the damp and cold of Manchester.

Sissi made weekend trips from Cambridge to do shopping for her and clean up the apartment as best as she could but Mam who had gained weight in old age was too heavy to be carried to the bathroom. Terry had to take leave of absence to be with his mother.

How the city had changed! The entire Rusholme area was unrecognizable. Once past St Mary's Hospital you saw Indian and Pakistani shops standing on either side all the way to the intersection with Dickinson Road. Cars and double-deckers moved sluggishly through crowds along Oxford Road. Manchester was no longer the home he used to long for when trapped in some alien place on the other side of the world. Ringway was a bustling international airport.

The quiet MGS campus in Fallowfield was lost behind the roar of traffic.

Rushholme was now something like Southall congested with women in cardigans worn over a sari or salwar khameej. For a moment he felt as though he had been transported to the main bazaar in the old section of Umeednagar. *A Tale of Two Princely Cities* languished on his desk.

Mam died as unobtrusively as she had lived. One by one her organs shut down until she could not retain food or water. She went into a coma holding Terry's hand and never opened her eyes again. Her burial was a quiet affair. A few fellow parishioners from St Mark's Church; two surviving friends from the Beam Bleaching days turned up with posies and stood shivering in the cold November air until she was lowered into the grave.

Back in the house Aunt Elsie served ham sandwiches and tea to Rev. Perkins and others. That night while Jeanette and Sissi slept in the old lodger's room upstairs Terry lighted the fire in the kitchen and sat in Mam's favorite rocker, tears streaming down his cheeks. He had not expected to feel so lonely in Manchester. Now that Mam was no more he couldn't bear to linger there even for a moment. The house had too many memories. Once he dozed off and heard footsteps on the stairs. His eyes snapped open but the staircase was shrouded in darkness.

He had to get out.

After a month spent staring at mounds of blind skulls in Rwanda Terry could understand why Conrad had Marlow narrate his story. English was Conrad's third language; in French his second language 'histoire' meant both 'history' and 'story.' Conflating the darkness of Roman London with that of 19th century Belgian Congo was Conrad's way of asserting that history does repeat itself to become a story. Packing tumuli of skulls into a brief segment for the evening news was not possible anymore, each bush and scorched field was the same yet somehow different, there was always some unidentifiable jagged piece that couldn't be pressed into a coherent mosaic without triggering a collapse.

There were clues missed according to a local headmaster whose Hutu pupils had scrawled on latrine walls "Tutsis are bad and they should be killed." Hitler had scribbled something similar on the walls about killing Jews in his prisoner of war days but no one had paid it serious attention.

The Rwandans followed the Serbs in taking a page out of *Mein Kampf* and staging a copycat massacre of the innocents at Srebrenitza. Was it ever going to stop? Hitler's autobiography was being issued in new editions with new additions. Terry was confused. Conrad was right; under different layers with different signs of wear and tear lay the same sacked Persepolis.

He was restless and decided to go with Jeanette to Connecticut to spend Christmas with her mother. Jeanette's presence helped mute the pain of losing Mam. She never tried to console him but with quiet efficiency helped him put Mam's house on the market through an estate agent. By Christmas time when Jeanette was getting ready to visit her mother, Terry knew that he must not be without her.

The following week he found himself standing in a separate line at JFK awaiting scrutiny of foreign visitors by Immigration while Jeanette sailed through. The twin towers had vanished at the other end of Manhattan but their ghosts blew like icy winds through every nook and cranny. Mam had come down with pneumonia and Terry had spent that entire August shuttling between London and Manchester. On 9/11 he'd clung to her bedside like a cowering schoolboy. The streets were deserted with people petrified around the telly. Mam kept pressing his hand reassuringly with her fingers not knowing what had happened, sensing something had frightened her lad.

By the time his passport was stamped Jeanette had already collected their bags. Late at night driving through snow-covered Connecticut roads his head began to droop. Snow was everywhere white during the day, bluish-gray at night. Miles and miles of it, with a church spire rearing high enough to be seen from some distance in small town Connecticut. The rest of the town lay smothered in snow. Peace at last, broken by church bells faintly pealing in that unstained whiteness. Ground Zero might as well be a crater on Mars not visible from here. Jeanette drove expertly along the slippery roads with six-foot high snow banks on either side. Then suddenly a green exit sign bearing the name Quinnipiac University jumped out of the morning mist like a grinning skull on a pirate ship.

Earlier driving up from JFK they had passed exit signs for New Haven, New Britain, New London and Windsor, names early settlers had assuaged their nostalgia with for the worlds they had left behind but Quinnipiac, Paugusset, Cockenoe, Housatonic were family secrets blurted out by naughty children at a dinner party, suggesting other losses that lay buried under the snow, gray branches knocked down by the previous night's storm.

His hippie mates in Beirut sported a Native American headband; some even claimed a dash of Mohawk blood. Heaven knows how much of it was an effort to wipe out an ancestral stigma with a skewed genealogy. Jeanette's eyes were on the road, her face framed by a cap of soft Merino wool was radiant in the morning light. Terry thought, but for Jeanette's land-grabbing Mayflower ancestors he wouldn't be driving through this pure New England snow. Perhaps at the heart of every darkness was an invisible statute of limitation that lifted the ban on past cruelty and let you enjoy its fruits in the here and now.

"A penny for your thoughts," Jeanette said as Terry sighed, rubbing his eyes.

"Nothing, I am sleepy but cannot take my eyes off this winter wonderland. It's so utterly peaceful."

"We're nearly there," Jeanette said reaching out to squeeze his hand.

The wheels lost traction on an icy patch and the car suddenly began to slide sideways, but Jeanette managed to steer it back slowly to the middle of road without braking.

"Sorry," she said, "should've been careful."

Martha, his mother-in-law, was a tall woman with gray hair tied in a bun. In the hands of those two self-sufficient Yankee women Terry felt like a schoolboy on a holiday. They pampered him but also kept him occupied. Martha asked him to help her bring in logs for the fireplace, took him out shopping to the local country store where she addressed him as son-in-law so that none of her neighbors would be left in any doubt that Jeanette had at last been sensibly married to a BBC man. Suburban Connecticut brimmed with nostalgia for Masterpiece Theatre.

Terry made his way to New York one day to visit Gabby. She seemed to have lost most of her teeth and her cheeks had caved, loose skin pouched over toothless mouth. Her eyes had sunk deeper and her speech did not flow unimpeded as before recalling her time as a young girl in Vienna. Reports of her city's degradation during the Nazi occupation were all based on what she had heard and read. On her recent visit Vienna had seemed like a parolee dressed in civilian garb, trying hard to blend with commuters on the U-Bahn, face buried in *Neue Kronen Zeitung*. Almost all traces of past misdemeanor had been surgically removed or swept under the carpet.

Back in the mid-Nineties she had written to Cy warning him of some horrible news coming out of Spiegelgrund, the psychiatric wing of Steinhof. She'd asked him to prepare his wife before revealing the true nature of scientific experiments conducted by the Nazi doctors in charge of the children's ward. The latest report was from a man who when he was about Rudi's age had managed to escape from Steinhof to avoid getting euthanized by a Nazi doctor.

"I withheld the information for some time," Gabby said. "I thought the best person to break the news would be Dr Sorabji. I thought he would know how to handle this obscene news. He had steered my cousin through the worst period in her life. For a long while there was no reply from him, than this arrived just before he passed away."

Terry recognized Cy's graceful sloping hand.

Dear Cousin Gabriella,

Thank you for your letter addressed to me. Please forgive me for taking so long to write back. May I say how touched I am by your confidence in my discretion and judgment to undertake this painful mission?

My only excuse for not honoring it is that being in a state of shock myself after reading your letter I felt I must wait until I was absolutely convinced I was equal to the task assigned to me.

However that opportunity never offered itself, and now it is too late. I am not of this world for much longer and do not believe as you seem to think that my imparting the news to Gisela would in any way dilute her suffering.

I have therefore decided to burn your letter but will try to convey the essence of it to her before I bid adieu. Your faith in me is certainly justified; I have watched my dear wife endure years of agony without letting the world get a whiff of it. However, I must confess this particular matter has driven me to the brink of despair.

'After such knowledge, what forgiveness!'

After reading Cy's letter Terry handed it back to Gabby. Tears were rolling down her cheeks. She got up slowly poured a drink for herself and went and stood at the window looking out at the snowflakes scattering like white feathers in the wind.

Terry could understand Cy's refusal to reveal the truth about Rudi to Gisela. He knew he wouldn't be around much longer and didn't want his wife to be left alone with a grief of unimaginable magnitude.

Gabby said, "Last year my niece Leslie was invited to Vienna to attend a seminar on 'the ethics of stem cell research' which is put on the backburner in this country thanks to Bush and his team of hardliners. The smoke from 9/11 had dispersed but its smell still made breathing difficult. The doctor said a change of scenery would do me good. Leslie insisted I join her on the trip and I gave in."

"She had grown up listening to stories about old Vienna from elders in the family. She had heard about the way we had been hounded out by the Nazis but our combined nostalgia for Wien had also painted a picture of the city which was attractive. Some of our friends after sampling Viennese fare at Café Saharsky at the Neue Galerie near the Guggenheim would go on and on about our winter holidays in the Tyrol, Sunday picnics in the Vienna Woods or evenings at the Staatsoper."

Gabby came and sat down on the sofa.

"We old folks filled Leslie's ears with all the good gossipy stuff that ex-Viennese talk about especially those who have lived for long in the congested world of Lower Eastside. We judged everything produced in the US, food, music, painting, clothes, and furniture by Viennese criteria. If somebody had a new sofa set in their living room, it was not deemed elegant enough by Biedermeier standards. Delmonico's was a pale copy of Demel and Carnegie Hall just a country cousin of Vienna's Musikverein. The loud, bustling New York was no match for good old Wien; the Hudson had no waltzes written in its honor. It was strange how even those who'd been sent packing from Vienna by Nazi goons were quick to put down New York and raise Viennese banners in immigrant neighborhoods."

She leaned back and closed her eyes.

"Listening to us, our gentile neighbors must have thought all of us snacked at Café Central and had tea with Empress Elisabeth at Hofburg. Nostalgia when not tempered with reason can play havoc with one's imagination."

**** ****

The city Gabby visited had been sanitized, Stephansdom had been spruced up, its roof damaged during the War repaired. The whole place seemed lost in a trance, crowds swaying rapturously to André Rieu and his orchestra playing Johann Strauss waltzes against the baroque façade of the Hofburg, busloads of tourists packing the Schoenbrunn. Modern Vienna lived as an epilogue to the vanished empire.

It was now like any other town in the world with only a nominal connection to the Nazis. The Gestapo were an aberration in this otherwise flawless city, the red gondolas on the Reisenrad rose in the sky illuminated in the evening, and the U-Bahn packed with commuters just as weary as anywhere else in the workaday world.

Gabby stopped at her old apartment on Ringstrasse only long enough to run her hand over the door like a blind mother feeling her son's face. Strauss was still in the park, Prince Eugen and Archduke Karl Viktor continued to guard the entrance to the Imperial Palace and Sacher-torts flew off the trays at Demel's just as soon as they came out of the kitchen. On the streets were young people with European faces and manners that knew London and Paris like the back of their hand.

"How could I explain," Gabby said, "to all the teenage girls in our family that for us Kaiserein Elisabeth was the perfect blend of beauty and intellectual elegance; we spent hours just staring at her pictures the way today's girls gawk at rock stars."

Next day the two women sat down in Café Gloriette looking at the city unfolding beyond imperial Schoenbrunn, eating Kaiserschmarrn mit Zwetschkenröster. Later they walked through the Stadtpark, a light breeze swishing through the leaves.

"Taking a tour bus in one's hometown," Gabby continued, "seeing it at once through the bifocal lens of a native and a first time tourist is creepy; one feels like a grave robber stumbling on a headstone bearing her last name. The prodigal walks gingerly, looking over the shoulder, ears straining to catch the sound of ghostly footsteps. One has to be careful not to seem better informed than some poor student earning her penny as a tour guide and getting her dates wrong."

Vienna seemed to be saying those six years of Nazi occupation were a mere drop in its long history stretching back to Roman times, never mind if like an acid drop it left a big burn mark.

Gabby remembered those happy years before the *Anschluss* when you could go window-shopping along lonely streets at night. One day her father took his family for what turned out to be an after-dinner educational tour of Innere Stadt. They strolled past St. Stephen's Cathedral into a narrow alley and stopped in front of an old house where Mozart had scored *The Marriage of Figaro*. Somewhere among those shadows was the Haydn House where the master had composed the Austrian National Hymn.

Father moved as if in a trance to another old building, a baroque church for its neighbor where the *7th Symphony* had premiered with the deaf Beethoven in attendance. There was yet another encounter with Mozart under a ghost of a house on the crowded Graben where *The Abduction from the Seralgio* had been crafted. By then little Gabby was tired and sleepy but so engrossed was Herr Rumplemayor in his musical dream that neither she nor her Mutti had the heart to suggest that they return to Stephansplatz, hop into a fiacre and head for home.

Instead they'd followed him to the little theatre clinging to the Imperial Palace, there he'd paused, putting a finger to his lips, "If you two stop chattering for a moment," he whispered, "you'd be able to hear Gluck's Orpheus singing *Che faro senza Euridice.*"

Fortunately the Beethoven and Schubert houses were not within walking distance so the trio had turned homewards. Gabby's eyes fluttered as though she were trying to keep focused on something, a door crashing, a child's shriek suddenly cut off by a smothering hand, feet marching on cobbles, a crowd frozen in abject silence.

Other than that, Vienna was just your normal modern city trying to keep up with the European Union in these fast moving times. Nasty bits of history had been plucked out like moles from the city's fair skin. It was churlish to bring up past mistakes when everyone was having such fun.

Gabby said, "The following day we wandered through Judenplatz where my oldest aunt had lived in squalor and was found dead in her small apartment not far from the new Holocaust Memorial. I couldn't take my eyes off those petrified books on the square monument; it was as if Papili's firebombed bookstore had become a tombstone of a lost civilization."

Gabby's throat was dry from all that walking and she had to sit down in the hallway of the Misrachi Haus while Leslie asked the Curator if the Museum had any records that might reveal what might have happened to Rudi at Steinhof.

The Curator said a current exhibition being held at Spiegelgrund by the Documentation Center of Austrian Resistance might be worth a visit.

Back in March a jury trial had begun against Gross, the Nazi doctor, but was soon suspended because the defendant was old and considered unfit for trial. For many years after the War he'd been the busiest and highest paid and most renowned psychiatrist in Austria.

A young woman who sat at a desk in the foyer seemed eager to answer specific questions related to the Children's Ward. Gabby didn't want to see any more pictures of Holocaust victims. But she was intrigued by a plaque she'd seen outside the white Church on the grounds of the Psychiatric Hospital, which suggested that the place had doubled as a school for disabled children in earlier times. The young woman's face clouded with pain.

"That is the next part of the tour," she said. "The Church stood in the part of the hospital once reserved for children with learning disability, those with mental or physical handicaps. While Austria was a Christian monarchy, such children were taught manual skills manageable by the handicapped. In those days the State really took good care of the 'Lebensunwertes Leben', or life unworthy of life."

Under Gross, am Spiegelgrund was restructured to facilitate experimentation. Gross killed those who wet their beds, as well as those deemed unsociable. Then he removed their brains for examination. Children were killed because they stuttered, had a harelip, or if their eyes were too far apart. They died by injection, were left outdoors to freeze or were simply starved.

Gross saved the children's brains for research. Years after the War row upon row of formaldehyde-filled glass jars containing the brains of children stood in the underground vault witness to the clinic's grisly past. The brains had now been laid to rest.

"Currently am Spiegelgrund clinic is part of an ultramodern psychiatric hospital. But," the young woman paused as if unable to continue. Then she looked up at Gabby and said in a resolute tone, "Though its name has gone, it cannot escape its past."

All Terry could do was to promise half-heartedly to try and write a historical account, depersonalized in the manner of a journalistic report on a collective tragedy and send it to Gisela. But walking down the steps from Gabby's apartment he couldn't help feeling that he had committed himself to finding words for an evil that scorched his imagination.

**** ****

BOOK V

(i)

Singapore, December 2004.

Almost an hour since the BA flight with his crew on board took off for London leaving a clear view of the avian sideshow, Chinese crackers shooting stars in the evening sky.

The Air India 747 to Bombay is still at the jet-bridge.

The firebirds' plumes sparkle and blink. Some rich Singaporean celebrating his daughter's wedding or a new grandson at Marina Bay.

Brisk to-ing and fro-ing of cabin crew, overhead lockers snapping shut.

Catching that connecting flight to Umeednagar is a must. Can't bear the thought of spending the night in a hard metal chair at Bombay airport, 'like a hen shut up in a pen, beating her wings.'

There's always the last minute, nudge n' wink bunk on the air-conditioned mail if you are not squeamish about bribe-stained sheets. Not cricket, but as Pat Aspel would have said in his plummy voice, 'palm-greasing is to the mid-night mail what the sola topi used to be to the midday sun — a bloody necessity.'

A week's sleep deprivation pries open his mouth.

In his dream he has walked that hospital corridor several times with Herr Doctor Gross, with his blonde hair brushed back from his broad shiny forehead behind which glowed the exceptionally brilliant mind of a scientist. He enters a cold, sterilized room where two nurses hover around an emaciated body of a boy weakened with hunger. The room explodes in brisk activity, a syringe is filled, it squirts, the nurses hold the body down and the doctor injects.

The boy opens his eyes, they are still remarkably bright; his body convulses then suddenly relaxes.

The nurse wraps a surgical mask around the doctor's face setting into relief blue eyes calm as a millpond. He needs all the concentration he can muster to reach down to the inner being of the boy's brain. He is trained to lift the sponge-like object in one swift motion like a milliner removing her latest creation from a hatbox. They say a good surgeon must have hands steady as a woman's, the eye of an eagle and heart of a lion.

He tells the adoring nurses how his two-year-old is already able to say 'Mami' and 'Papi.'

The blonde nurse beams; the doctor draws a circle around the boy's head with a crayon, the other places into his waiting hand what in the glow of the overhead light looks like a surgical saw with extremely fine teeth. At that point Terry's eyes snap open. He stumbles to the pitcher on the stool and drinks water spilling some of it on his nightgown.

He sits in a chair unable to sleep, staring out from the balony.

Perched atop a cliff Hotel Paradise is sodden but intact.

The tsunami had tolled the bell for a quarter of a million inhabitants without shrinking the mosquito population of Banda Ache.

Shredded remains of towns and villages stretch three miles to the sea from where the giant wave had spent itself half way up the escarpment. The day after the Indian Ocean almost absentmindedly bulldozed Banda Ache and piled up its crumpled remains deep inland, the BBC had managed to assemble a motley crew from its various Far Eastern Units and wired Terry who was in Singapore with Jeanette to head straight to Indonesia.

His team had shot the early relief efforts: aid-helicopters dropping packaged food and potable water to the marooned on rooftops, retrieving bloated corpses lodged in trees.

The last sardine winkled out of the emergency chow-kit, it was lumpy rice and sweetened tea the rest of the week, goat's milk being optional.

Shooting the same desolate scene again and again at different locations, it no longer felt odd to see a large ferry boat, its red stern and white funnel intact, squatting in the middle of a highway, mangled cars upended like nursery toys or a hijab-clad woman staring at the sheared remains of a fully furnished bedroom over a kitchen.

At nightfall, the Outback rumbled up the dirt road winding through thickets of bamboo and straggly brush. Twitching with lacerations an occasional figure on its way to the village froze in the headlights.

Next morning, his last in Banda Ache, Terry spots a solitary trawler cast off for the day's catch. The one that got away. You couldn't move across the shoreline without stepping on a limp hand or foot, or bumping into listless survivors staring at the ocean. The rest were buried under the sand, with an occasional hand or foot sticking out. As far as eye could see, there was nothing but hulls of upturned trawlers, waterfront shacks entangled in fishing nets and wind whistling through ribcages picked clean by bloated vultures. Wings clasped in front, they looked like prosperous Flemish burghers posing for a group portrait.

According to the gaunt middle-aged manager, the hotel cat had gone missing. Perhaps oriental moggies came equipped with occult sensors. His old mouser Buttons, had no such foreknowledge. Mam said Buttons was the first to clamber out of the shelter but was deaf to the sirens blaring in the night. Sudden long ago vista the morning after a Luftwaffe raid. Listing drunkenly in the smoke, the lonely spire of St. Mark's Church.

Last night, mobile jingling in the stillness had made him jump, Sissi in Cambridge sounded as though she were in the next room; funny how quickly she'd acquired that bone-in-the-neck estuary voice.

"Dad, I think Oma is dying, Juno is stuck in Dallas. You'll probably reach Umeed before I do. Will catch the first available flight next week."

Typically, Juno was stranded in Texas with her latest yummy man; some last minute hiccup with her Green Card.

"Least said, soonest mended," Mam would have snorted.

'Reaching Bombay in the evening.'

Terry likes his e-mail messages terse but cannot get used to Sissi's short hand, '2' for 'to' and such, favored by her generation.

If only he'd not made that promise to Gabby.

He tries to imagine how a human brain can be removed; scooped out of the skull like a sponge cake?

What was he thinking? And how could he have even thought of asking Sissi to speak to Gisela about it?

Packing the portable digital Beta Cam and accessories in mud-spattered cases that morning was 'no sweat' as old Harry Knickerbockers would've said. The days of slogging through loamy scenes of carnage like Jonestown, with Harry hefting the 16mm were mercifully behind him. The only diversion was the foul-mouthed, Bronx-reared stringer, peeling off Laocoön-like thick black cables slithering out of his unwieldy sound recorder.

Despite long experience in rummaging through the aftermath of disasters overturning dying embers, his own brain shuts down like an engine when he tries to find words for relaying Gabby's message.

Dragging him home from a smoldering site, Mam used to say her son had a covenant with the devil. As a three-year-old, he used to follow his cousin, Marty everywhere. Uncle Tom's threats to take a strap to his son's back never stopped them from playing hide-and-seek in a condemned building. Unexploded wartime incendiaries had blown three lads to smithereens.

Bones stiffened in the beam-bleaching plant; Mam would slump in her rocker and again mumble, "I reckon our Terry has a covenant with the Devil."

By the time Bhopal turned into a gas chamber, Terry had graduated from a rustler-up of crucial footage of remote catastrophes to a documentary maker sniffing out a cover-up from the faintest wrinkle on a faded photograph. Gabby's revelation had gutted his brain.

The tsunami's pugmarks are everywhere, the remains of Banda Ache fester in brazen sands; he has no wish to know how such things happen.

****

Umeednagar Station at six in the morning. Terry walks straight into a Banda Ache moment, little bundles of weary travelers strewn across the foyer, rhythmic gliding of freight trains on sidings.

Back prickling with sweat he crams into an auto-rickshaw; it soon begins to career, axle to axle with scooters and lorries. Bundles of supine roadside dwellers swing in and out of the rear-view mirror like the dead trussed up at Bhopal Junction.

After a twenty-minute chariot race the rickshaw stops under a neon sign, 'New Jersey Housing Complex.'

Across the road, where once stood mannerly, red-tiled bungalows with wrought-iron gates, flagstone paths running through slivers of lawn to wooden grilled front doors, is the membered aluminum hulk of a new mall with in-fills of tinted glass.

A yawning guard opens the gateway. The rickshaw rattles past silhouettes of apartment blocks hoist on thickets of stilts across Gisela's old parkland. Recessed at the far end is the sagging façade of Kunj Bungalow.

Somewhere inside, a grandfather clock suddenly expands its chest and lets off a series of catarrhal chimes.

Housekeeper Subhadra stumps through empty chambers, upstairs and downstairs, in ceaseless bouts of dusting. Terry Sahib and Sissi Baba are coming. The tiny slit-eyed, wooden-doll bride, freshly plucked from the garrets of Kathmandu forty years before, greets him with a toothless smile. Husband Bahadur is curled up on a charpoy far side of the veranda, groaning and muttering under the quilt. Of the thirty strong household staff, including syces who kept the stables brassage-clean and the lawns lush as moss even in summer, only the Gurkha pair remains.

A crumbling stone post is all that's left of the fan-shaped veranda. A pile of crooked slabs serves as steps to the main doorway.

****

(ii)

Gisela to Subhadra.

"Sissi Baba come?"

"Terry saab come. Sissi Baba come next week. Sleep sleep now." Subhadra plumps up her pillow, gently brushes aside strands fallen over closed eyes.

According to Subhadra it was Terry tiptoeing up cautiously. Kind soul, always mindful of my comfort. I was spoiled by my men, beginning with Papili, then Cy, and last but not least dear Terry, friend and ally, even after Juno walked out on him. Can't wait to see him. It's impossible to break the cordon thrown round by Subhadra and Bahadur — my praetorian guard. Weak as a kitten. If only my eyes would stay open. Subhadra won't let him come near me till she has fed me porridge.

Two more hours of tossing in bed.

It's twenty past ten by the time Terry showers. The smell of fried eggs and toast draws him to the kitchen where Subhadra is busy loading a tray for his breakfast. The pallav of her crumpled sari keeps slipping down her almost bald head as she sets down the tray on the table by the window. Her eyes have receded further back in the skull, but she manages a withered smile of a Sybil.

Gisela has dozed off after taking her pills. Juicy gossip from the world of make-believe captioned below the *Times of India* masthead. The new jet-age India reads with relish tearful confessions of errant Holywood celebrities reinstated in the public domain through the midwifery of Oprah while debt-ridden farmers commit mass suicide in small print three hundred miles to the east of Bombay. As Subhadra limps to the sink with the empty tray, Pat Aspel's words about the Umeed Dynamite Case of thirty years before come back to Terry.

"These poor wretches have pinned their hopes on the BBC for carrying their story across the world."

****

Terry's eyes are full of questions. I wish I could explain how the house sank and the award roses festered. Called to account I could crunch the numbers.

Paid staff salaries including Gopal's and Savita's yearly increments for six years.

Defrayed expenses of seven thousand difficult pregnancies.

Tuition for Subhdra's grandchildren.

Car repair, driver Mahamud's salary and on and on and on.

Pessy our neighbor's son never forgave Juno for marrying you. I see him now as a little boy in short pants come to retrieve his ball from the rose bushes.

Instead of the ball, he took away the entire garden. His mother, Behroz my friend of many years, lost her mind early and turned spiritual: weekly séances with her late husband. Rest of the time she just sat on the veranda, smiling to herself till her mind cracked.

The garden was Cy's legacy to his daughter against a rainy day. She sold it off to Pessy, needed cash to be with that two-bit actor in Colombo. Pessy employed thugs to chase off old Parsi and Goan Catholic families from those pretty bungalows along Post-Office Road. Only Col Mehra held out for five more years till offered a price he couldn't refuse. They say Pessy plays golf with the police commissioner, cards with the mayor and at election time bankrolls the most obliging politicians.

The leafy, foresty Umeed of Pessy's schooldays of short pants and unruly mop of hair gradually disappeared behind ugly glass and steel monsters; he went prematurely bald and developed a paunch. Cy used to take Juno and Pessy on hunting trips, we both had much affection for the boy. But along came Chanda Singh, a crack shot when sober and cousin to royalty five times removed. Seven years his senior Juno married him over my objections. The day Chanda's jeep overturned and he died of a broken neck, Pessy was there like a shot by her side, but she kept him dangling for a long time and married you.

You were her passport to England. With your kind eyes and ready smile —

a sitting duck. I should have warned you when I saw her unleash her charm. But what could I do? You liked being escorted by someone with pretty white legs, red skirt and yellow blouse of Japanese silk.

Cigarette holder in mouth, she watched you like a dog trainer, playing the maiden desperate to be rescued. Living in a monsoon-drenched bungalow, invention came thick as fungi to Juno.

You were such an English gentleman despite that funny North Country lilt; I thought she would settle down for good. Cy with his bad heart wanted to see a grandchild before his 'ticker packed up' as he used to say. And my liebling Sissi was like a china doll when she arrived.

Poor Terry, I can see you are appalled I can only whistle, should have warned you they had to remove my sound box to prevent metastasis. Now here I am ready to tell all and even sing for you lieder from my young Gymnasium days, but can only produce meaningless sound. Melodies well up, recoil before reaching the throat.

I keep seeing Mutti, eyes closed, doubled over her cello like an expectant mother, Papili at the piano caressing the keys. Next moment, their eyes snap open and Lied ohne Worte erupts in an auto-biography of speaking shadows.

"Language would be an intrusion," said Mendelssohn when a meddling poet offered to replenish his voice-flushed D major with words.

****

(iii)

One day while pottering around the backyard of Kunj Terry came upon a door he'd never seen before. A flight of steps led down to a sparsely furnished room with a low ceiling. Judging from its contents Terry assumed it was some kind of hideout for Gisela when she needed to be alone. Perhaps no one save Cy and Subhadra knew of it. It was cool in that almost soundproof room with two air-ducts in the wall. There was a Thoren turntable and a stack of LPs, a settee with curved legs and beige leather upholstery. Music and silence must have been the only companions absorbing large portions of Gisela's private pain.

Now she could retain without retching or vomiting chicken broth spooned to her by Subhadra every afternoon, and her face lost some of its deathly pallor. She was able to speak in short high-pitched disembodied snatches without dribbling or coughing, her voice rebounding from some point on the wall behind her bed.

As the day of Sissi's arrival drew closer there was a marked improvement in Gisela's condition. With each passing day her eyes turned to the door expectantly as if to accelerate her granddaughter's homecoming.

Sissi had gone to Cambridge to read for the English tripos but had switched to Linguistics. She was now at the final stage of qualifying for an M.Phil. in the Education of the Disabled; Terry had told her to be strong and make her Oma proud by completing all the requirements for the degree before leaving England.

At 43 Pessy's childless wife Laxmi who'd been one of the teachers during Sissi's early years at the Convent of Jesus and Mary had given up her job and spent two years with her mother's family in Bombay obtaining a Diploma in Teaching Handicapped Children. During her earlier trips back to Umeed Sissi had noticed that Laxmi's impaired hearing found it difficult to distinguish between singular and plural nouns and struggled with pronouns not knowing when to use them.

Kirpal has gone to the airport to receive Sissi. Terry remembers him running errands around the house hitching up his shorts to fetch something for his mother. Gisela had done everything to keep him in school but he had fallen into bad company and kept failing till in desperation Subhadra and Bahadur bought him an auto-rickshaw with all their savings. He was married and had three children in quick succession but his wife had died recently and Gisela was saddled with their upkeep and education.

In the mid-Seventies when Terry first arrived here Umeed was a town skirted by a railway track half-smothered in grass during the monsoon with an occasional whistle from a passing night mail as a reminder of the world elsewhere. Now the drone of aircraft constantly filled the skies over the city. In a few years the old princely capital would be reduced to a departure lounge with international flights landing and taking off night and day, a true city of the 21st century, caught in a tangled network of flyovers, traffic seething like chemical fluid choking all roads leading to the airport.

The minute hand makes a sound like a hiccup as it moves, the polished mahogany frame of the Grandfather clock convulses when it beats out the hour. Now the autos come up the pathways just wide enough to let one medium-sized vehicle squeeze through, twisting and turning as it screechingly works its way to the front of the house. Pessy had in fact merely replicated the narrow gullies of the old township, setting apartment houses so tightly next to each other as to blot out all light and air. It was now beginning to take on the musty smell of hoary lanes from where the moneyed class had moved out to what was euphemistically called a modern housing complex.

Subhadra wheeled her mistress out to the veranda in the evening when the breeze was cool. She would peer through the housing complex to catch a glimpse of the high tower of the Palace, which in the old days held aloft a red beacon to signify that the His Highness was in town and all was well with the world. After constant badgering, Subhadra yields to Gisela and rolls her out to the edge of the veranda to wait for Sissi. She lifts one thin hand, skin lolling like an empty pouch, till she can spot the rickshaw rattling up to her barb-wired compound.

Sissi's arrival reopens the passes buried under Gisela's avalanched voice. The two of them cling to each other laughing through tears. Then Sissi begins to sing, Gisela hums along swaying to the rhythm, Subhadra squeaking in the background. The veranda at Kunj is a rendezvous site, a murmuration of starlings in the air; Terry recognizes the melody, her first year in England Sissi used to sing it at bedtime, eyelids drooping, voice trailing.

Am Brunnen vor dem Tore,
Da steht ein Lindenbaum.
Ich träumt in seinem Schatten
So manchen süßen Traum.
Ich schnitt in seine Rinde
So manches liebe Wort;
Es zog in Freud und Leide
Zu ihm mich immerfort.

Sissi had been Gisela's audience even when she was too little to understand what she heard. Subhadra was her other listener, and lately into her uncomprehending ear her mistress had been pouring snatches of Hölderlin and Rilke. Subhadra would smile and make little sounds and laugh her rasping country woman laugh. The three of them were in league; Terry had no idea how their secret non-lingual communication apparatus worked; birds flying in tight formation using low-frequency infrasound.

After they had been in Gisela's bedroom for about twenty minutes his daughter would whisper, "Let's go out now Dad, Oma wants to sleep."

As if she had only been waiting for her, Gisela died peacefully in Sissi's arms. But those four days before she drew her breath for the last time her face glowed with happiness, her blue gray eyes regained some of their old sparkle. The contentment on her face as she fell asleep holding Sissi's hand had such ageless grandeur that it made Steinhof and its murderous history seem tawdry and inert like nuclear waste.

In talking about it to Sissi the night before, Terry had tried to place Rudi's final moments in a historical context. There on the veranda, with Bahadur coughing and muttering in his corner, Terry recounted the gruesome story to Sissi. For a long while neither of them stirred.

"You must understand that even in England there were experiments that required opening of the human skull," he said tentatively. "We know that Einstein's brain had been studied for uncovering the secret source of his superhuman intelligence. By the same token an attempt to discover the seeds of insanity before they sprouted might have seemed quite legitimate to someone with a sick Nazi mentality."

"But Daddy," Sissi interrupted him, "that is mere hair-splitting. Sticking your fingers into someone else's brain after they had died may not be considered unethical but I still think it's disgusting. More to the point, how can any one justify killing an innocent boy as if he were a laboratory animal? That's obscene."

Terry was appalled that in trying to shield his daughter's eyes while escorting her through hell he'd fallen into the same Faustian trap as Dr Gross, the Nazi doctor.

The silence was broken by a sudden discharge of breath by Bahadur's lungs.

"That sounds like apnea doesn't it?" Sissi said looking at the sleeping figure at the far end of the veranda. "I must report it to uncle Gopal when he comes in the morning to check Oma's blood pressure." Then she hugged Terry and said, "Off you go to bed Daddy. It's past midnight."

"What about you?"

"I'll be all right. You look tired and need rest. I'll sit here for a while."

Slowly and without fuss his daughter was taking charge of her Oma's house.

At five in the morning he stepped out, tiptoed down the staircase to find Sissi sitting in the same position he had left her.

"I have been thinking about what you told me last night. I felt nailed to this chair, couldn't get up or do anything."

"I should have told you earlier," Terry said, "I've been carrying it with me for over a month, ever since I left New York and it was driving me out of my mind. Telling you was like telling Gisela. She loves you so much, you are her natural heir."

"Quite right, Dad. I am glad you told me instead of her."

Both of them heard Subhadra scuttle into the kitchen. In a little while she emerged carrying a carafe of water and disappeared into Gisela's bedroom. Sissi darted in after her and found Gisela sitting up, face flushed, beads of perspiration dotting her forehead. She caressed Sissi's face, mumbling "mein Bienchen, mein Schaetzchen,' again and again. Then her body arched as another coughing fit seized her frail frame, a tremendous rasping sound rose from her throat, her cheeks puffed up suddenly and eyes snapped open. Fixing her gaze on Sissi's face like a waking child's, she said in a clear voice,

Mein kleiner Engel

Meine Füße haben mich verlassen

Meine Füße sind verschwunden.

Then her body relaxed and her lifeless hands dropped down by her side, her eyelids closing as though she were falling asleep.

"She is gone," said Sissi, placing her grandmother's head gently down on the pillow. With an animal cry Subhadra flung herself on the crumpled body of her mistress. Gisela's lips were wrenched open by the escaping breath, leaving a tender smile in its wake.

The first hours after her passing were like the silence that spreads across a lonely shore after the tide recedes and the last bird has fluttered into its nest. Sissi's eyes were dry and she was composed as she took charge of the cremation, ringing Dr Trivedi and Matron Savita.

The Matron now gray-haired and limping, Dr Trivedi a little heavier and Mahmud leaning on a cane, came in one by one and stood whispering on the veranda until Sissi and Subhdra brought out wicker chairs for them to sit in as they waited for the ambulance.

As the news of Gisela's end spread through the town a large number of her old patients almost all of them walking slowly gathered outside Kunj to convey their 'Sorabji Madam' to the crematorium. Those who were on scooters followed the ambulance driven slowly through the afternoon traffic. Pereira and two other waiters from the Club cycled down and there was a man in Palace livery with a note and a bouquet. The note simply said 'Rest in peace dear Gisela,' signed Maharani of Umeednagar.

Those who were without any vehicle followed the ambulance on foot.

Terry who'd driven ahead with Dr Trivedi was already at the crematorium to receive Gisela and her mourners. There was no loud wailing of the sort Terry had heard in the past when someone had died. Even in her death Gisela commanded love with dignity from those whose lives she had touched.

A loud chant went up from those assembled, "Hamara Memsahib Zindabad."

Gisela had been most unmemsahib-like during her lifetime and in the crowd's chant the expression was purged of its entire colonial *hauteur*. Once the body arrived Dr Trivedi asked the officials to wait to allow the walking crowd to catch up. Then Gisela was put on a sliding shelf, which pulled her into what was essentially an oven; with a soft swoosh electric flames enveloped her body.

Afterwards Dr Trivedi and the Matron drove all the way to Lake Pushkar in Rajasthan to empty the urn of ash.

It was when Kirpal drove them back in his rickshaw that Sissi broke down and sobbed uncontrollably. Terry had never seen her cry that way before in London. She clung to Subhadra and Kirpal and all three of them cried together.

Terry felt excluded from that group pulled into a tight huddle by a primal bond. For a few minutes, he was a stranger watching a family grieve together. It was a revelation to him that his daughter was not only deeply attached to Subhadra but also to her son. They had been children growing up in that great house but Sissi's long years in England had erected practically no barriers between the two. At thirty Kirpal was already a widower with three children. His wife had died giving birth to their youngest girl, who ducked behind a door every time Sissi looked at her and smiled. The two older children were at school.

***** *****

For the rest of his stay Terry saw Sissi only at dinner. She left early with Kirpal and his son to Laxmi's school for the handicapped.

In many ways Sissi was like her Oma -- quiet of movement and voice. As a child she simply surged forward when in a hurry, never breaking into a jog.

Surprisingly she had no great ambition. Other Indian girls and boys her age were literally fleeing to the West as her own mother had done earlier but Sissi, in 'reverse migration', was determined to make Umeed her final home.

Terry asked her if she had been unhappy in England.

"No, on the contrary, but there are many in England who can do the work I am going to do in Umeed. And truth to tell I never left here."

When Sissi and Kirpal were together in the same room each seemed to know what the other was thinking. If Sissi took a step forward to move a piece of furniture Kirpal was already there to lend a hand.

Unlike her mother, Sissi had a self which belonged to Umeed. Terry could actually feel a silent panic rise within him, a sense of being banished from his daughter's private world. For the first time he understood Lear's hysteria at the recognition that his favorite child was kin to someone else. And although Kirpal was older by three or four years he acted as though he had learned in childhood to defer to Sissi in every decision.

No matter how hard Terry tried to be part of their world he was still a Sahib to children and adults alike whereas Sissi walked into that throng as to a family reunion. Kirpal's children called her Sissi Massi (Aunt Sissi).

The following week Gisela's will was read in the presence of Dr Trivedi and the Matron. She had left Kunj, her only worldly possession, to her granddaughter, the two-room outhouse to Subhadra's family, a priceless diamond necklace and gold broach to Matron Savita, and the clinic with its medical library to Dr Trivedi.

For transferring the title to Sissi the death certificate issued by Dr Trivedi was not deemed adequate. One had to make an application to the Mamlatdar who would issue an official document needed to effect the change in the title deed. It was a mere formality. Since Laxmi had come in to discuss how to implement changes at her school Sissi gave the application form along with Dr Trivedi's certificate to Kirpal and asked him to fetch the document from the Mamlatdar's office in town.

But Kirpal was gone for a long time and returned empty-handed. He told Sissi that the Mamlatdar Sahib's assistant had demanded Rs 10,000 for releasing the certificate. There followed a lot of whispering and looking over the shoulder before Laxmi's driver came to take her home. Next day Sissi accompanied by Laxmi and Kirpal went to the Mamlatdar's office and demanded to see him.

At this point the story stumbled into a beguiling animal fable. It had to do, as Terry gathered, with Sissi impersonating a member of an International NGO unit working in tandem with a local charity. Kirpal's humble, errand boy appearance and distinctly Nepalese features were so out of sync with Sissi's European touristy look, the assistant failed to notice that far from being strangers to each other his visitors belonged to a pack hunting together. Being thrown off the scent he requested Sissi to take a seat and brazenly ordered Kirpal in Hindi to put the 'cash donation' in the right-hand drawer of his desk. The rest of the account involved a nifty use of a palm-sized tape recorder, the sudden appearance of Laxmi on the scene, the Mamlatdar confronted with two irate women sheepishly signing the certificate to avoid a corruption scandal.

Kirpal's recounting of the episode had Sissi and Laxmi marching to the flapdoor, flinging it open and playing the rewound tape to the Mamlatdar. The voice of the assistant asking Kirpal if he had procured the 'dakshina' (gift) for his Sahib came over loud and clear.

Before a captive audience of his teetering children and beaming parents Kirpal rendered the flabbergasted Mamlatdar gagging on a half-bitten pakora while Laxmi clicked her camera. His reenactment of the slimy underling and his bewildered adipose boss standing drop-jawed as the women gathered their things and swept out of the office had his hearing-impaired youngest daughter in stitches.

Later that day Terry heard Sissi telling the agents of Sunrise Builders she won't be intimidated into selling Kunj under threat to anyone. She was not interested in their money and she had no intention of disposing of her grandmother's property. With the help of Aunty Laxmi she planned to open a school for hearing-and-speech-impaired children. Laxmi had been using a space provided by the government at one of their schools in the old section of town but it was available only in the evening. Terry realized finally that Sissi was not going back to England.

After Laxmi went home Sissi came and sat down on the sofa with her father.

"Dad, you look terrible. Don't be sad, mine is not a sudden decision. I have been helping Aunty Laxmi for the last three summers. Oma never said I should return to Umeed for good but I knew she wanted me to. Last week when you told me what had happened to Oma's brother I sat and thought for a long time. Not telling her was a good decision but something else had to be done to balance that evasion. At that time I had no idea that Oma was going to leave her house to me although she used to say 'whatever I have is yours.' I think it is only right that I should stay and carry on her work. She and Granddad gave so much to people who needed their help and support. England can get along without me. There are many people all over the UK qualified to work with the differently-abled as we say in our field. Here this work is just beginning. I have been working with Kirpal's youngest. She was born deaf. She has been attending Laxmi's school and now is ready for proper education."

But the really stunning blow came at the end.

"And Dad listen carefully. I intend to marry Kirpal if I succeed in turning his life around and be a mother to his children. I don't want to keep anything from you. No more surprises. You have been a wonderful parent but also a true friend. I love you and am extremely fond of Juno for all her strange ways. I know what many people would think. They would say how could someone like me be in love with a man like Kirpal, a servant's son? But Subhadra has never been a servant to me. Even Oma thought of her as family. I certainly did. When Juno left me here, and Oma and Granddaddy at the clinic the whole day, who do you think gave me love? The sort of love a child yearns for but can never articulate. It was Subhadra and Kirpal. Her family became my family. She would interrupt her work in the kitchen and with the smell of freshly-ground coriander still on her hands soap my back because I wouldn't let any other servant touch me while taking a bath. That smell followed me to England. I realized I couldn't live without Kirpal. I did go out with friends in Cambridge and some of them were first-rate chaps but in the end there was something that always held me back. Perhaps despite my white skin I am at heart too Indian to feel at home anywhere else."

"I can understand that, but why rush into this marriage, what's the hurry?"

Sissi looked at her father for a long while then said, "When we were younger Kirpal was far ahead of me in maths and used to help me out with my homework. If he goes back to college, qualifies in Computer Science – he is very good at it, there is no reason why I shouldn't marry him. I know in my heart that it was my going away that turned him into a recluse. He lost interest in everything including studies, began smoking pot, got into fights. I am sure he sees how wrong it was to hurt his parents and especially Oma. If he proves me wrong I shall be sad but I'll still have my work with the children."

Terry was stunned. He thought her Oma's passing had frayed Sissi's nerves. The ebbing of all that ocean of love must have left a vacuum in Sissi that only someone she had known all her life could fill.

My poor girl is confused, he thought. She wants to emulate her Oma, but Gisela had married Cy, a prince among men. To give yourself to a rickshaw-wala on the assumption that some day somehow he would rise to your level seemed too rash in a preternaturally mature girl like Sissi. It sounded too much like a mission, a gesture of self-abnegation, something she had to do to appease the spirit of the dead. She had never met Rudi but had felt his presence all the time growing up under his invisible shadow.

Terry tried to fight his prejudices. How easy it was to preach class and caste blindness? What was his class? Hadn't he always been a working class lad from Salford?

He needed Jeanette. She would know what to do. He'd get her to speak to Sissi. The very thought of Sissi marrying Kirpal filled him with horror. The suddenness with which his daughter was taking these most unexpected decisions was too much for him. As a child Sissi must have felt exiled in a deeply wounding way.

She was full of plans for her new school.

"We'll call the school Dr Gisela Sorabji Academy. Ranjana my old dancing partner and friend from the convent has also decided to join us. We'll open the rest of the rooms on the ground floor as well as upstairs. Uncle Pessy has promised to reinforce the columns on the veranda, repair the broken windows. We are all set. Next time you come down bring Mum, I mean Jeanette with you. I'm sure she would be very proud of me."

Once again Terry had that feeling of being ejected from the life of his daughter. Sissi and her friends were interconnected in a manner he had never been with anyone in England except Mam. Sissi and her generation were street smart in a way Cy's had never been. The young wanted a fighting chance to be self-sufficient in a world where might was right. And above all they were impatient for change, knew how to fight dirty when required — judging from that mini sting-operation carried out by Sissi and Kirpal to catch the Mamlatdar red-handed. A modest start perhaps but Terry hoped it was the beginning of the great springtime in India and not just youthful idealism flashing in the pan.

For the next two days Sissi's eyes would well up if she tried to speak to her old friends from school who came in the evening for a quiet sit-in with her. It was a form of mourning for the dead but also a renewal of friendship.

Soon it was time for Terry to head for Hong Kong where Jeanette was waiting for him.

**** ****

(iv)

Terry's last day in Umeed.

One of the few banyan trees still standing in Umeed is in the backyard of Kunj. It is like an old elephant come back droopingly to die by the herd's waterhole.

That giant banyan belonged to Cy and Gisela's world. Soon it too will be extinct like the dinosaurs of the past, the world needs space for its exploding population.

The spirit of the city, its statuary, masonry, its alternating colors from monsoon green to winter gray, the parched lips of its earth, all these live somewhere in the memory of elephants too old to walk in Royal processions. The here-today-gone-tomorrow winters of Umeed are getting shorter every year owing to global warming. It is now a town of factories with assembly lines practically ending in the bellies of air-cargo warehouses.

The airport is the true city of the 21st century. The new Umeed with its intricate network of arterial roads is already on its way to becoming a suburb of the invisible world-capital, a virtual metropolis, its population forever circling its dark heart, not godless judging from the crowds swelling outside temples and mosques but perhaps god-free.

Sissi and her friends would know how to find their way in it.

The 'No Smoking' sign goes off with a ping. An enormous weariness closes on him; he can barely open his eyes. All around him there is sound of bodies unfolding, overhead lockers snapping open.

What had taken him by surprise was the way Sissi had planned her future. In that she was like her Oma, the young medical student who'd gone to London to complete her studies when the Nazis began to foul Vienna.

He was never in charge of her anyway and now it was too late to start meddling in her affairs, to start playing Daddy. That way lay madness.

God, how it rained in Bombay when they touched down. You could see nothing through sheets of water cascading down the windows of the hotel. Even though they made a dash for the hotel lobby once out of the taxi their fingers dripped afterwards like the ferule of a rain-soaked brolly. But today the skies are clear over the Arabian Sea with a few fleecy clouds sashaying away like dancing girls in a Bollywood item number.

Gratified, he watches them drift away to the distant horizon from where at midnight a jumbo jet will carry him to Hong Kong.

Outside, the sea rolls smoothly, fronds hang like yards of torn drapery from glistening palms and everywhere it is so green that leprechauns might step out of grass. But who believes in them these days?

Sissi is really here to see him off.

"Dad" she says over breakfast, "Why Hong Kong?"

"My dad was stationed in Singapore when it fell to the Japanese. There had been rumors that some Kim Philby-like figure had betrayed our men and caused them to surrender. But it proved to be a wild goose chase. No one at the University of Singapore had heard of such a thing. Jeanette's assignment in Singapore is over, she is guest lecturing at the University in Hong Kong. It was the last bit of Empire severed without much heartbreak on either side. Now that Gisela and Cy are no more I know how to end the tale of princely cities."

Sissi hands him a buttered toast.

"I don't know how to say this," Sissi says, "I can't promise you anything. Some expats in England are still hung up on roots and make money writing about them from their comfortable homes in Highgate or Camden Town. These days you can buy roots from vendors on Oxford Street. If it gets too hot for me in Umeed I know Jeanette and you will have room for me to crash in the attic."

Buses and taxis are scarce in the waterlogged city the day after a heavy downpour so like other tourists they ride in a hooded Victoria that goes clip-clopping through Sunday silence where ghosts of the Strand and Aldwych haunt the crescents and squares under colonial facades of South Bombay. Sissi hums softly,

Alle meine Entchen

Schwimmen auf dem See,

Köpfchen in das Wasser,

Schwänzchen in die Höh.

Finally they pull up at the giant Gateway where masseurs, conmen, peddlers of biros, watches, blades, shampoos, Japanese silks and electronic gadgets hawk and hiss, rubbing shoulders with other dispensers of dreams, longevity and aphrodisiacs.

Out in the bay wobble buoys amidst ferries, tankers and smugglers' dhows rakishly tilted by trade winds, which had once escorted ashore ships loaded with tropical twill and poplin from Salford, locomotives from Sheffield and smoothed the passage of P. & O. liners. Over the horizon to the right is Karachi and far beyond that England. Several hundred miles to the North beyond the ruck of hills lies Umeed.

A tug at his sleeve and a clucking gremlin presses a grisly aphrodisiac into Terry's hand while Sissi clicks her camera. He chucks the mess into the sea but before it can land a crow swoops down and wings off with it. The gabble continues non-stop followed by more tugging at the sleeve. Terry parts with a ten-rupee note to keep the tout from starving. With the Gateway for home, he has nowhere to go. His way out is the way in.

Perhaps a fugitive has to inhabit an unending series of reincarnated cities, before he can rest. He hurries back past the wheedling voice to Sissi waiting in the victoria. The masseur offers him instant remedy for all his aches and pains.

But the horses are fractious and neigh impatiently, stomping their hooves. Terry jumps in and away they go clattering down the road. The masseur scrabbles after the carriage with promises of permanent cure.

But ... but how can he explain? It would take more than mere pampering the flesh to put the fires out, to encase him like a song-bird in a gilded cage or a ship, a delicately carved ship in a bottle, with sheared gunwale and sails trimmed to suit the scale of the quack's shrinking empire.

English translation of German text

46 Excuse me, actually I am on my way to the library. It's on the upper
    deck. I'll be happy to show you where it is.

46 All my little ducklings
    Swimming on the lake
    Heads in the water,
    Tails up in the air.

49 This is our home, this is where we come to rest after toiling in the
    field like you. Please do not plow us under.
    Your friend,
    Ant.

96 They shall not have them, the green banks of the Danube.

144 Will you send me a picture postcard?

145 I am going to Rome with Papili and Mutti when I am discharged.

145 I've been a good boy.

145 Yes, indeed Rudolf is a good boy.

170 My father. My father, and do you not see there

170 Shimmer of willows so gray.

223 The Linden tree
    By the well, past the ramparts
    there stands a linden tree
    While sleeping in its shadow
    sweet dreams it sent to me.
    And in its bark I chiseled
    my messages of love:
    My pleasures and my sorrows
    were welcomed from above.

225 My little angel
    My feet have left me
    My feet are gone

A Select Glossary of Indian terms

Ayah	Nanny
Agiyari	Parsi Fire Temple
Anglo-Indian	Person of Indo-British parentage
Aulia	Originally, Elahi Hazrat Khwaja Nizamuddin, a Sufi saint of Delhi but now applied routinely to a saintly person who administers 'karamat' or miracle cure.
Baas	That's enough
Baba	Term of endearment for a baby boy or girl
Baap	Father
Baccha	A kid or a toddler
Balaji	An incarnation of the Hindu deity Hanuman
Bapuji or Bapu	A term of respect for a father
Beedi	A hand-rolled cigarette
Bengan	Aubergine, American eggplant
Bevakoof	Idiot
Bharat Mata	Mother India
Bhujia	Crispy chick-pea and onion patties
Bhootani	A female ghost
Bustees	Shanties
Chakram	Gone round the bend
Chamcha	Minion or side-kick
Chela	Acolyte
Chodo ye sab kuch	Forget all this
Chowk	Market Square or Plaza
Darzi	Tailor
Dhamala	Riot
Dhobi	One who takes in washing clothes
Farishta	Messenger of God
Hamara memsaab	Long live our Memsahib
Harim	Variation of Harem

Katha	A ritualistic recitation of epics and scriptures
Katta	A derogatory term for a circumcised man
Kutteki Aula	Dog sired
Kurukshetra	The famous battlefield from the Mahabharata
Lakh	One lakh is equivalent to one hundred thousand
Lakshman Rekha	To disregard a warning. Refers to the symbolic line drawn in the forecourt of Sita's cottage
Mai	Mother
Maya	Illusion
Memsaab	A corruption of Memsahib used mostly by uneducated poor class
Meetha	Sweet/ American dessert
Mofussil	Rural district
Munna	Son
Munni	Daughter
Nathji	An incarnation of Krishna
Pahelwan	A wrestler
Palanquin	A covered litter carried on shoulders of four men
Panchayat	A council of elders
Pallav or Pallu	Loose end of a sari with which traditional Indian women cover their head
Resident	A senior British Official representing the
Samosa	A fried snack stuffed with vegetables
Samjhota	Reconciliation through compromise, a truce.
Shetan	Satan
Shikara	A houseboat
Tonga	A horse drawn carriage
Vidharbha	An underdeveloped region in the Western part of Maharashtra

About the Author

Until recently, Jaysinh Birjépatil taught English Literature at Marlboro College in Vermont. He was born in the city of Baroda, India, when it was an elegant princely capital. His background includes private schooling and academic training (MA, PhD) at the University of Manchester (UK) and Yale. Before settling down in Vermont he taught at M.S. University, Baroda and Brown University in Providence, Rhode Island. He is the author of *Beyond The Axle Tree*, a study of T.S. Eliot and has contributed articles to scholarly journals in India, England and the United States. At Manchester, he also trained in theatre and directed plays at Brown and Marlboro College. In 1965 he was selected to play a tiny role in an experimental film called *The White Bus* directed by Lindsay Anderson.

His first novel *Chinnery's Hotel* was published by Bodiam Books (U.K), and by Ravi Dayal / Penguin India. *The Good Muslim of Jackson Heights* released in the US by Fomite was earlier published by Ravi Dayal-Penguin, India. His short stories have been included in *The Way We Were: an Anglo-Indian Anthology* and in the fiction issue of *South Asian Review*. His poetry has appeared in *Critical Quarterly*, and *Acumen* in England and in an anthology of *Indian Poetry in English*, edited by Kaiser Haq for Ohio State University Press.

Fomite

A fomite is a medium capable of transmitting infectious organisms from one individual to another.

"The activity of art is based on the capacity of people to be infected by the feelings of others." Tolstoy, *What Is Art?*

Writing a review on Amazon, Good Reads, Shelfari, Library Thing or other social media sites for readers will help the progress of independent publishing. To submit a review, go to the book page on any of the sites and follow the links for reviews. Books from independent presses rely on reader to reader communications.

Visit http://www.fomitepress.com/FOMITE/Our_Books.html for more information or to order any of our books.

As It Is On Earth
Peter M Wheelwright

Dons of Time
Greg Guma

Loisaida
Dan Chodorkoff

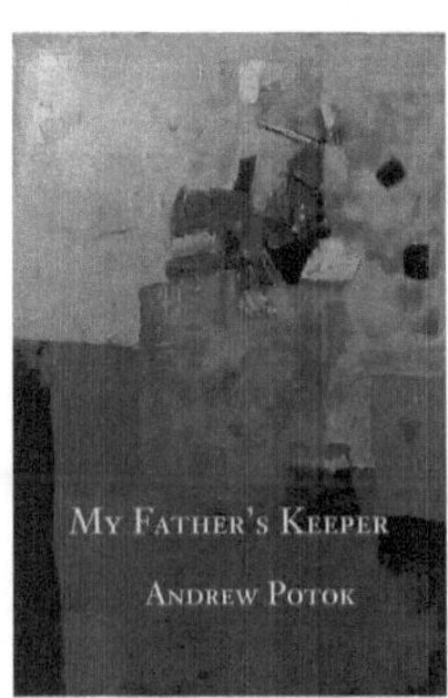

My Father's Keeper
Andrew Potok

My God, What Have We Done
Susan V Weiss

Rafi's World
Fred Russell

The Co-Conspirator's Tale
Ron Jacobs

Short Order Frame Up
Ron Jacobs

All the Sinners Saints
Ron Jacobs

Travers' Inferno
L. E. Smith

The Consequence of Gesture
L. E. Smith

Raven or Crow
Joshua Amses

Sinfonia Bulgarica
Zdravka Evtimova

The Good Muslim
of Jackson Heights
Jaysinh Birjépatil

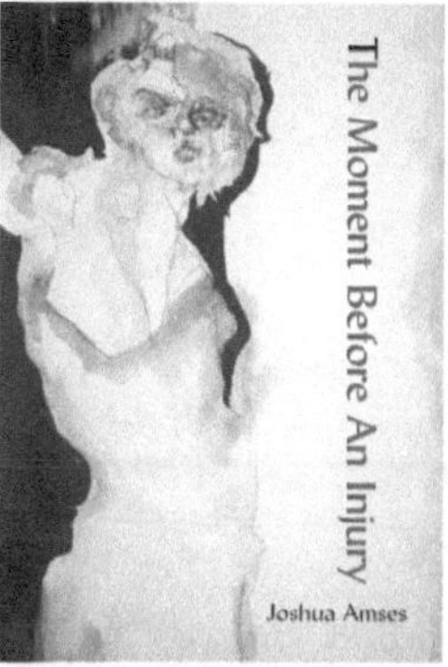

The Moment Before an Injury
Joshua Amses

Fomite

The Return of
Jason Green
Suzi Wizowaty

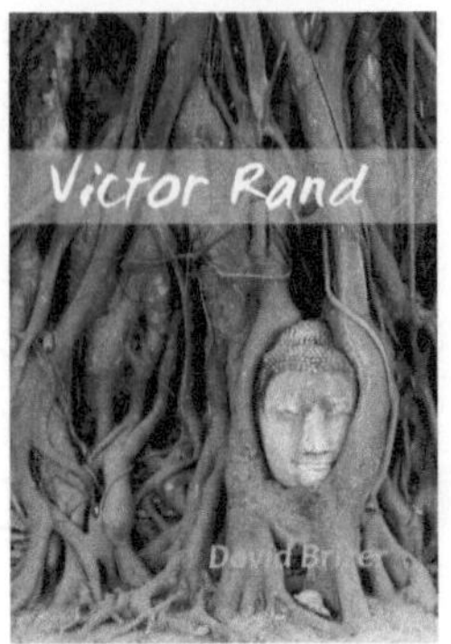

Victor Rand
David Brizeri

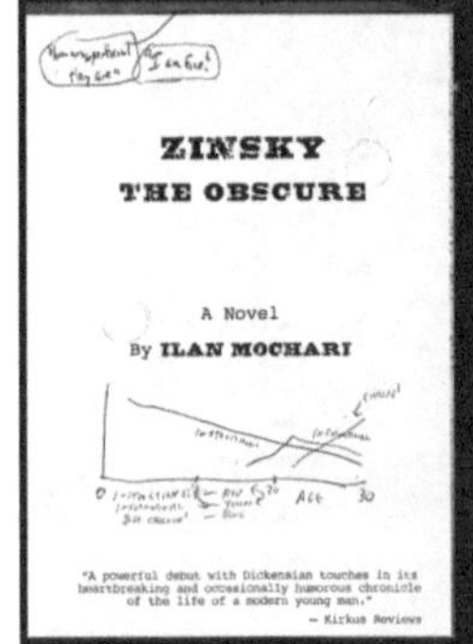

Zinsky the Obscure
Ilan Mochari

Body of Work
Andrei Guruianu

Carts and Other Stories
Zdravka Evtimova

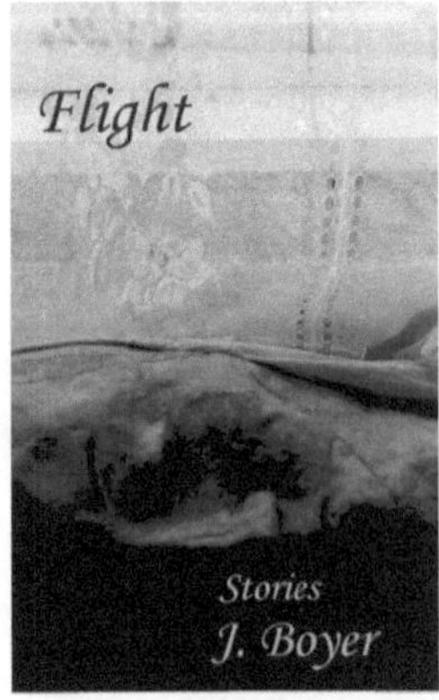

Flight
Jay Boyer

Love's Labours
Jack Pulaski

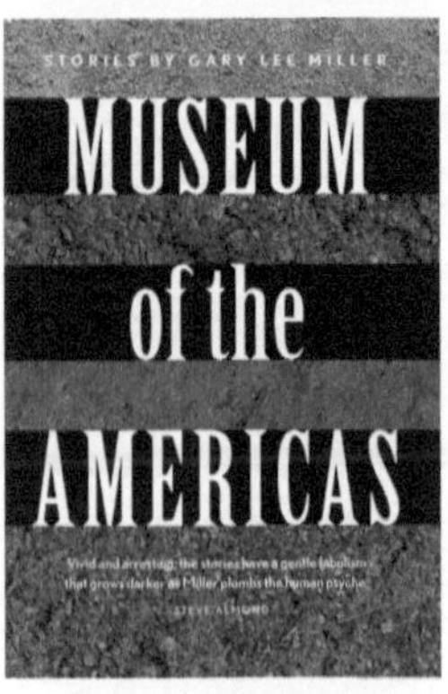

Museum of the Americas
Gary Lee Miller

Saturday Night at Magellan's
Charles Rafferty

Fomite

Signed Confessions
Tom Walker

Still Time
Michael Cocchiarale

Suite for Three Voices
Derek Furr

Unfinished Stories of Girls
Catherine Zobal Dent

Views Cost Extra
L. E. Smith

Visiting Hours
Jennifer Anne Moses

When You Remeber
Deir Yassin
R. L. Green

Alfabestiaro
Antonello Borra

Cycling in Plato's Cave
David Cavanagh

Fomite

AlphaBetaBestiario
Antonello Borra

Entanglements
Tony Magistrale

Everyone Lives Here
Sharon Webster

Four-Way Stop
Sherry Olson

Improvisational
Arguments
Anna Faktorovitch

Loosestrife
Greg Delanty

Meanwell
Janice Miller Potter

Roadworthy Creature
Roadworth Craft
Kate Magill

The Derivation of
Cowboys & Indians
Joseph D. Reich

Fomite

The Housing Market
Joseph D. Reich

The Empty Notebook
Interrogates Itself
Susan Thomas

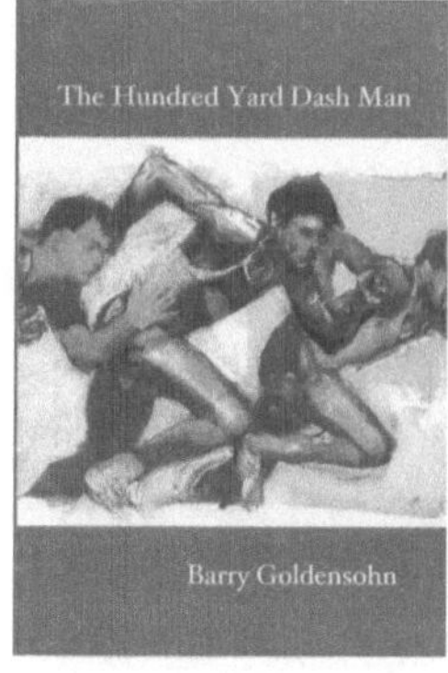

The Hundred Yard
Dash Man
Barry Goldensohn

The Listener Aspires
to the Condition of Music
Barry Goldensohn

The Way None
of This Happened
Mike Breiner

Screwed
Stephen Goldberg

Planet Kasper
Peter Schumann

My Murder
and Other Local News
David Schein

Picking Up the Bodies
James F. Connolly

Fomite

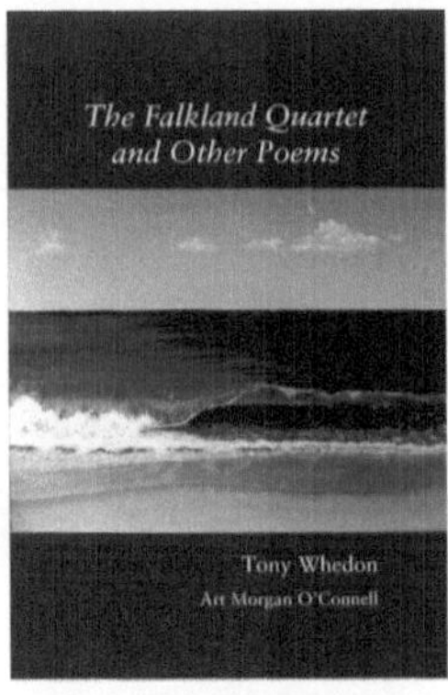

The Falkland Quartet
Tony Whedon

Drawing on Life
Mason Drukman

Among Angelic Orders
Susan Thoma

Confessions of a Carnivore
Diane Lefer

Principles of Navigation
Lynn Sloan

Derail Thie Train Wreck
Daniel Forbes

Free Fall/Caída libre
Tina Escaja

A Guide
to the Western Slopes
Roger Lebovitz

Planet Kasper
Volume Two
Peter Schumann

Fomite

Foreign Tales of
Exemplum and Woe
J. C. Ellefson

Where There Are Two
or More
Elizabeth Genovise

The Inconveniece
of the Wings
Silas Dent Zobal